LOVE ONCE MORE

Love Once More

THE ABUNDANCE SERIES BOOK 4

SALLY BAYLESS

KIMBERLIN BELLE PUBLISHING

Printed in the United States of America
First Printing, 2020
ISBN: 978-1-946034-11-3

Kimberlin Belle Publishing
Contact: admin@kimberlinbelle.com

Scripture taken from the Holy Bible, NEW INTERNATIONAL VERSION®, NIV® Copyright © 1973, 1978, 1984, 2011 by Biblica, Inc.® Used by permission. All rights reserved worldwide. NEW INTERNATIONAL VERSION® and NIV® are registered trademarks of Biblica, Inc. Use of either trademark for the offering of goods or services requires the prior written consent of Biblica US, Inc.

Cover Design © Jennifer Zemanek/Seedlings Design Studio

"Forget the former things; do not dwell on the past. See, I am doing a new thing! Now it springs up; do you not perceive it? I am making a way in the wilderness and streams in the wasteland.

Isaiah 43:18-19

Chapter One

Anyone could—if he or she put half a mind to it—leave the past behind and focus on the future. At least that's what the self-help books all said.

It's also what Kristen Hamlin kept telling herself as she climbed the porch steps of her sister's antique shop.

And what she'd told herself for weeks, ever since she finished reading *A Better You in Ninety Days.*

But it didn't feel like anything about her had changed.

At least not yet.

She blew out a long breath and opened the door of the shop, forcing her mood to lighten. After all, her sister was back in Missouri after her honeymoon, and it would be great to catch up with her again.

She stepped over the threshold, entering the former Victorian home that was now a shop filled with antiques. A blur of pink satin sped toward her.

"Aunt Kristen!" Five-year-old Emma, wearing a

princess dress, long white gloves, and silver flip-flops, barreled down the hallway from the kitchen.

Kristen's heart swelled with love as she knelt and gathered Emma into a hug, pressing a kiss into her red curls. "Hey, there, cutie pie."

"Mommy and Nate are back!" Emma's blue eyes danced. "They brought me seashells and a T-shirt and—"

"And she's decided we should go on a honeymoon every June." Abby came around a display of milk glass. "I get the impression Mom might have spoiled her a little while we were away."

Yeah, Mom might have. Kristen might even have helped. But she wasn't about to confess that to Abby.

"I've been sworn to secrecy," Kristen said. "All I can report is that I watered the plants at your new house and kept the shop." Which she'd enjoyed. The store was soothing, with its artfully arranged reminders of a simpler time, faint scent of furniture polish, and the gentle tick of the mantle clock in the front. No wonder customers frequently stopped in simply to look once more at a beautiful dresser or peruse the glass cases of antique costume jewelry.

"But I'm here, as promised, bright and early Monday morning, to give you an update on how sales went," she said.

And putting her own work schedule on hold for a few hours while she did so. But since she worked as a freelance textbook editor, her hours were fairly flexible. If she couldn't make time for her sister, what was the point of having that freedom?

Abby straightened a set of milk-glass punch cups that

surrounded a matching punch bowl on a large Demilune table.

Kristen peered closer at her older sister. Shouldn't Abby be glowing after a whole week alone with her handsome groom? And be happy that she and Nate and Emma had moved into their new house on the outskirts of Abundance?

Abby adjusted one more cup, then rested a hand on Emma's shoulder and smiled down at her. "Sweetheart, why don't you run upstairs and show your stuffed animals all your pretty new shells?"

"Okay, Mommy." Emma picked up a turquoise beach pail and scampered up the stairs.

Abby's gaze followed her, but her smile faded as the slap of Emma's flip-flops grew fainter. "We need to talk," she said quietly.

"Was there a problem on your trip?"

Abby's hazel eyes lit. "No, it was lovely. Really lovely, but..." She led the way to a small seating area near the front of the store, a spot designed for weary shoppers to rest. "I popped over to Cassidy's Diner to get us a treat." She gestured to a carry-out container and glasses of ice tea on the coffee table. "And I heard all the latest here in Abundance. Including some bad news."

Kristen sat on one end of a maroon velvet loveseat and picked up a napkin. "What is it?" She opened the carry-out box and put a cinnamon roll on a delicate, flowered plate.

Abby pulled her light-brown hair—almost blond after a week at the beach—between her hands at the base of her neck and smoothed it over one shoulder. "It's about Gwen." She sat down next to Kristen.

"Gwen?" Kristen put her plate on the table. Her high school best friend had recently planned a trip to Hawaii for her family and parents. "Was it the flight over? Was it too exhausting for her mom? Too hard with the babies?"

Abby shook her head, glanced down, then looked back up at Kristen, her eyes troubled. "I don't know how to tell you this, sis, but Gwen...Gwen and her husband were both killed."

Kristen's mouth gaped. "What?"

"I'm so sorry." Abby rested a hand on Kristen's arm.

Kristen's throat tightened, and her eyes stung. She numbly wiped frosting off the side of one finger and onto a napkin. "Killed? How?" This had to be a horrible mistake.

"They were on a helicopter tour with her parents, and the helicopter crashed. Her parents and the pilot survived, but Gwen and John...didn't."

Kristen's eyes filled with tears.

Abby pulled her into a hug, holding her as teardrops streamed down her cheeks.

How could this be true? How could Gwen and John be gone? Just like that? She tried to recall her last words to her best friend. Maybe something like "Have a good time in Hawaii. Remember, I want a video of you trying to do the hula!" The last time they'd spoken, and she'd made fun of Gwen's lack of dancing skills? Why couldn't she have said how much their friendship meant to her?

After a few moments, Kristen drew in a ragged breath and scooted back. "Did you learn anything more?"

"Grace at the diner said Gwen's dad broke both his legs. Her mom was pretty much okay. I mean, as okay as she was before."

Kristen nodded slowly. Mrs. Norris had multiple sclerosis and had been having more issues lately. Gwen had planned the trip because her mom had always wanted to see Hawaii but wasn't sure she'd have the energy or mobility to enjoy some of the sights for much longer.

"I—I—" Kristen dug a tissue from her pocket and wiped her eyes. "I can't believe Gwen's gone. What about the babies?"

"They're fine. Apparently Gwen and her family were staying with one of her mom's oldest friends. The woman was watching the twins while the rest of the family went up in the helicopter."

Kristen's mouth fell open. If the twins had survived and Gwen and John were both dead, that meant... meant...

Her pulse began to pound. Snippets of a recent conversation with Gwen swirled through her mind. Gwen had been so angry with her brother, Clay. So concerned about her girls' future after she saw a story online about a young couple who tragically died within two months of each other, both from rare medical conditions, leaving three children. With Gwen's being such a close friend, there was no way Kristen could refuse when Gwen asked. With her own history with Clay, with the way he'd broken off their engagement, Kristen could understand perfectly...but—

She swallowed, her mouth suddenly dry.

"Are you okay?"

"Yeah." Kristen grabbed a glass of iced tea from the table and took a drink.

"You've gone kind of pale."

"With good reason." She set the glass on the table and watched a rivulet of condensation race down the side. "I...I think I'm supposed to be raising Gwen and John's girls." She looked back up at Abby.

"You?" Abby leaned forward. "Why not her parents? Or Clay?"

"Gwen told me her mom's health is too unpredictable to ask her parents to care for small children."

Abby dipped her chin slightly, as if she understood. "But what about Clay? He's her brother."

"Gwen and John listed Clay as the guardian when they made up wills right after the girls were born. But lately Gwen's realized he's too wrapped up in his work to be a good parent."

"Oh." Abby's voice held an awkward note.

Even after ten years, it *was* awkward. Clay's obsession with work hadn't been a newsflash to Kristen. She, more than anyone, knew that Clay Norris cared more about computers than he did about people. But even for Clay, losing his sister and almost losing his parents had to be hard. The whole situation was simply awful.

"What about Gwen's husband's family?"

"He doesn't—I mean, didn't—really have any family. He was an only child, and his parents were both only children, and they died while he was in college."

"So she asked you to be the guardian?"

"Yeah." Kristen took another drink of her tea, put the glass back on the table, and wiped the moisture from her fingers on her shorts. "About a week ago. And I agreed. I mean, I never thought it would matter. I just thought it would give her some peace of mind if I said yes. But she took it really seriously, talking about how they had a big life insurance policy and how I wouldn't need to worry about money for housing or clothes or food or college. She sounded as if they were going to make the changes immediately."

"Wow," Abby said, "that's a lot to ask of someone who doesn't already have kids."

"I was honored." Kristen sank back in her chair. "But it is a pretty big thing to wrap my mind around."

Abby grabbed her hands. "I'll help you. Mom and Dad will too. You'll do a great job."

"Thanks. That means a lot coming from you, the World's Most Perfect Mom."

Abby gave a soft laugh. "Hardly."

Kristen lowered her chin and looked her sister in the eye. The question wasn't worth debating. Abby was an amazing mom and the nicest sister a person could have.

If Kristen sometimes felt a little less than in comparison, if her chest had ached as she watched Abby get married last weekend, it certainly wasn't Abby's fault.

Besides, the inadequacies in Kristen's life wouldn't really matter now. She would be too busy managing her editing projects and figuring out how to take care of twins.

But how could Gwen and John be gone? John was such a nice guy, and Gwen... Gwen had been so special, the kind of person who lived life to the fullest, who believed in others and encouraged them to chase their dreams. Just being around her always made Kristen happier. And now she'd never get to talk to her again...

She sat up taller. Her grief would have to wait. "Gwen wouldn't have asked me if she didn't think I could do this.

And I can. I can make sure those little girls are brought up with love and attention. Exactly how she wanted."

Abby squeezed Kristen's hand, her eyes filled with what looked like a spark of approval. "You'll be wonderful with them."

"Thank you." Kristen got up. One thing at a time. "The only number I know for Gwen's mom is their old landline from when they used to live here in Abundance. But I'm pretty sure a friend of mine has a cell number from when we were planning her shower. I'll text her."

Then she'd call Mrs. Norris and figure out what to do next.

Two nine-month-old girls were counting on her.

Chapter Two

Monday afternoon, Clay Norris stepped off the elevator and studied the sign on the wall of the Best Health Medical Center in Honolulu, Hawaii.

Room 607 was to the right.

He turned and headed down the hall, tennis shoes squeaking on the gleaming tile floor.

He was exhausted. The day had gone on forever. To his body, it was already Monday night. He'd tried to rest, but barely slept on either plane during his flight from Kansas City, his mind swirling with memories of his sister. Eighteen months younger, she'd been a year behind him in school. Sure, they'd fought like all kids do, but mostly they'd gotten along. He remembered her, when she was about six, helping him build a giant snow fort. Remembered her when she was eight, sobbing at his side when they found their dog run over in the road. Remembered her laughing out loud that time when she was about twelve and he'd been scraping seeds out of a pumpkin and accidentally sent a spoonful flying into her hair. She'd been a good sport.

And she'd found her perfect calling as an ICU nurse in a huge academic medical center. She'd met her husband, John, in the same hospital.

John, a pharmacist, had been quiet, the kind of guy who hated parties and got to know people gradually. Gwen had been crazy about him, even charmed by his goofy laugh and his love of the Cubs.

Clay had found the Cubs thing unfortunate, but he'd tried to ignore it because, overall, John had been a great guy.

A nurse looked up from a desk. "Can I help you?" Behind her, halls branched off in three directions.

"Room 607?"

She tipped her head toward one of the halls.

Clay nodded his thanks and kept walking, still thinking of Gwen and John.

It was such a tragedy, especially to happen now. They'd tried for years to have kids and had been so thrilled when they finally had their two little girls. At Christmas, John's face had lit up at the sight of his daughters. Gwen seemed incapable of having a conversation, in person or on the phone, without bragging about them.

Except, of course, that last phone call Clay had with her.

She'd been furious when he canceled on the trip to Hawaii. Said he was in denial about Mom's illness. Said he was a workaholic whose only priority was "stupid computer games."

He wasn't.

He'd wanted to be in Hawaii with them. Really. If he had been, maybe things would have turned out differently. Maybe he could have talked them out of that helicopter tour. But he had his company, Norware Games, to run, a new product about to launch, employees who needed to keep their jobs... And, when his chief development officer and administrative assistant ran off to California, no way to make sure the game made it to market and keep the business afloat except by working more hours himself.

He'd tried to explain, but Gwen hadn't listened. She'd said she couldn't believe that if something happened to her and John, he'd be the one responsible for Lark and Lea. Said he barely noticed the girls when he was in the same room with them. Said he'd missed the family Thanksgiving last year. And said—conveniently forgetting that a giant snowstorm had grounded planes out of Kansas City—that he'd almost missed Christmas.

So when he canceled on Hawaii, she was furious. Their last conversation ever, a giant fight.

And now, if she was here, she'd be even madder.

Because...he hadn't really thought the guardian thing through when he agreed before the twins were born. When Mom called to tell him about the helicopter crash, reality set in, fast and hard. There was no way he could be a guardian to two baby girls. Maybe, just maybe, he could handle one ten-year-old boy. They could throw a baseball around and play video games. Clay would even let him win sometimes.

But two baby girls? When he'd seen them at Christmas, his nieces had been nothing more than sleepy lumps. Gwen had offered to let him hold one, but he'd backed away. Babies had those soft spots in their skulls. What if he somehow dropped Lark and damaged her brain? Or maybe it had been Lea that Gwen had held out toward him. It wasn't as if he could tell them apart.

No, he was completely unqualified to be an instant parent. So he'd come up with a much better plan. He could be the legal guardian on paper but pay for a full-time nanny at his parent's house. Mom could oversee the care of her granddaughters without having to do the physical work. He usually plowed most of his profits back into the company, but once this new product successfully launched, Norware Games would be on firmer footing. Hopefully, he could easily afford full-time nanny care then.

Plus, think how it would comfort Mom to see Gwen's little girls take their first steps and hear them say their first words. Or whatever big achievements they were doing these days.

He had no idea. Gwen posted so much about the girls on social media that he'd discreetly shut off her updates.

He certainly didn't know anything about babies, which was why his plan was the best option. If there was a problem, like if one of the girls wasn't sleeping well at night, Mom or the nanny would know what to do.

When he couldn't sleep at night, he played video games.

There was always someone online who was willing to do battle in another galaxy. But watching Uncle Clay kill aliens probably wouldn't put one of the twins to sleep. All those images of violence might give a baby nightmares. Besides, even he knew that children weren't supposed to interact with strangers online.

603. 605. Here it was—room 607.

The door was closed, and hushed voices came from inside.

Clay knocked. "Mom? Dad?" he called out as he pushed the door slightly open.

There was a rustling sound, and then Mom opened the door wide. "You made it." Her eyes filled with tears, and she let out a sob and pulled him close, burying her head on his shoulder.

Pain twisted in his chest, growing sharper with each shudder of her body. He patted her back and tried to blink away his own tears.

At last she moved away, pulled a tissue from her pocket, and blew her nose.

Her blue eyes were bloodshot, her normally fluffy grayish brown hair hung limp, and a line of stitches ran across her forehead, connecting a string of purple bruises. She'd said on the phone that she hadn't been hurt at all. If she looked this bad, how was Dad?

"Come. Sit down. We've got an extra chair." Mom led the way, limping. Was that the MS or an injury she'd suffered in the crash?

Clay followed her into the room. With every detail that came into view, his stomach grew heavier.

"Hey, son." Dad's voice sounded off, as if he was heavily medicated, and his brown eyes didn't quite focus.

Nearby, a monitor beeped and jagged green lines ran across the screen.

Mom had told him Dad had broken both his legs. She hadn't said they were in casts from foot to hip. She hadn't said his skin was ashen. And she hadn't said he had all sorts of wires and tubes hooked up to him.

"Dad, I'm so sorry about all this." Clay waved an open, helpless hand toward the casts.

"Now, Clay, it's nothing to worry about." Mom's tone was falsely bright. "The doctors assure us that in a couple of weeks, Dad can be transferred to a hospital back home in Denver. After a while, if we get someone to come in and help me, he'll be able to come home."

Nothing to worry about?

Right.

Had Mom taken a good look at Dad?

She shot Clay a sharp glance. There was an odd light in her eyes, as if nothing more than sheer will was keeping her going. As if she'd never forgive him if he didn't agree with her.

Was this all just an act so Dad wouldn't understand how bad things were? Was he so drugged up that he didn't know that after the casts came off, he might need months of physical therapy before he could walk again?

Did he even know about Gwen?

"Uh, I'm sure going home would be good," Clay said, trying to sound upbeat. He approached the bed and attempted to hug his dad, but was stopped by all the wires. Instead, he grabbed his hand and sank into the empty chair.

Dad gave a vague smile and weakly squeezed Clay's hand.

"Knock, knock, kno—ock," an overly cheery voice called from the hallway.

Clay turned toward the door.

A tall woman pushed a stroller into the room. Her hair was an unnatural shade of red, and she wore a bright-green tent of a dress. "Clay," she said. "Your plane arrived."

He stood and walked toward her. "It did. Nice to see you, Mrs. Cochran."

"Call me Noreen, please. My goodness, I haven't seen you in what? Thirteen years? You were about fifteen." She reached for his hands. "I'm so very sorry about Gwen and John," she added softly, as if she didn't want Dad to hear.

"Thank you," Clay murmured.

"Your mom's been counting the hours since your plane left the mainland. I'm pretty happy you're here myself. Things are crazy at the resort where I work. It's been a treat taking care of these two little sweeties, but they really need me in the catering center."

Clay nodded wordlessly.

Noreen touched his arm. "Don't you worry. Before I leave, I'll teach you all about bottles and how to change diapers."

He gulped. Would it be wrong to beg her to stay? He hadn't even considered who had been taking care of the twins. Somehow, he'd pictured them in the hospital. But they weren't hurt. Not like Mom and Dad.

Mom and Dad... Their injuries had seemed so much more manageable from far away. Plus, they seemed so much older and frailer now than they had six months ago at Christmas.

There was no way he could tell them what he'd been thinking as he flew out, that they should keep the twins. Simply surviving the next few months was going to take all the energy and stamina they had. He couldn't possibly ask them to have the additional responsibility of Lark and Lea, even with help.

No. That was going to be his job. No matter what it cost him.

He swallowed, stood, and slipped past Mom to move closer to the stroller. The contraption was huge, holding each of the girls in one of those car seat carrier things he'd seen Gwen and John hauling around.

Noreen pushed back the canopies that partly covered the twins.

The girls stared up at him, looking bigger and more alert than he remembered.

"Don't just peek in at them," Noreen said. "Pick up those little loves. Here, let me help you."

"Uh..." Clay took a step back and ran into the wall behind him.

Two seconds later, she positioned one of the twins in his arms, the one wearing a pink outfit with a cartoon rabbit on the front.

"Hi," he mumbled. "Uh..."

"That's Lark." Noreen adjusted his arms so that he held Lark in his left arm and tucked the other twin, this one wearing an outfit covered in green turtles, into his right arm. "And here's Lea."

A sweet, vaguely familiar fragrance that might be some kind of lotion filled the air. One of the girls wiggled, and some of her wispy brown hair brushed against his arm, as soft as the feathers that came out that time he got a hole in his down vest. And, unlike at the holidays, the twins peered at him like real little people, studying him as if not sure who he was.

Clay looked from one small face to the other. Their eyes were brown. Like Dad's. And Gwen's. And his.

The wiggly one—uh, Lea—reached out and touched Clay's nose.

He jerked his head back.

Lark giggled, and Lea gave him a drooly, unrepentant grin.

Somewhere deep inside, Clay felt warmth bubbling up, filling his heart.

He didn't have a clue how to work those car seat things, or how to change a diaper, or even what to feed a baby. He didn't know how he could possibly run a computer game company and manage life with twins. But he knew the most important thing.

He knew he was supposed to take care of these two little girls. He owed it to Gwen. And he wasn't going to let her and John—or the twins—down.

Late Monday, after eight texts to three different people, Kristen was finally ready to call Mrs. Norris. It was unbelievable that it had taken so long to get a current phone number after hearing about Gwen's death early this morning. Hopefully, it wouldn't seem rude that she hadn't reached out sooner. But was it now too late in the day to call?

She retied the sash of her bright-purple bathrobe, then sat at her kitchen table and took out her phone.

Here in Missouri, in Central Daylight Time, it was almost ten o'clock at night. That meant in California it was eight, and Hawaii had to be at least two hours earlier than that. So...not the middle of the night. Not a bad time to call.

But this call wasn't going to be easy to make. She was still reeling from the thought of losing Gwen.

Kristen had been a grade ahead in school, but they had been great friends, ever since that day when Gwen was in second grade and Paige Albright, one of Kristen's third-grade classmates, had made fun of a doll Gwen brought to school. Kristen, who'd herself been on the receiving end of Paige's nasty comments, overheard and threw a big, hairy caterpillar on the bully. That was all it took to cement a friendship.

Gwen had been one of a kind. She had a way of coming up with ideas that, although they might sound crazy at first, ended up being the most fun. Like the time she and Kristen had gone to a state park at the Lake of the Ozarks for the day. Gwen decided they had to stop and buy matching pairs of the biggest, gaudiest sunglasses the tourist shop sold. They'd ended up wearing those sunglasses all summer, every time they were together. Kristen still had hers in her top dresser drawer.

It just wasn't fair that Gwen was gone. Oh, Kristen had heard sermons on suffering. She knew that sometimes bad things happened to good people because God gave man free will. But it didn't make her feel any better at the moment.

It probably wouldn't help Gwen's parents feel better either. As much as she was going to miss Gwen, the loss for them had to be much, much worse.

She looked down once more at the paper where she'd written Mrs. Norris's number. What did one say to a woman who had lost her daughter and son-in-law and whose husband had been severely injured? And Gwen's mom and dad were such sweet people. Everyone in town had missed them when they moved to Denver after Gwen graduated from Abundance High.

Kristen swallowed. No more stalling. She needed to do this. She put the phone on the table, set it to speaker, and tapped the screen to place the call.

After five rings, a familiar voice answered.

"Mrs. Norris?" she said gently.

"Yes?"

"This is Kristen Hamlin. I heard about the accident. I'm so very, very sorry."

"Kristen, dear, thank you." Mrs. Norris sounded tired but steady.

"Gwen meant the world to me. I can't—" She forced herself to hold it together. "I can't really believe she's gone. And John..."

"I... I know." Mrs. Norris's voice grew shaky.

Kristen hunched forward, leaning over the phone, hands clasped in her lap. She'd said the wrong thing and upset the poor woman. She was terrible at this. But she had to continue. "Uh, how are the twins?"

"Okay, I guess. Not sleeping that well." There was a pause, and Mrs. Norris blew her nose. "I can't believe Gwen won't get to raise them."

Pain cut into the back of Kristen's throat. "I know." Did everything she say have to make things worse? She hesitated, trying to think of a way to ask her next question delicately, but none of the words that came to mind made the situation any better.

Maybe she should plunge right in. Probably Gwen's mom was waiting for her to act, waiting for her to take responsibility for the girls. If what Grace Cassidy had said about Mr. Norris's injuries was true, his wife probably had her hands full. Kristen needed to show she was eager to help, proud that Gwen had asked her to be the guardian. "Actually, Mrs. Norris…it's the twins I'm calling about. I mean, since Gwen asked me to raise them if anything should happen to her and John."

"Raise them?" Mrs. Norris sounded bewildered.

"She didn't tell you? We talked about it before she left for Hawaii. She was very adamant I agree to take them if anything happened to her and John. I'm ready to help, any time you need me. I can—I can fly right out." She didn't have money for the airfare in checking, but she could put it on her credit card.

"I'm sorry, Kristen, but I don't have any idea what you're talking about. Clay's going to be raising Lea and Lark. Gwen and John set that up right after the girls were born."

Kristen's stomach suddenly went queasy. She fingered the fuzzy sash of her bathrobe. "I guess Gwen didn't have time to discuss with you that she and John were changing that. I'm sure her lawyer can—"

"I just got off the phone with their lawyer. Clay arrived in Hawaii earlier today, and he's with the girls right now. I wanted to be sure he had documentation in case it was needed for the flight back. The lawyer said he'd email it to me. He didn't say a word about you." Mrs. Norris paused, then spoke more slowly. "He did mention that Gwen and John had made an appointment for next week, but he wasn't sure what it was about."

"Oh." Kristen sat back in her chair. "I guess they hadn't changed things yet. But, Mrs. Norris, she made me promise I would raise the girls."

"You must have misunderstood. I know Gwen was really mad when Clay didn't come to Hawaii, but I'm sure she was just blowing off steam when she talked with you. She and John were probably seeing the lawyer about that plumbing problem that wasn't disclosed when they bought their new house."

Kristen pressed her lips together. That didn't make a bit of sense. Gwen might have been venting her anger when she listed example after example of times Clay had acted like his family didn't matter, but the timing of the appointment with the lawyer was too soon to be a coincidence. No one made an appointment with a lawyer if she was just blowing off steam. Plus, Gwen had talked about how she and John had agreed that Kristen was the best choice, and Gwen had brought up that insurance policy and other financial information that she wouldn't have shared without a reason.

"Gwen was lucky to have a friend like you, someone who would even consider taking on the responsibility of raising her children. But," Mrs. Norris said firmly, "the girls will be staying with Clay."

Given how nervous Kristen had been about caring for the girls, she should feel relieved. Instead, she felt a wave of guilt. She'd made a solemn promise to Gwen, but the paperwork needed to allow her to keep that promise had never been done. What was she supposed to do now?

For one thing she should get off the phone. This

conversation wasn't going to get any better. "Uh…I'm… I'm sorry for your loss, Mrs. Norris. I'll be praying that Mr. Norris recovers quickly."

"Thank you, dear."

The line went dead.

Chapter Three

"I can't thank you enough, Lucas." Clay led the way down his townhouse stairs Wednesday afternoon. He undid the baby gate at the bottom and went into the living room, where the twins were playing on the carpet.

"No problem." Lucas walked through the gate and closed it behind him. "You were never going to get all that stuff into your little hybrid car."

"That's the truth. By themselves, the car seats took up most of the back seat." In fact, when he arrived in Missouri this morning after taking the red-eye from Hawaii, it might have been easier if he and the twins had taken up residence in the store. The shopping list the hospital social worker had given him had been two pages long. Two pages of baby supplies, all of which Gwen and John probably had in their house. But their house was in Connecticut, more than a thousand miles away. A couple of friends who lived nearby would be sending some of the twins' things, but that would take a while. The memorial service for Gwen and John, decisions about clearing out their house, all of that would have to wait until Dad was better and Clay was out of crisis mode. So he'd worked his way down that shopping list. And what a list.

So. Much. Stuff.

At least, thanks to Mom, he'd known that he only needed one crib. Gwen had made that decision at the start, thinking the girls would be happier together.

Even so, halfway down page one of the shopping list, he'd realized the baby gear was never going to fit in his little gold car. He'd called Lucas Stiner, who lived a couple of townhouses down and owned a pickup truck.

"I'm really grateful for you helping me haul all this home," Clay said, trying to cover a yawn. "And for staying to help me install the gates and put the crib and the changing table together."

"No problem." Lucas lifted his long hair off his neck, secured it with a ponytail holder from the pocket of his cutoffs, and walked toward the front door. "I don't see how one person could have assembled that crib."

"Especially not someone who got about three hours of sleep last night on the plane. Even though Lark and Lea are starting to get used to me, neither of them seems fond of air travel." He was pretty sure, though, that each of the girls had gotten more sleep than he had. Every time they were quiet, his mind had swirled with memories of Gwen and worries about how to get the twins through the next stage of the trip home.

But they'd made it to Abundance and, thanks to his neighbor, had things relatively well set up.

Clay waved goodbye to Lucas and looked around, stretching his back as he mentally itemized all they'd accomplished. His desk and file cabinet had been wedged into the living room. His former home office—now the girls' room—held the crib, changing table, and a tower of diapers and wipes. Two high chairs sat ready in the kitchen, and the countertop was stacked with baby food. Every outlet in the living room was covered, and every cord tucked as far out of reach as possible. The coffee table, with its pointy corners, was stored in his garage along with a bookcase and some boxes of computer hardware, basically making it impossible to fit in his car. He and Lucas had even put up baby gates blocking access from the living room to the stairs and the hall. He'd baby proof more later, but for today the girls could sleep in their crib and play in the living room.

Now seemed like a good time for a late afternoon snack. Clay let himself through the gate into the kitchen and grabbed a box of banana-flavored teething biscuits. He returned to the living room, sat on the couch near the twins, and opened the box.

"What do you think, Lark and Lea? Would either of you like one?"

The girls ignored him, more interested in a plush star that made crinkling sounds when they squeezed it.

He pulled a biscuit from the box and took a bite. Not bad.

Lark let out a gurgling coo, and Lea waved the star in the air. Neither of them seemed to want a biscuit, but they appeared happy.

Maybe now, if he could stay awake enough to focus,

he could figure out how to get his life back on track. He grabbed his laptop and opened it.

Daytime child care was covered starting tomorrow, thanks to Midge, the secretary at the Abundance Community Church.

Clay was irregular at best in his church attendance, but he had helped Midge with computer issues a few times. Minor things, none of them worth sending a bill, at least in his opinion. But Midge had been quite grateful and promised to pay him back one day. Right after he landed in Kansas City, he'd gotten a text from her saying that she'd gotten him two slots at the day-care center run by her sister, Marianne Quigley.

He'd debated how soon to put the twins in day care, thinking perhaps he should take a week off work to spend more time with them. The social worker at the hospital said that during this transition they needed to be held a lot and have their needs met quickly. To be honest, that last part, even more than the back-load of work at Norware Games, was what made him decide to start them in day care right away. Most of the time he didn't have a clue what their needs were. From his conversation with Marianne, he felt sure the day-care owner would know better than he.

Unfortunately, the day-care center closed promptly at five thirty. A fine option in the short term, but as soon as possible, he'd need to hire a full-time nanny. Ever since Blake and Brynn took off for California and left Norware Games shorthanded, he'd been working well past a normal closing time.

Until he found a nanny, in the evenings the girls could hang out in the living room, eat those biscuits, and play with toys while he worked. Once he got back to full staff and the new game launched, things should get better. The game—"Hidden Pirate Treasure: Caribbean," or "Caribbean Treasure," as he and the team referred to it—was going to be a hit. He just knew it. When it was, they could roll out sequels set on the Atlantic Coast or in the Mediterranean or in the Indian Ocean.

Then his position as CEO would be perfect. Perfect for him, and for the girls. He could be the success he'd always dreamed of, and he'd be able to control his own schedule, allowing him to spend more time with the twins.

In the meantime, now that they weren't mad about being on the airplane, the girls were so sweet. He knew they'd get along fine once they got into a routine. The more he was around Lark and Lea, the more they wormed their way into his heart. He opened an email and tried to read it, but instead yawned and sank back against the couch, gazing at the twins. How had he not realized at Christmas that they were real people, who had real personalities? Already, he could tell that Lark was the more adventurous one. Lea was more of a cuddler...

Snuggly...

Like this couch pillow...

The doorbell rang, and Clay jerked upright, dropping his laptop as he scrambled up from a prone position.

"Ouch." He reached down and picked the laptop off his left foot.

The doorbell rang again.

Probably one of his employees or, in spite of his spotty attendance, someone else from the church dropping off a casserole. He'd received five while he and Lucas were building the crib and baby-proofing.

Clay stumbled toward the door, glancing back to check on the twins.

Lea sat near the gate to the hall, sucking her thumb, eyelids sinking. Lark was turned away but sitting up near his recliner.

He scrubbed a hand over his face and opened the door. "Hi, Clay."

Not an employee. Not someone he only knew from church.

Kristen Hamlin.

His stomach twisted into a hard knot. He'd been afraid she'd stop by.

Her hair seemed blonder, falling in waves over her shoulders. But those gorgeous hazel eyes were exactly the same.

She took a step closer and the flowery scent that still filled his dreams wafted toward him.

"I wanted to stop by and give you my condolences. I'm really sorry about everything that happened. My whole family is." Her voice was gentle, and she held a foil-wrapped package and a plastic container toward him. "Mom made a cold chicken and pasta salad for you, and I baked a loaf of zucchini bread."

"Uh, come in." He took the food and backed away from the door, glancing in the living room. Were the twins still okay? Yep. Lea was watching Kristen as if fascinated. Not that he could blame the little girl. He'd done that a lot himself in high school.

"Oh, look how darling they are." Kristen's eyes grew teary, and she blinked rapidly. "I can't...I can't believe

Gwen is gone."

The urge to pull Kristen into his arms was almost too hard for Clay to resist. But he didn't have the right to hold her. Not anymore.

"I know. It doesn't seem real." His voice broke, and he cleared his throat, then gestured awkwardly toward the couch.

"Do you think I could hold one of the girls?"

"Sure." Would questions like that always feel odd? It didn't seem right that he was the one who was supposed to know what Lark and Lea would want. "Be right back." He made his way through the baby gate and stuck the food in the fridge.

When he returned, Kristen was kneeling beside Lea, totally absorbed. She carefully picked her up and sat on the couch, nestling the baby into the crook of her arm as if it came naturally.

Lea said something unintelligible and grabbed Kristen's necklace.

The twins liked shiny things. He'd already figured that out.

Should he pick up Lark? Did she feel left out? No, she seemed happy, playing with something.

He looked back at Kristen. "Thanks for the food, and thanks for calling my mom to tell her how much you'd miss Gwen. It meant a lot to her."

Kristen tipped her head, and her hair shifted to one side. "It did?" Her voice held an odd note. "Did, um, did she tell you why else I called?"

"Yeah." Clay sat on the couch next to her. "I'm sorry there was a misunderstanding."

Lea squirmed.

Kristen set the baby back on the floor, and Lea quickly crawled over near her sister. "I'm not sure there was." She paused and straightened her necklace. "Gwen was pretty clear that she wanted me to be the twins' guardian."

Clay sat upright, more awake than he'd been all day. "Why would Gwen and John do that?"

Kristen jerked back.

Okay, he might have been a little loud there.

Loud enough that the sympathetic look cooled in Kristen's eyes. "I understand that she hadn't discussed it with you all. Or even made the official arrangements. But Gwen asked me to promise I would be their guardian." Kristen's chin jutted out a little. "And I *am* good with kids."

"I know you are. But since Mom and Dad can't take care of the twins, they belong with me. I'm their uncle."

"Gwen was afraid that you'd be too busy with your work. Computers are"—Kristen pressed her lips together—"really important to you."

Clay winced at the reference to their breakup. Even after all these years, they still hadn't moved past it.

Kristen stood. "If Gwen and John had made an earlier appointment with their lawyer, I'd have been raising the girls."

Clay's body tensed. "The lawyer didn't say a word about you. And a conversation is not a legal document. Besides, the girls and I are doing fine."

She leaned her head slightly to one side, looking at Lark and Lea. "Really? Since when are you supposed to let babies eat cardboard?"

Cardboard?

Kristen sped across the room, picked up Lark, and removed the remains of the banana biscuit box from her hands.

Clay's throat tightened, and he peered at Lark. Was she all right? Yes, she seemed fine. "I fell asleep, okay?" He took Lark from Kristen's arms, holding her close. "I didn't mean to, but the flight back was grueling and—"

"What if she'd eaten the plastic bag inside? She could have choked."

Clay's throat grew even tighter. Kristen was right. Lark could have died, all because he couldn't stay awake.

Something warm oozed onto his arm. He looked down. Lark had spit out a big glob of well-chewed cardboard, and Lea had crawled over to sit at his feet, her face bright red, as if she was about to cry.

"You know as well as I do, Clay, that I'm the last person in the world you'll ever convince that you'll be a good guardian. How are you going to spend the time with them that they need?" She shook her head. "Lark and Lea would have been better off with me." She left, shutting the door behind her with a sharp *thunk.*

His stomach clenched. What if she was right?

The twins' little faces appeared frozen, their mouths slightly open. Then, bit by bit, Lark's cheeks became as red as Lea's, and both their mouths pursed up.

A second later, as if on cue, they began to wail.

Clay groaned. What if he *was* too wrapped up in his work? What if Gwen and John did mean to change their will and make Kristen the guardian? What if setting up the crib and the changing table and putting covers on all the outlets was the easy part?

Or what if he spent so much time with the twins that the product launch failed and Norware went bankrupt?

He had the sinking feeling he was in way over his head.

Still mulling over her visit to Clay's, Kristen drove home and pulled into the parking lot outside her apartment complex. She snagged the last shaded spot and tried to accept the situation.

But it didn't seem right.

Gwen and John hadn't wanted Clay to raise the girls. They had wanted them to be with her. That should matter.

Granted, Clay seemed like he was doing pretty well taking care of the twins. Kristen had noticed the baby gates and spotted stacks of baby food on the kitchen counter. And she had to give him the benefit of the doubt about Lark eating cardboard. Emma had eaten a page of a board book once when Kristen was watching her.

But what if Clay wasn't a good guardian? What if the cardboard wasn't a fluke? What if he got so wrapped up in his work that something bad happened to the girls?

She blew out a long breath and got out of her car.

"Hey, Kristen." Deanna, a woman who lived one building over, waved and walked toward her. "I haven't seen you in ages."

"Hi, Deanna. It has been a while."

The two of them weren't good friends, but they had gone to the movies together a couple of times. Deanna, who was in her forties and was a caseworker for social services in the children's division, was a big fan of matinees.

"What's new with you?" Deanna met her in the shade.

"Not much." Kristen hesitated. "Except a really dear friend and her husband were killed in a freak accident. I'm still trying to accept that she's gone." She explained about the helicopter wreck.

"Kristen, I'm so sorry. How horrible." Softhearted Deanna had grown teary just hearing about what happened.

"I know." Kristen looked away and told herself not to cry again. "Anyway, I almost became the guardian for their twin baby girls. Gwen had asked me, but she and her husband never changed the legal paperwork, so the girls are with their uncle."

"Wow."

"I'll still get to see them, but..." At least she hoped she'd be welcome to visit. She hadn't handled things as well as she could have with Clay.

"Is the uncle local?"

"Clay Norris. Do you know him?"

"I know of him. He runs that computer game company, right?"

"Yeah. It's his whole life, according to Gwen. I can't help but feel that I would have been a better guardian."

"He is family, though." Deanna frowned. "If there's no legal paperwork, I don't see how you can get custody."

Kristen shrugged. "That's pretty much what my brother-in-law, Nate Redmond, told me when I called him last night. He said if I don't have a signed document, it doesn't matter what Gwen said she planned to do."

Deanna hitched her purse higher on her shoulder. "Nate's a lawyer here in town, isn't he?"

"Yeah, with Redmond and Associates."

"I imagine he knows what he's talking about." A note of sympathy sounded in her voice. "Maybe Clay will do better than you think." She pursed her lips and looked off to one side. "You could always offer to baby-sit. With twins, I can guarantee he'll need a break. That way you can see how they're doing." She angled her head toward her car. "I've got to go. I'm meeting a friend for dinner. Call me sometime and we'll get together."

"Will do." Kristen waved and walked toward her apartment.

Deanna's suggestion wasn't a bad idea. The thought of assuring herself that everything was fine with the twins would help ease the guilt of not being able to follow through on her promise. Even though the conversation with Clay had been awkward, he was bound to need help. Who would turn down free baby-sitting? Would offering for only one afternoon a week really be enough time to find out how Lark and Lea were doing?

She stared for a long moment at the door to her apartment, then unlocked the door. She couldn't just ignore what Gwen had wanted. She'd made a promise to love the twins and care for them, a promise that had mattered a lot to Gwen. If Kristen couldn't be the girls' guardian, the least she could do was keep an eye on them. And she just might have a way to do that.

But it would mean seeing Clay.

Every day.

It was the last thing she wanted, but she could do it... For Gwen.

Chapter Four

"Did you want me to continue watching the twins next month?" Marianne Quigley bent, put a brightly colored plastic toy on a shelf, then looked up at Clay.

He tried once more to get one of Lark's feet into a sock. She'd had two shoes and two socks on a minute ago when he got to the day-care center. How did she manage to get one foot bare so fast? And how was he going to put that shoe and sock back on with Marianne watching? The process was like trying to dress an eel. Not something he needed to attempt in front of an audience after a long, hard Monday at the office.

"You know I adore having these girls here, and I think the extra time I've spent with them has helped them adjust." Marianne knelt down beside Lark and took the sock from Clay's hands. In three seconds, she had the sock and shoe both on. "I had a call from a new family in town, though, and they wanted to know if I had a vacancy. You seemed unsure of your plans when the girls started here last week, so…"

Clay wasn't surprised that the new family had called. Probably the minute they'd asked for the best child care in town, someone had recommended Marianne.

When he'd first talked to her on the phone and she said that she watched kids in her basement, he'd pictured something small, dark, and crowded. She assured him it was nice and, since she was Midge's sister, he believed her. It turned out Marianne had an excellent space for kids that took up the whole lower floor of her home—a walkout level with lots of windows and a doorway. There was a big playroom, a quiet bedroom where children could nap, and even a full kitchen with little tables and chairs, as well as high chairs. No wonder all four kids in her care seemed happy. Even Lark and Lea, who had so much to get used to.

Which made Marianne's question tricky. What if she stopped taking care of the girls the minute he told her his plans? But he couldn't lie to the woman. Best to get it over with.

"I've been so grateful that you've been keeping the twins for me. You've been wonderful." Really wonderful. A lifesaver. "But I have been advertising for a full-time nanny. It would make my life a lot easier, though I don't have anyone lined up yet. Would you be willing to keep them through the end of July, and I'll try to find someone to start then?"

Marianne raised one eyebrow. "Have you gotten any responses to your ad?"

"No one I'd consider." Clay tried to keep the

frustration out of his voice. Each of the three people he'd interviewed had been terrible, a total waste of his time.

"I don't want you to think I'm simply trying to keep your business," Marianne said, "but I doubt you're going to have any luck."

Clay carried the diaper bag over to the double stroller he'd parked near the door, tucked it in the storage area, then strapped Lark in. "Why?"

"I just haven't heard of a lot of people working as full-time nannies in Abundance. I think they're easier to find in bigger cities, where more people can afford the expense of a caregiver for only one family. Most of the child-care providers in Abundance have home-based centers like mine."

Clay frowned. What she said made sense, and clearly, Marianne didn't need to lie to him to keep her numbers up. She had parents eager for her to take care of their children.

Plus, when he'd been thinking full time, he'd meant from six in the morning until whenever the twins went to sleep. Maybe the only people who worked those hours in child care were stay-at-home parents.

Just like being a business owner, being a guardian apparently meant a guy needed to face reality, take in new information, and adapt.

"I appreciate what you're telling me." He picked up Lea, strapped her in, and then looked at Marianne. "I'd like you to keep Lark and Lea long term. They seem so happy here. I'll have to find another answer for what to do after five thirty."

Marianne walked over to the stroller and rested a hand on the arm of each girl. "Nothing could make me happier than having them stay. I fell in love with these two within the first few minutes they were here. I would have been so disappointed if you'd left."

Yes, this definitely was the right place for Lark and Lea. "Thank you. I guess that other family is out of luck."

"I'll recommend another child-care center. Give them a Plan B."

Clay said goodbye and took the girls out to his car to head home. If the nanny idea wasn't going to work, he needed his own Plan B. He couldn't continue as he was, caught between the duty to spend more time with the girls today and his need to make the new game a success so he could spend more time with them later.

He'd had the twins in Abundance for five days, and each day he'd fallen further behind in preparing for the launch of Norware's new game on September 1, just over two months away. He could work each night after the girls went to bed, but he also needed time for doing laundry, picking up toys, and packing the diaper bag for the next day. And sometimes, if Lark or Lea had a particularly bad time the previous night, he collapsed into bed an hour after he got them to sleep.

All while launch day crept closer.

He needed to get ahead of the demands of the job, and that meant a renewed effort to fill both the chief development officer and the administrative assistant positions. He'd been so busy dealing with every crisis that arose that he hadn't taken time for the hiring that would actually let him get his head above water. No more. First, he'd advertise more broadly for someone to head up product development, then he'd go back through the applicants for the administrative assistant position. Surely he could fill that slot, even if he couldn't find someone as good as Brynn. Whomever he hired could help screen the candidates for the other position and schedule the interviews.

No more running around frantically, doing all three jobs himself. It wouldn't be easy, but he should be able to manage the twins by himself after five thirty.

It was time—past time—to hire a new administrative assistant.

"Let me tell you more about the job." Clay picked up his notepad from the edge of his office desk and scanned through the bulleted points he'd made before the first interview. In the two days since he vowed to get his life together by hiring a new administrative assistant, he'd picked the top five candidates and done three interviews yesterday, plus one earlier today. Only this last interview by Skype remained. He looked back up at the camera attached to his main computer screen. "I would expect you to answer the office phone, keep my calendar, coordinate meetings, and organize files."

"Organization won't be a problem. Color-coded folders are very near and dear to my heart." The brown eyes of the woman on the other end of the video call twinkled, as if she realized her love of office supplies was quirky.

"Good." Clay scanned the file on his screen. So far, he really liked this candidate, Samantha Wyler. She seemed bright, articulate, and more professional than the other people he'd interviewed. "I must be missing something in your file. I don't see your job experience for the past six years, just volunteer work."

"Unfortunately, that's accurate. I've been out of the workforce a few years for, um, personal reasons. But my volunteer role as president of the hospital guild was a lot like running a small business."

"Hmm." He found that kind of hard to believe, at least based on the hospital guild in Abundance. From what he knew, it was a bunch of nice, older women who took turns staffing the information desk, but maybe there was more to it or things were different in Texas or in a bigger hospital. When he looked Samantha in the eye through the camera, she calmly returned his gaze, and at this stage of the search for a new administrative assistant, he was getting a bit desperate. "You'd be moving from…Dallas?" He glanced out his office window, then back at the camera. He enjoyed the view of row after row of cornstalks, gleaming green in the summer sun, but someone from a big city might find it boring. Might find everything about his little town boring.

"I'd be quite excited to move to Abundance. I grew up there."

"You did?" Clay knew he wasn't supposed to ask personal details in a job interview, but if she was from the area, she might be more motivated to stay. Not run off to California with his next head of development. "I mean, if you don't mind telling me."

"I don't mind at all. I was born and raised in Abundance, and I've been wanting to move back home. That's why this job appealed to me. Wyler is my ex-husband's name. I'm a Hamlin."

"Samantha Hamlin?" He didn't remember a Samantha.

"Maybe you know my brother, Jack, or my cousin Abby? Jack's older, but Abby and I were in the same grade in school. She runs an antique shop on Main Street."

A heaviness settled in Clay's stomach, and he struggled to keep his emotions from showing. Abby was Kristen's older sister and, he was pretty sure, the person Kristen had complained to the most about him.

Which meant he needed to be as forthcoming as Samantha had been. "I…" He was going to come across as an idiot. "This is going to sound weird, but I don't want any issues later on. I grew up in Abundance, and your cousin Kristen and I dated pretty seriously. I moved back here after college. I was the guy…"

"O—hhh." Samantha drew the word out, understanding filling both syllables. "I did hear about that. But that was a long time ago. You must have been, what, eighteen?"

"Yeah."

She tipped her head and gazed off to one side, her mouth drawn up.

Then she looked back at him. "I appreciate your telling me. Honesty is vital to a good working relationship. But I don't think what happened between you and Kristen changes anything," she said in a matter-of-fact tone. "I want this job. I certainly wouldn't give up the opportunity based on a high school romance gone bad. And the good thing about me not having a paid position somewhere is that if you hired me, I could start sooner. I know my background isn't typical, but I believe I can do a really good job, and I think I'd love the position."

Clay studied her. Dark-brown hair, pulled up in a knot on top of her head. An easy smile. All in all, she seemed calm, classy, and capable. Norware could use a big dose of all three of those qualities.

His stomach eased and he let out a silent breath. "Let me check your references and get back with you."

"Sounds great. Thank you."

"Thank you. I'll email you later today one way or the other."

He gave a quick wave, said goodbye, and disconnected the call.

Barring a horrible reference, he'd found his new administrative assistant. Step one in his plan to grow his business, do a good job raising the twins, and stay sane.

Kristen pulled her silver Ford Escape into the driveway on the right side of the first duplex and parked behind Earl Ray's truck. She couldn't see the words "Hamlin Auctioneer Service" painted on the side door, but she knew it was her cousin's red vehicle as soon as she saw the Guns N' Roses bumper sticker.

She climbed out and could smell burgers grilling, as if someone might be having a picnic for Friday dinner. The street was quiet, and the buildings seemed nice. Four two-story duplexes, each with two driveways, each leading to a one-car garage on the outer edge of the building. Twin front doors stood side by side in the middle of each duplex.

Unit one, on the left of this first building, was Clay's. When Kristen had moved back to town a year ago, she'd asked around until she learned where he lived, then picked a different complex. At the time, she'd wished that after he finished college, he'd moved close to his parents in Denver instead of returning to Abundance.

But now, with Gwen gone, having Clay in Abundance was actually convenient. If she moved into one of these townhouses, she'd be in the perfect position to keep an eye on him and the twins. Oh, she loved her apartment across town and had been about to sign a lease for another year, but she had yet to return the paperwork. And the rent Earl Ray's wife, Stacey, had mentioned for these townhouses was less than what she was currently paying. The coincidence seemed too perfect, almost like a sign that moving here would be the right thing to do.

"Hey, Kristen, how's my favorite cousin?" Earl Ray, wearing a Kansas City Royals T-shirt, jeans, and a cap advertising his auctioneering business, strolled toward her.

She raised her eyebrows at him. "I have it on good authority that you tell Abby she's your favorite cousin."

Earl Ray grinned, and the skin around his green eyes crinkled. "When your family members are as beautiful and talented as mine, it's hard to pick a favorite."

Kristen gave a soft snort. "I have no idea how Stacey puts up with you."

"Neither do I," he said in a more serious tone as he pushed his glasses up his nose. "But I'm grateful every day that she does." He opened the passenger-side door of his truck and pulled out a bag from the hardware store. "So, you said you're interested in renting?"

"I remembered that Stacey said you had a townhouse or two that would be open soon. Is that right?"

"We've got one that will be available August first. You want to see a unit? I was going in to install this new mini-blind." He held up the hardware store bag.

"Lead the way." She hadn't really paid much attention to what the townhouses looked like when she'd dropped the food off with Clay. She'd been too focused on the twins.

Earl Ray grabbed a toolbox from inside the truck bed and walked toward the buildings. "I tell you, it wasn't a month after Stacey and I remarried that she said we needed to invest in some rental property. The minute this place came on the market, she wanted it. She was right. These are nice. Let me show you unit two."

"Unit two?" This one, the one right next to Clay's, was going to be available? That would be absolutely perfect.

Earl Ray unlocked the door and swung it open, waving her inside.

Kristen wandered through the downstairs. She'd thought she liked where she was, but this place had newer carpet. Bigger windows. A cute little extra half bath. A lovely kitchen with a stacked washer-dryer and granite countertops, not gray laminate. And a nice patio off the kitchen. Beyond the patio, the backyard consisted of well-kept grass with a few trees here and there. At the rear of the yard, a thicker stretch of trees gave privacy from the houses on the next block. She turned back toward the stairs, eager to explore the second floor.

"You like it so far?" Earl Ray ripped the plastic packaging off the new window blind.

"Like it? I love it." She named the price Stacey had mentioned. "Is that correct?

"Yep. That's with a ten percent discount, because you're family. Stacey and I want long-term, quality renters. We're not trying to rob people blind, just make a decent profit and provide a nice place to live."

"How soon is it available?"

"This unit's already rented. Number five, though, is the same as this one only a mirror image, you know, because it's on the left side. It'll be available August first, like I said."

Kristen stopped halfway up the stairs. "Earl Ray, I want this one."

"Unit five will be really nice once we're done with it."

She came back down the stairs. "No. This unit is perfect. There has to be a way."

"Why?" Earl Ray drew the word out and angled his head to one side.

"I just do."

"Uh-huh," he said in a tone that dripped skepticism. "It doesn't have anything to do with who lives in unit one, does it?"

"That's none of your business." Kristen walked toward him. "What do I have to do to get this unit?"

Earl Ray set down the window blind, and spread his hands, palms up. "Even if I wanted to, I can't rent you unit two. Have you heard that Samantha is moving back to town?"

"Really?"

"Yep. Said she'd had enough of Dallas. Probably has something to do with that scum ball she married and their divorce. Anyway, she called me last night, and the place is hers. I promised her it would be ready July twelfth."

Kristen drew in a quick breath. "Our cousin Samantha is the new tenant?"

Earl Ray nodded.

Since she'd moved back to Abundance, Kristen had noticed that living so close to all her relatives could sometimes be a little stifling, a little too much of everyone knowing your business. But for today at least, the fact that her dad and Earl Ray's dad and Samantha's dad were all brothers was going to solve everything. "I'm sure Samantha would be perfectly happy with unit five, and I could move in here. You said they're the same."

"They're the same except for the fact that unit five is a pit. I told Stacey that it didn't matter how much her friend begged, we shouldn't rent to her son and his two friends. We had to evict them last week. Three months without paying their rent and they trashed the place. The cleaning crew we use isn't available until mid-month. There's no way to have unit five ready when Sam's moving van arrives."

"I could clean it," Kristen burst out. It wasn't how she had planned to spend her free time for the next several days, and she'd probably have to work on her edits into the evenings and skip the big family Fourth of July picnic, but it would be worth it.

"Ooh, trust me, you don't want to do that. Seriously, unit five is bad. I've got a guy coming in tomorrow to replace one of the kitchen cabinets that's completely ruined. Dealing with the filth in the rest of the place will be a big job for our cleaning team, and there's three of them. You'd have to scour every inch of that kitchen, shampoo all the carpets, get out the stains, and repaint all the walls, as well as some of the baseboards. And—bear in mind I say this as a man who was single for many years, that whole time Stacey and I were divorced—the bathrooms are disgusting."

"But—"

"Stacey's going to insist that the place be up to her standards. Which, let me tell you, are pretty high."

"I don't care," Kristen said. "I can do all that." Yes, she'd have to edit quickly, but she could manage it. She could adjust her hours as she needed to, doing the cleaning early in the morning before it got steamy, then editing in the afternoon and evening.

"Why don't you wait until August first, let somebody else clean unit five, and move in there yourself? I'm sure from a few doors down you can run into Clay Norris just as often as you could from next door. I bet you can win him back."

Kristen's mouth fell open. "Win him back?"

Earl Ray gave an exaggerated shrug. "Hey, I understand how it is, having a romance end badly before you're twenty and never getting over it."

Seriously, was that what people would think if she moved in next to Clay?

No, of course not. It was Earl Ray, projecting his own experience.

"That's not it at all." Quickly, she explained about the twins. "You know good and well that if I tell Stacey this is about the welfare of those two little girls, she'll let me have unit two."

Earl Ray sniffed. "Fine. We can ask Samantha if she minds. If she does, though, unit two stays hers."

Kristen raised both fists overhead in victory. "Yes!" This was going to work. She just knew it. Why would Samantha care?

"Remember, even if Samantha does say yes, we'll be checking over unit five the evening of July eleventh. If it's not spotless, we're moving Sam into unit two and you'll just have to wait."

Kristen brushed aside Earl Ray's words. "Spotless won't be a problem."

If it meant she could keep an eye on the twins, unit five would be the cleanest rental in all of Abundance. She wasn't letting Clay's obsession with his career goals hurt Lark and Lea the way it had hurt her.

Chapter Five

Planning. Efficiency. Optimization.

The first time Clay had gone shopping with the twins, shortly after he'd gotten off the plane from Hawaii, he'd found the customer service counter at the store and thrown himself on the mercy of the older woman working there. She asked an associate to help him, a young mom who'd known what to buy and how to keep the twins happy while the four of them worked their way through the store. Since then, he'd been dashing to the nearby grocery to grab a few items at a time over his lunch hour, when the twins were at day care. Not in any way efficient.

That strategy was changing. Last night he'd made a detailed list of everything he and the girls needed to get through the next week. Top of the list, of course, was diapers. He'd added frozen pizza, diaper wipes, soda, and baby food, but he hadn't stopped there. He'd also included the things he had to make emergency lunchtime trips to get in the past week, like toilet paper, and added some healthy stuff for himself, like fresh fruit. This crisis lifestyle was going to stop. He would solve it all with one big Saturday morning shopping trip.

Then, after the household was well supplied, he'd feed the girls some lunch, tuck them in for their afternoon naps, and reread the resumes of the applicants for the head of development. Another step toward getting things under control.

"Okay, Lark, let's get those shoes on." He scooped her up from the living room floor, where she'd been studying her toes, and sat her on the couch. With almost as much skill as Marianne Quigley, he slid on her shoes and socks. "See? Uncle Clay is getting the hang of this."

Lark grabbed a handful of his T-shirt and brought it toward her mouth.

"Hey there, my goal was to get to the store drool-free." He handed her a bright pink teething toy. "How about this?"

Fifteen minutes later, after a last-minute diaper change and a search through the townhouse to find his keys, which were in his pocket the whole time, Clay carried Lea, then Lark, out to his car in the driveway.

"Hi, Clay. Hi, Lark and Lea." Kristen waved from in front of the duplex where Lucas lived. She set something in the open trunk of her car and walked toward him. "Where are you all off to this Saturday morning?"

"We're headed out to get groceries and supplies for the week." What was she doing here? He leaned down and made sure each of the girls had a toy to play with while he drove. Then he backed his way out of the car and stood up.

"I've got the list all made."

"You didn't order it ahead of time for pick up?"

"No. The store's website is too slow." The search engine brought up useless results all the time. Frankly, he'd recommend a complete redesign. "Besides, I want to see the full selection of baby-food flavors. Some of the ones I got before are sort of disgusting. Lea will eat anything, but Lark's pickier."

"Are you sure? I mean, the store's going to be swamped, two days before the Fourth of July. Couldn't you see all the flavors if you went to the baby-food website?"

Clay opened his car door. "No need to worry. I've got it all under control." He waved, climbed in his car, and started the electric engine. He even had the car's battery fully charged. Talk about good planning.

Kristen scrunched her mouth into a frown, waved, and walked toward Lucas's place.

Clay gave a sniff in her direction. *That's fine, Kristen. Take your disapproval to Lucas.* It was weird, though. He hadn't realized they knew each other.

But he couldn't worry about that now. It was already nine fifteen, and he'd hoped to be back right after ten, in time for the twins' morning snack. "Get ready, girls. We're going to do some speedy shopping."

They let out happy little coos.

He glanced at them in the rearview mirror with a bittersweet smile. They were definitely Gwen's daughters. His sister had loved to shop.

Once they reached the store, Clay found the last available cart with two seats for children and strapped the girls in. He even remembered to wipe off the seats in case the previous occupants had sneezed. Or drooled.

Drooling, he'd learned, was pretty much a constant with babies.

Then, despite the fact that the aisles were crammed with shoppers, he squeezed his groceries in around the diaper bag in the cart, rapidly working down his list.

Until he got to baby food. The number of choices was staggering. He gazed at the shelves, eyes glazing over. Would the one that looked like chopped up lasagna actually be tasty? He put two jars in the cart just as Lea began chewing on the strap of her seat. Clay tried tucking it behind her, but the instant he looked away, she had it back in her mouth. Though he'd wiped the seat, he hadn't even thought to clean the strap. There were probably germs all over it, germs that were stuck in between the fibers where a diaper wipe couldn't reach. Lark must have felt left out, not being part of the game of Hide the Strap, because she started fussing.

Clay made his baby food selections fast, but not fast enough. Lark's fussing escalated to crying. Not just a tear or two, but red-faced, tightfisted wailing. He rolled the cart back and forth a little in a motion he hoped was soothing.

Apparently, it wasn't.

Lea joined the fussing and began making a high, screeching cry, a cry that sounded remarkably similar to an angry chimpanzee Clay had once seen at the zoo. He unstrapped her and bounced her on one hip while pushing the cart and tossing items in with one hand.

Less than a minute later, both girls were screaming.

A woman walked by, pushing a cart holding a happy

toddler. She grabbed a large package of diapers and gave him a pitying look.

He gritted his teeth. It was so reassuring to know that fellow shoppers thought he was incompetent.

He put Lea back in the seat, strapped her in, and ripped open a package from inside the cart.

"Look! Yummy banana biscuits!" he said, putting a bright, happy note in his voice. He handed one to each girl.

Lark threw hers on the floor.

Lea crumbled hers and dropped it.

He opened his mouth, but then clamped his lips shut. His ability to fake anything close to a happy tone was gone. Yelling at the girls was not going to help.

He jerked a wipe from the bulging diaper bag and tried to clean up the crumbs from the floor. The screaming grew louder and was now punctuated with angry kicks against the plastic seat.

Clay crammed the wipe and the banana biscuit mess in an empty pocket of the diaper bag, then scanned his list. He hadn't even made it to frozen pizza or the soda aisle.

It didn't matter.

He grabbed two packages of diapers and a box of wipes, hesitating for a split second. There'd been that one epic diaper change that took five wipes. He tossed a second box of wipes in the cart and sped toward the checkout.

Ten minutes later both girls were strapped in their car seats, the groceries were thrown in the trunk, and Clay was headed home.

If he'd listened to Kristen, he could have pulled into one of the order-ahead spots. Someone would have brought his groceries out—all his groceries, including the pizza he'd planned to eat for lunch—and he wouldn't have even needed to take the girls out of the car.

Why did Kristen always have to be right?

At least they were on the road. Gray clouds were gathering on the horizon, but the crying had stopped and—

An icy frisson spread through his chest, and he jerked his head to look in the rearview mirror.

"Lark, Lea," he said loudly. "You girls don't want to take your naps in the car. Wait until...please, wait until..."

His heart sank. It was no use. All that crying must have worn them out. They were both fast asleep.

Which meant there wouldn't be any naps this afternoon.

No break for him. No time to read resumes. No chance to get his life under control.

Kristen gave an extra hard push as she tried to scrub a glob of goo off one of the kitchen cabinet shelves.

The goo remained firmly attached.

If only she'd listened to Earl Ray. Or asked to see unit five before she offered to clean it.

"A pit," he'd said. "They trashed the place."

Talk about an understatement. That was comparable to saying that the Piggy Platter from Whole Hog Barbecue was a large portion.

She'd never seen an apartment like unit five—ever. None of the apartments of her male friends in college had been this bad.

The air conditioning in the unit, which had sat empty for four days, hadn't been on until she came in this morning. The air was still sticky, and the heat only enhanced the smell, a hovering stink of stale beer, body odor, and rotting garbage.

The smell was only the beginning. Today, according to her plan, she needed to clean the kitchen. Before she'd seen unit five, she'd estimated that it would take about three hours.

Right.

Three hours wasn't going to make a dent. She'd spent the past hour and a half on these filthy cabinets alone.

Which meant she was falling behind the schedule she'd created, and that wasn't like her at all. She loved planning out her time, keeping to her schedule, and delivering her editing jobs on time or even a day or two early. But when she got a book to edit, she knew how to estimate how long it would take. She was good at her job and had lots of experience.

She had zero experience cleaning a place like this. Something she probably should consider a blessing.

She pushed back her sweaty hair with her upper arm, trying to keep her rubber glove away from her face. Disinfectant couldn't be good for her skin, and this stuff she was scrubbing out of the cabinets might well be a biohazard. With a sigh, she surveyed what was left to do.

The counters were covered in crumbs and stains. The linoleum looked as if the former tenants had poured a new sticky substance over it each week, experimenting to see which would create the most mess. One spill she could identify as spaghetti sauce, but the other dried puddles were—perhaps luckily—a mystery. A baked-on black crust encircled each burner on the stovetop. She hadn't even been brave enough to peek in the oven. The inside of the refrigerator smelled so bad she could barely stand to open the door. Couldn't the losers who lived here at least have unloaded the fridge before they moved out?

Maybe she should take a break from scrubbing and empty the fridge.

She stripped off her rubber gloves and threw them on the counter. Then she scrubbed her hands and dried them on a paper towel, texted Deirdre a photo of the stovetop, and headed out the front door toward her car. Thank goodness she'd thrown a box of trash bags in her trunk.

A crack of lightning lit the sky, and thunder rumbled. She quickly opened her trunk and pulled out a trash bag. Would one be enough? She draped it over the side of the trunk and peeled another bag off the roll. Better to have two, just in—

A gust of wind grabbed the trash bag she'd set aside and blew it across the lawn.

Kristen grabbed the other one, slammed her trunk shut, and chased after the escaped bag. The wind picked up, whistling through the trees, and the bag unfurled and went tumbling across the front lawns of the townhouses.

At last, half a block past Clay's unit, the bag lay on the grass as if worn out from its escape.

She planted one foot on it. "Ha!" Captured.

A second later, huge raindrops began spattering down. Great. Could this day get any worse? She wadded up the trash bag in her hand and stuck it in one of the back pockets of her shorts. Then she grabbed the bag from the grass, spread it over her head, and turned to sprint toward unit five.

"Hey, Kristen." Clay had pulled into his driveway, apparently done with his shopping. She'd been so busy chasing the stupid bag that she hadn't even heard him drive up.

His brown eyes held what might have looked like neighborly kindness to someone else. To her it looked like pity.

"Hi." She gripped the trash bag with both hands and dashed toward unit five.

Exactly what she needed when she'd been rained on, to see Clay looking completely dry and even more handsome than he'd been in high school. His brown hair was brushed back from his face, and his beard had a couple of days of stubble, drawing attention to his firm jaw.

Inside unit five, she slammed the door behind her and stomped into the kitchen.

Not fast enough, though, to avoid catching a glimpse of herself in the powder room mirror.

She stiffened.

Had Clay really seen her like this? The man who'd broken her heart?

Her makeup had sweated off, revealing every flaw in her complexion. Her hair went every direction, including straight up, as if it had been stirred. And she was pretty sure she smelled like that goo she'd been scrubbing out of the kitchen cabinets.

Oh, she was over Clay. Wouldn't have him back if he begged. Not with the way he'd hurt her.

Yet she wouldn't want anyone to see her looking this scary.

Especially not Clay.

A week later, on Saturday morning, Kristen stood outside unit five. She slid the key to her new townhouse, unit two, the one right next to Clay, onto her keyring, and she waved goodbye to Earl Ray and Stacey as they drove away.

Her back hurt from using the carpet scrubber, she may have lost some of her sense of smell from all the chemicals she'd used, and her nails were completely ruined, but unit five was ready for Samantha, and even finished a couple of days early. Stacey had given Kristen's cleaning her full approval, told her to consider her first month's rent paid, and said she'd be happy to hire her in the future if Kristen ever wanted to earn extra money. Kristen had been thrilled to get a free month of rent, but politely declined future cleaning. There had been a certain pleasure in making the grungy apartment shine, but she'd rather spend her time editing.

Which, except for church, was what she'd be doing the rest of the weekend. She had a lot to do to get caught up on her job, and hours of packing ahead of her. But before she went home, she wanted to spend a moment alone, soaking in the feel of her future home. She cut across the grass and climbed up the single step to her new front porch. She wouldn't have time to move in until next weekend, but she could at least walk through the unit and start to think of it as home.

Just as she fit the key into the lock, the door to Clay's apartment opened.

"Kristen...hi." His brows drew together. "What are you doing here?"

"Taking a quick look at my new home."

"You're moving in?"

"Next weekend."

He ran a hand along the side of his neck. "Next weekend?" A note of disbelief laced his words.

"I'm really looking forward to it. These are such nice places. Better than where I've been living across town."

Clay nodded, and she could see acceptance growing in his eyes. Not full-blown, I'm-ready-to-throw-you-a-housewarming-party acceptance, but some modicum of understanding.

"I'll be right next door, so maybe sometime I can baby-sit for the twins, if you'd like," she said, trying to keep her tone light, as if it was something that just happened to occur to her, not the whole reason she'd spent the past week testing the power of bleach.

"Yeah, maybe." He nodded stiffly, as if he wasn't buying her casual suggestion.

So much for his acceptance.

"I've got to get something out of my car." He gestured to where it sat in the drive.

"Any time you need help with the girls, I'm only a door away." She gave what she hoped was an encouraging smile, unlocked the door, and stepped inside. Really, this could work. It might seem a little awkward now, but it was the best way she could think of to keep her promise to Gwen.

She just had to give it time to feel normal.

"Shhh, Lark, you've got to quiet down." Clay patted her back as he held her over his shoulder and paced across the kitchen floor late Sunday night. "You'll wake up Lea."

Lark's concern for her sister's sleep was apparently minimal because, if anything, she got louder. Her little body was sweaty from being so worked up, and her face was flushed.

"This is ridiculous. How have they not come up with some way to run a diagnostic to see why you're so unhappy? I think you and Lea are getting used to me. Your diaper is fine. You're not hungry. You don't have a temperature. You don't seem to need to burp. I even changed you into lighter pajamas." He slid Lark down to where he could look her in the face. "Why are you so upset?"

No reply, only more wailing.

How long could a baby cry? This had been going on for almost an hour.

It felt like days.

Eventually, Lark had to run out of energy and want to sleep. He certainly did. He had to be awake in—he gave the clock on the microwave a pained glance—five and a half hours. It was going to be a hard day, with back-to-back meetings.

Should he call his mom to ask for advice? No, she and Dad had only gotten back to Denver yesterday. Dad was doing well, even better than the doctors had hoped, but Mom was probably asleep, exhausted. And he'd been trying not to bombard her with questions. She had enough to deal with without worrying about the twins or him.

Maybe Kristen was right. Maybe the twins would be better off with her. And now she was moving in next door, where she'd notice his every mistake.

He had to figure this out. What if all this crying wasn't

just frustrating to him, but equally frustrating for Lark because something was seriously wrong and he wasn't smart enough to know what to do?

His phone let out a *ding.*

He pulled it from his pocket. Some app he didn't even remember installing had sent a notification. He'd have to change that in Settings, and—

Lark had stopped crying.

The sound had startled her.

Her mouth pursed up again, and she made her angry face.

"No, don't cry. If all you need is a sound to distract you, listen to this." Awkwardly using the phone while holding her, he started his favorite playlist.

Her mouth grew tighter.

"Wait—I'll—I'll sing." People sang lullabies to babies all the time. But he didn't know any. He tried a popular song.

Lark's head tilted to one side. She didn't cry, but she didn't actually look happy, more like someone who'd ordered a half-pound burger and been served grilled fish.

Maybe she didn't know that song. What would Gwen have sung?

"Hamilton!" he said aloud. Gwen probably sang from the musical *Hamilton.* Thanks to the fact that she had insisted on loading the entire soundtrack onto his phone a couple of years ago, even he had been hooked on it for a while.

He scrounged through his memories and came up with a chorus. Probably off-key, and not sung too loudly because of Lea, but certainly identifiable as music from *Hamilton.*

Almost instantly, Lark's brow smoothed, her face grew less red, and, after a second, she rested her head on his shoulder.

Clay repeated the chorus, softer and slower, and moved toward the stairs.

She gave a sigh and nestled in closer.

A few moments later, he crept into the girls' room, and, in the dim glow of the night-light, he carefully—incredibly carefully—laid her in the crib next to Lea.

He took a step back and—

Banged his foot into the diaper pail, which he hadn't put back in the corner after he emptied it.

His body rigid, he glanced from Lark to Lea. *Please, please, please, don't wake up. Please don't cry.*

Neither one stirred.

He let out a huge sigh.

Lark was fine.

Lea was fine.

Nothing else really mattered.

For a long moment he stood there. His muscles relaxed, and he gazed at one girl, then the other. They were beautiful. The soft curves of their cheeks, the gentle swoop of their eyelashes, the way Lea had her right thumb in her mouth and Lark had her left thumb in her mouth, making them the cutest mirror images ever.

At last, he made sure the baby monitor was on.

"I love you guys," he whispered.

Then he went into the hall and quietly shut the door.

Chapter Six

At a quarter to eleven, Samantha Wyler collapsed on top of the comforter she'd tossed over the bare mattress in her new townhouse. She tucked one long edge of the comforter over herself and rolled, snuggling in as if she were the filling in a giant burrito.

Sometimes being a grownup meant having permission to do things the easy way.

Yes, she'd probably sleep better if she'd found a pillowcase and her sheets and blankets. But going to sleep wouldn't be a problem.

Tuesday, July 12, felt as if it had been eighty hours long.

She'd gotten up when it was still dark and driven five hours, the last leg up from Dallas, expecting to arrive at her new townhouse a half an hour before the moving van. The movers had texted her along the way, telling her when the GPS said they would arrive.

In theory.

Instead, after they had a flat tire and realized that the spare was missing, the movers had arrived three hours late, after two in the afternoon. And she started her new job tomorrow.

So she'd carried in the lighter boxes, ordered the movers pizza for dinner, even searched around for the little blue stickers that indicated the number of each box or piece of furniture.

When the van finally was unloaded, she'd waved off the evening offers from her family to come by to help her unpack. She was too tired to care about the boxes that meant she couldn't park in her garage or about getting her kitchen set up properly. And too exhausted to explain to the whole Hamlin clan why she'd come back to her hometown.

Sure, some of the family knew. Her parents down in Florida, where they'd moved years ago. Here in Abundance, her brother, Jack, and her favorite cousin, Abby. For now, that was enough. Tonight was not the time to discuss the fact that she had some trust issues with... well, everyone she wasn't related to.

So she'd found her clothes for tomorrow, her coffee pot, her pillow, and her comforter. Not her sheets or pillowcases or blankets, which didn't seem to matter a bit.

She let out a long sigh and pulled the comforter tighter around her. Her body grew heavy. Sleep. Wonderful...sleep.

"Oup-oup-ou-ooooooooooooo."

She sat bolt upright in bed. What was that noise?

"Oup-oup-ou-ooooooooooooo." Louder this time.

How could the barking—no, it could only be called

howling—be so loud? Was the dog the size of a horse?

Samantha had next-door neighbors with dogs back in Dallas, two of the most adorable pugs on the planet, little fellows who occasionally let out a bark or two. But she couldn't even hear them unless she was outside at the same time they were.

This was no pug.

And it was still howling.

She laid back down with one ear mashed into her pillow, the other covered with two layers of the comforter.

It didn't help.

Okay, maybe the dog/horse/coyote had been let out for one last potty trip before bed. Give it ten minutes and the disturbance should be over. She could use this time productively and mentally go through all the places where she needed to change her address again, since she'd switched units with Kristen.

Speaking of which, if she'd been in unit two like she was supposed to have been, she probably wouldn't even hear this dog. Kristen never had said why she wanted to trade when she called. She'd better—

The howling stopped.

Hallelujah, the owner must have taken the dog inside. Samantha nestled back down under the covers, turned her pillow cool side up, and willed her body to relax.

"Oup-oup-oup-oup-ou-ooooooooooooo!"

She hadn't thought it could be louder. It was.

She jerked up and scrambled to find her phone on the nightstand. 11:07. Weren't there any noise standards in this town? Rules that said that after ten o'clock people— and their pets—had to be quiet?

Surely, it would end soon.

She opened the notes app on her phone and typed in a few of the places she'd given her new, or what should have been her new, address. She'd have to send an email or go online to update them that she was not in the unit she'd expected to be in, but in the one next to the dog.

Now it was 11:15, and the beast was still howling.

All right. She'd had enough. Was the owner planning to leave the animal out all night? She couldn't go pounding on doors randomly, but if someone had a light on, she could at least ask if the dog was theirs.

She climbed out of bed, slipped on her flip-flops, and—

Her bathrobe was nowhere to be found. It was probably in one of the boxes she had yet to unpack. She dug out her rain slicker, pulled it on over her short nightgown, and stomped down the stairs toward the front door.

Outside, insects hummed, and the air was thick with humidity, but she didn't see any dog.

Another howl, sounding as if it came from behind the duplex.

She tucked her hair behind her ears and tromped through the dewy grass around her side of the building to the back.

There it was. No fences separated the yards of the individual units, and the creature was making that racket right under her bedroom window.

It wasn't as big as she'd expected. Since there wasn't much light back here, only moonlight, she couldn't quite tell what breed it was. A beagle, maybe? No. A basset hound. Big ears, stubble legs, and really strong lungs.

"Elvira, get back here."

Samantha jerked back.

The whisper seemed to have come from the far corner of the building, but she couldn't see anyone.

She edged closer, her feet sliding a little where the dew had dampened her flip-flops. But now was not the time to worry about wet feet. It was time to have a serious discussion with the dog's owner about the need for quiet when it was nearly midnight.

She took one more step, and the dog galloped toward her, barking at full volume, pulling out its leash with a metallic whine.

"Be quiet, dog. People are trying to sleep," came another loud whisper. A flashlight beam appeared on the grass, and a tall figure moved toward Samantha.

In spite of the leash, the dog still came closer.

Adrenaline shot through her. What if it bit her? "Stay," she shouted. "Sit."

The dog obeyed.

"Whoa," the owner of the flashlight said, no longer whispering. "No wonder she's making such a fuss. Who are you?" He shone the light in Samantha's face.

She covered her eyes. "I'm the person who just moved into unit five and can't sleep. And your dog was barking and howling long before I came outside to see what was going on." She shoved her hands on her hips. "You can't let her out when it's almost midnight. She's too loud."

The man lowered the flashlight beam and moved closer. "I'm sorry. The people who live in seven are never home, and the guys who used to live in five never really seemed to care."

She almost growled. "Maybe they didn't just move in and have to get up and start a new job first thing in the morning."

"Aww, man, again, I apologize. Those guys did stay up pretty late. You know, college kids."

This guy didn't seem that much older than a college student himself. Again, though, it was hard to see in the darkness. She could only tell that he was tall with long hair, longer than hers.

"Lucas Stiner." He held out his hand.

"Samantha Wyler." She shook it.

"I live in six. This is, uh, this is Elvira."

She wasn't sure, but she thought he rolled his eyes.

"I didn't name her."

The dog's name wasn't the problem. But hopefully Samantha had already made her point about the noise. She took a step back. "I've got to go to bed."

"Right. We'll try to be quieter." He tugged on Elvira's leash. "Let's go in, girl." The two of them headed around the far corner of the building, Elvira's dog tags jingling.

Samantha squished her way back through the grass to the door of her home, arriving just as the door to the next unit shut behind a wagging tail.

She went back into her new townhouse, kicked off her flip-flops, and rubbed her wet toes dry on the carpet. Probably, down at unit two, all was quiet. Plus, Kristen worked from home. If she needed to sleep in a little because she was kept up by the neighbor's dog, it was no big deal. Agreeing to trade units had been a mistake.

Just like so many of her decisions in Dallas.

Probably including her plan to move back to

Abundance. Sure, it was nice to be around family, but coming home felt like an admission of failure and, with her lack of work experience, might be an even bigger nightmare when she started her new job tomorrow.

Ugggggh. She ran her hands over her face as she trudged up the stairs. That was a train of thought she'd been trying not to take. She needed rest, and she needed to keep telling herself she could handle this job and make a new life for herself here in Abundance.

Now, with her mind headed straight down the track toward regret and worry and self-doubt, it wouldn't matter how quiet her new townhouse was.

She was never going to get to sleep.

Elvira raised her nose into the morning breeze and turned to peer past Lucas, toward the townhouses.

There, coming out of next door, was the woman from last night. She walked out to the blue Nissan parked in her driveway, opened the front passenger-side door, and leaned into the vehicle.

Lucas hadn't heard her come out, but he wasn't Elvira. He bent down, scratched the basset hound behind each large brown ear, and studied his new neighbor.

Last night, he thought she'd been wearing a polka-dotted raincoat and flip-flops. Now, she appeared ready for the workday in tan pants and a shirt that was a vivid blue, the very shade he'd envisioned for the uniform of Lexi Ballard, the sexy heroine in the book he was writing. And without the raincoat, his neighbor had curves that definitely made the July morning better.

Clearly, another apology on behalf of Elvira was in order.

"C'mon, big mouth." He gave the leash a tug and started toward the Nissan.

Elvira trotted along beside him, occasionally dawdling to sniff the ground.

Lucas hadn't gotten a very good look at the woman last night in the dark, but she was striking, really striking. Shoulder-length brown hair. Tanned skin. The most striking thing about her, though? How much she resembled Lexi, his fictional heroine.

Not something he planned to mention.

"Hi there." He came up closer to her car.

She backed out of the vehicle, turned, and gave a smile that didn't quite reach her big brown eyes. "Hi," she said quickly.

"Um, I wanted to apologize again for Elvira's barking last night. Tell me when you normally go to sleep, and I'll make sure to take her out before then. She and I are still getting our routine figured out."

Samantha bent down, let Elvira sniff her fingers, and rubbed her head.

Elvira moved closer, eager for more.

"That would be wonderful. I'm in bed by ten thirty."

Ten thirty? He was just getting settled in at his computer about then. Sometimes, if inspiration struck, he might be up writing until three.

Samantha rubbed one of Elvira's ears for a moment and stood back up. "You said you're getting your routine figured out. Did you get her recently?"

"An old guy who's a friend of mine wasn't able to keep

her anymore because of medical issues. I told him she could live with me, and I'd bring her over to visit him sometimes."

Samantha's features softened. "That's very kind of you." She glanced at her car. "I'm sorry, but I need to get to work." Her gaze ran down Lucas's outfit and her forehead crinkled.

A ratty T-shirt from a cosplay convention, cutoffs, and his oldest tennis shoes without socks. "I don't go in until later," he said.

"What do you do?"

His stomach twitched. "I—" For a second, the urge to tell her the truth, the whole truth, was almost overwhelming. But it was best to stick with the same thing he told everyone else. "I work at Whole Hog Barbecue. Most nights as a server, but on the weekends I'm in charge of the pit."

"I've eaten there. It's really good."

Her tone was polite, but it lacked the interest he'd hoped to hear. But what was he thinking? That she'd be as excited by brisket and dry rub recipes as he was? That she'd understand how long he'd worked at Whole Hog before Jordan let him handle the pit, especially on weekends when the crowds were the heaviest? No, he wasn't a corporate executive, but he was proud of what he did in his day job. "What about you?"

"I'm working for Clay Norris over at Norware Games."

"He's a good guy, a friend of mine. Did you know he lives in the unit on the end?" Lucas gestured toward the first building.

"Really?" She glanced over. "Kind of weird, but I guess there aren't that many apartment complexes in Abundance. Anyway, Norware seems like a nice place to work." She took a step back. "Well, thanks..." She gestured toward Elvira, waved, and got in her car.

Nothing about her body language said she was impressed with a twenty-seven-year-old man who cooked barbecued ribs. No matter how incredible those ribs were.

Would she possibly be impressed if he told her about his other job, as a science fiction writer? Would she find him fascinating, creative, irresistible?

Probably not.

It wasn't as if he was ever going to take the chance to find out.

Chapter Seven

Clay hurried down the hall on Wednesday morning, arriving at his office ten minutes late.

Samantha sat in the lobby near what would be her work area.

"Come in, come in. Sorry I kept you waiting." He ushered her past her desk and into his office, then gestured to the guest chair and sat down at his desk. "I got delayed dropping my nieces off at day care."

"Abby told me about your sister." Samantha sat down. "I'm so sorry for your loss."

"Thank you." He picked up a folder from the side of his desk and placed it in front of him. "Did she tell you about the twins?"

Samantha nodded. "I imagine the adjustment has been pretty challenging."

"Yes, and it's been an adjustment for them too, of course. The learning curve has been steep for me, but I'm getting the hang of it." He opened the folder. "Let's get you started here."

Samantha looked past him, eyes widening at the monitors that lined the corner and side of his desk. She wasn't used to working in the tech industry, so four huge screens probably did seem like a lot.

"I'll need you to sign these papers to get payroll started." He slid them across the desk. "And"—he dug into his top drawer—"these are the keys for the front door and your desk."

For the next half an hour, Clay showed Samantha around Norware Games, which took up part of a building put up a few years ago on the outskirts of Abundance. He introduced her to all the staff and showed her where their offices were. First, the empty office next to his, where hopefully he'd have a new head of development soon. Then he introduced Gareth and Heidi, the young programmers who, along with Clay and some freelancers, helped with development. Glen, the finance guy. And Julie M. and Julie C., who handled the marketing. After that he walked Samantha to her desk and went over her day-to-day responsibilities, telling her the software they used for email, scheduling, expense tracking, and the website.

Even though he had to explain a comment from Gareth, because she didn't know that a MMORPG was a Massive Multiplayer Online Role-Playing Game, she seemed as if she could handle the job. She asked good questions and, from her nonchalant expression, found most of what he said familiar. Bit by bit, the knot in his stomach eased.

Eventually, he checked his smart watch. Almost 10 a.m.

"I've got a phone call I need to take. I'll probably be on for almost an hour. Just let my calls roll to voice mail."

"I'll start on those emails you wanted sent."

"Excellent." He stood and went into his office. Already, he felt more optimistic.

Despite the delay this morning, day care was going well.

The Abundance Community Church seemed to have him on a weekly list for a casserole delivery. Someone had stopped by last night with a yummy-looking Mexican dish that he planned to eat tonight.

And hiring Samantha Wyler would work out fine.

His business could get back up to full staff, and he could get the hang of things with the twins. Any day now he'd have his life completely under control.

At ten thirty, as soon as she felt she could reasonably step away from her desk, Samantha found her way to the ladies' room. She locked the door, backed up against it, and bent forward at the waist, inhaling deeply.

She'd thought she could do this, thought she was prepared, but other than answering the phone and sending an email, she had no idea how to do this job. She didn't know how to schedule a meeting electronically, had no idea how the expense software worked, and had never even heard of the software they used for their website.

She never should have married Reg. Never should have dropped out of college to put the lying, cheating jerk through med school. Never should have quit working in retail when he got hired on with the orthopedic practice in

Dallas. And never should have spent her days currying favor with the wives of the heavy hitters at the hospital.

The only things her time on the auxiliary board had taught her were how to deal with massive egos, how to organize an event, and how to keep smiling, even when she wanted to strangle one of the fellow members.

But she'd moved back to Abundance. She'd taken this job. And she wasn't brainless.

Surely, if she drove home and searched for a YouTube video on her personal computer over lunch, she could figure out how to use that fancy calendar program. Tonight, she'd go back online and learn how to use that expense software.

No matter what, she couldn't go back to Dallas.

Sure, for a while at least, she could live on her alimony. But she needed a purpose here in Abundance, a reason to get out of bed each morning, and some kind of identity that wasn't tied to her ex-husband.

It wasn't like there were tons of jobs available in her hometown.

She had to make a success of this one.

"Hey, Kristen, get the door," Earl Ray shouted.

Kristen dashed over and opened the door to her new home, then scooted out of the way to allow her cousins Earl Ray and Jack to bring her couch into the living room. "Over there, please." She gestured to the longest wall in the room.

Coming in right behind them, Hank and Seth carried her mattress.

"Thanks, guys." She pointed upstairs. "Nate and Dad have the bed frame all set up in the bedroom on the right."

She was so lucky to have family willing to help her today. All it had taken was a couple of phone calls. Mom and Dad, of course, had volunteered as soon as she told them she was moving. But four of her cousins were also helping—Earl Ray, Hank, Jack, and even Samantha, who'd only recently moved in herself. Her cousin Becky had sent her husband, Seth. And of course, Abby, the world's sweetest sister, was here with her husband, Nate.

"Kristen," Mom called from the kitchen. "If you'll show me where you want things, I'll get your dishes unpacked."

"That would be great." Kristen hurried to the kitchen and answered Mom's questions.

"It's going fast, isn't it?" Mom pushed back her blond hair and unwrapped the newspaper from around a pitcher.

"It sure is," Kristen said. "By the end of the afternoon, everything should be unloaded from Hank's and Earl Ray's pickup trucks. I'll unpack more tomorrow after church, but I should be back at work on Monday." She could already picture herself, sitting at the table in her pretty new kitchen, editing that intro to calculus textbook, her latest project for Fibonacci Publishing. It had taken a while, after things fell apart in Chicago last spring, but now that she was freelancing forty hours a week for Fibonacci, her career was back on track.

And, starting today, she'd be right next door to Clay, where she could keep an eye on him and the twins.

"Where do you want this?" Samantha called from the hall.

Kristen walked to the doorway of the kitchen.

Samantha was carrying a small chest of drawers.

"In my bedroom. Here, let me help you." The chest wasn't that heavy, but it would be awkward for one person to get it up the stairs.

A few minutes later, they scooted it into position.

"Thank you," Kristen said. "I really appreciate you coming over to help. You only moved in a few days ago. You probably still have boxes of your own to unpack."

"I do." Samantha chuckled. "But some of them aren't very pressing. It's not like I need boots or my winter coat."

Kristen pulled her T-shirt away from her collarbone to let a bit of cool air in. "That's the truth." The high today was supposed to be 97°F. "But I bet it would have been at least as hot in Texas."

An odd expression passed through Samantha's eyes when Kristen said the word *Texas.* Sadness, or regret, or maybe a mixture of both. "Oh, yeah." Samantha brushed at the top of the chest of drawers as if she saw dust. "Texas is hot."

Kristen wasn't sure what to say next. She knew Samantha was working for Clay and knew she had gotten a divorce, but she didn't know the details. Even though they were cousins, Kristen really didn't know Samantha that well. She was Abby's age, seven years older.

"How's your new job?" Kristen finally said, picking up a box. Hopefully she'd found a safe topic.

"It's going well," Samantha said, but her shoulders stiffened. "Clay's a little stressed out with the twins, but Norware seems like a good place to work."

Kristen moved the box to the corner on the floor, out

of the way, and stood up. Samantha worked with Clay every day. She'd have a perfect window into his life, even better than Kristen would living next door. But...

It was a small thing to ask. They were family, and it was for a good cause. "You, uh, you wouldn't be willing to do me a favor, would you?"

"What?" Samantha walked toward the bedroom door.

"I'm concerned about the twins. I don't know if you knew this, but I was actually supposed to be their guardian. Their mom, Gwen, was a dear friend, and she talked with me about it but hadn't had time to change things with her lawyer."

"Oh." Samantha stopped, turned back, and looked at Kristen.

"I want to be sure the twins are well cared for, so if you ever hear anything that makes you nervous, will you tell me?" Kristen's words tumbled out too fast.

Samantha's eyebrows drew together, and her lips tightened as if Kristen had asked her to go through Clay's desk and steal any cash she found. "You mean...you want me to spy on my new boss?" Her voice held a note of incredulity.

"Not exactly spy," Kristen said slowly.

"Clay seems like a good guy. I understand that things didn't turn out the way you were expecting, but he is the girls' uncle. If I heard something that made me nervous, I'd tell him so he could fix it. He seems like he's trying to do the best job he can."

Kristen took a step back. "I guess that makes sense."

"I'm going to go bring in another box." Samantha headed out into the hall.

An ache built in the base of Kristen's throat. Really, she was trying to do a good thing, keep an eye on the twins. Gwen had seemed so earnest that day they'd talked. Kristen had agreed to take care of the girls. No matter what had or hadn't been set up legally, she couldn't ignore Lark and Lea.

And she needed—after the mistakes she'd made in Chicago with Dylan—to do something right. If she ignored her promise to Gwen, she'd be an even worse person than she already was. She had a responsibility, an obligation to the twins.

So why did everyone act as if she was interfering?

Chapter Eight

At five thirty on Wednesday, Kristen knocked on the door of Clay's townhouse. She'd been just about to end her work for the day and had been feeling quite pleased with her progress on the intro to calculus manuscript—particularly the errors she'd caught in the chapter on derivatives—when she'd gotten an urgent text from her cousin, asking her to come next door.

What was Sam doing at Clay's? And why did she need help?

Samantha threw the door open. "Can you please give them dinner?" She gestured to Lark and Lea, who sat on the living room carpet, taking things out of a diaper bag. "I almost forgot that Abby's husband, Nate, was staying late at his office today to review some legal matters related to my divorce."

"Sure, but—"

"You're a lifesaver." Samantha grabbed her purse from the couch.

"Where's Clay?"

"There was a fire in the office next to Norware. Nothing got burned on our side, but he has to stay until the fire department says everything is safe for our part of the building. He asked me to pick up the girls from child care and said he'd be home as soon as possible."

"Oh."

"Thanks so much. I owe you one." Samantha dashed out the door.

Kristen drew in a deep breath. Talk about unexpected. She glanced down at the twins, who were looking adorable, dressed in matching pink rompers.

Except that Lea was chewing on a diaper.

Kristen took it away from her, grabbed a toy beside the couch, and handed her that instead. Then she shoved all the other supplies back into the diaper bag and set it on the couch.

A small piece of paper remained on the floor. She picked it up.

"Diapers, wipes, changing pad, snacks, formula..." The list, in Clay's neat handwriting, went on for about fifteen items. The paper was creased, as if it had been folded many times, as if he might consult it whenever he got ready to leave the house. Kind of surprising. Personally, she had a deep appreciation of checklists, but that kind of attention to detail wasn't Clay. He was more of a big-picture thinker, a problem solver.

Possibly why he'd started his own company. Which, even though she'd never admit it out loud, impressed her.

She tucked the list into a mesh pocket on the outside of the diaper bag, where it would be easy to spot. Then she sat on the floor and talked to the girls and played with them, letting them get used to her for a few minutes until it was time to feed them dinner. Hopefully she could figure out what it should be. She'd taken care of her niece, Emma, when she was little, but every time Abby had told her what to do.

"That's why I have a cell phone," Kristen said to Lark and Lea. "If I need to call to ask what to feed you guys, I know Abby will help."

She let herself through the baby gate and walked into the kitchen.

Two high chairs stood at the ready, and on the table beside them sat two clean bowls and two sippy cups. Two jars of a pasta, tomato, and beef baby food, two smaller jars of pears and raspberries, and even a little spoon, as if Clay had laid everything out before he went to work. On the counter, she found formula, ready to mix. No need to call Abby. The dinner plan was obvious.

When she peeked in the fridge, though, it was pretty empty. Sure, there were lots of condiments on the door, but the only real food was some leftover pizza still in the box, a half-empty two-liter bottle of soda, the tail end of a loaf of bread, and some moldy grapes.

An odd tightness formed around Kristen's heart. Clay was working a lot harder at taking care of the twins' meals than his own.

Granted, he wasn't with them now, but even she couldn't blame him for a fire in the business next door to Norware. Emergencies happened.

Between that list in the diaper bag and the way he organized things in the kitchen, it was clear he was working hard at the details, as if he was trying to do the best job he could with the twins.

Maybe she was wrong. Maybe he really did love them. Maybe even with a forever kind of love—the kind she hadn't thought he was capable of.

She pressed her lips together and, following the directions on the package, prepared some formula. This was not the time to think about the past.

Soon, she had each girl strapped into a high chair and was feeding them dinner, a process all three of them enjoyed.

A spoonful for Lea, then a spoonful for Lark. Or maybe it was the other way around. She wasn't totally sure which twin was which.

"It really doesn't matter what your name is," Kristen said to the twin she thought of as Lea. She wiped a drip of baby food off the side of the little girl's mouth. "You and your sister are the cutest, sweetest babies in the whole world." She hesitated. "Except, of course, for Emma when she was a baby."

One of the twins reached for the spoon, and the other girl kicked her feet against her high chair and giggled.

Kristen let out a contented sigh as she scooped up more baby food with the spoon.

Her role in the twins' life might not be what she'd hoped, but right now, enjoying this moment with them, she was too happy to care.

At ten after six, Clay unlocked the front door of his townhouse. The soft sound of singing came from the living room, but it didn't sound like Samantha. It sounded like—

He opened the door.

Yep. It was her.

Kristen Hamlin sat on the floor, holding a stuffed toy elephant, making it dance from side to side, and singing along as "Come Dancing" by The Kinks played from her phone.

The back of his throat grew tight, and for a moment he stood there, silent. She'd loved that oldie back in high school, had played it when they were in the car, when they studied, and when they picnicked out at Hideaway Falls. Even made him dance with her by the picnic tables at the base of the path to the falls.

Not that he'd needed much convincing to take her into his arms that day.

Or would need much convincing to do the same today.

He swallowed, forcing himself back to the present, back to reality. "What are you doing here? Where's Samantha?"

Kristen spun toward him, eyes wide. "Oh, I didn't hear you come in." Her cheeks grew slightly pink. "Samantha forgot she had an appointment. She asked me to feed the girls."

Clay's chest tensed, as if armor plating were interlacing around his ribcage. Any second now, Kristen would accuse him of being a terrible parent, despite the fact that the fire hadn't even been at Norware and the fact that he had a responsibility to make sure things were safe for his employees. None of that would matter to Kristen.

"If you want to take a shower, I'm happy to stay with them a little longer."

Clay glanced down at his clothes. A fine layer of soot mixed with sweat covered everything he wore, and his shoes were damp where he'd stepped in a puddle of water from the fire hose. Yeah, a shower would be wonderful, especially one where he didn't have to put the girls in their crib, scrub his body as fast as humanly possible, and listen the entire time for one of them to start crying.

"If you really don't mind, a shower would be great," he said cautiously.

She looked up at him. Her face held no anger. "Really. I'd love to spend more time with them." She tipped her head toward the twins. "Especially if you'll tell me which one is which."

"This is Lark, and this is Lea." He pointed to them in turn.

"Thanks." She put the toy elephant in Lea's outstretched hands and then smiled up at him.

She was so beautiful that all he could do was stare.

Her golden hair gleamed in the evening light that came through the window, and her face was almost glowing.

She looked gorgeous and…right. As if she belonged in his apartment, belonged with the twins, belonged in his life.

The thought echoed through his mind the way the air sometimes shook after someone slammed a door hard.

What he wouldn't give to undo the past.

"You look incredible with them." The words tumbled out before he could stop them. "I mean, they seem so happy with you. You'll make a really good mom one day."

Her mouth fell slightly open. For a second she sat there, eyes narrowing.

He knew her, knew her so well, that he could tell what was in her mind. She was thinking that she should be the twins' guardian, that if they were with her, they'd be happy all the time.

She glanced down at the girls, then looked up at him again. The tension around her eyes eased, and her face held the same peaceful smile she'd had before. "Thanks. Now you go take your shower."

Kristen looked from one of the twins to the other, happily playing on the carpet.

Upstairs, the shower ran. Here, the twins babbled to each other.

Lark crawled away, grabbed a toy caterpillar, and rolled to her back, gnawing on one of the caterpillar's antennae.

Lea studied her sister, scooted toward Kristen, and started to climb onto her knee.

Kristen helped Lea onto her lap. She ran a hand gently over the little girl's head, then closed her eyes and buried her nose in Lea's light-brown wispy hair, sweet with the scent of baby shampoo. Her whole body felt light, relaxed, and peaceful. Was this what it was like to be a mom? To feel such completeness, such purpose in caring for someone?

She'd always dreamed of having children.

When Clay had come home, it had been almost as if they were a family.

But they weren't. She had to remember that.

Her stomach contracted, and a chill radiated out from

her core, shooting down her arms. She pulled Lea closer, but the contentment she'd felt was gone.

Clay had broken their engagement more than ten years ago. In spite of how much she'd loved him, in spite of the months they'd secretly made plans, in spite of the white dress hidden in the back of her closet, it had been over. They weren't running away to Vegas to get married as soon as she—who'd been a summer baby and graduated from high school at seventeen—turned eighteen.

He had thrown their love away. Thrown her away. Left her to be laughed at by the girls she'd so proudly sworn to secrecy about their plans. He probably thought he'd find some prettier, smarter, more sophisticated girl at college.

Before that day, she'd never known she could run so fast to get away from someone. She'd darted behind the shed where Dad kept his lawnmower, climbed the neighbor's fence, and raced across his cornfield, feet pounding on the hard earth between the hip-high rows until she collapsed. She'd never known a person could cry so much that her head throbbed, her eyes felt raw, and red blotches formed on her skin. Never known that the word *heartbreak* described a literal, physical pain that burned in her chest and her stomach and the back of her throat.

To say the breakup had been hard on her was like saying a tornado could mess up a woman's hair.

If that book she'd read, *A Better You in Ninety Days,* was right, that breakup had messed her up for years. She'd felt so worthless, so unlovable all through college. If she was fully honest with herself, she'd still felt unlovable last year when she got involved with Dylan. Whenever a guy had shown any interest in her, it had meant too much. It had meant, even if only for a few weeks, that the empty place inside her chest hollowed out by Clay had been filled.

But those relationships never lasted. With every guy who dumped her—and it was always the guy who ended things—the hollow place inside her grew larger. Year after year of bad decisions and feeling farther from God. Year after year of feeling more and more worthless.

All of which began with Clay.

So what was she doing pretending to be a member of his little family?

Hanging around him was like pressing a steam iron onto the tender skin exposed after a sunburn had peeled. Why would she do that to herself?

Oh, her former neighbor Deanna had probably been right. There would be times when Clay needed a break. Even days like today, when an emergency arose, that help was essential. Living so close, she could forge a role in the twins' lives, maybe even become like an aunt to them.

But the farther she went down that path, the more she'd be around Clay. She'd thought, by living next door, she'd have a front seat to all his mistakes.

What if, instead, she saw more of what she'd seen today, evidence that he loved the twins? The more she saw him in a good light, the more painful it would be.

Earl Ray and Stacey would let her out of her lease. She could move back to her old apartment complex. She could pretend, as she had since she returned to Abundance last year, that Clay had moved to Denver with his parents. She could avoid all this misery.

But—

She pulled Lea closer and gazed across the room at

Lark, who was now trying to put her foot in her mouth.

But she'd made a promise to Gwen.

"You two are what matters," she said.

And weren't there signs, like the fact that Clay had shoved the girls off on Samantha today and the way he barely had groceries in the fridge, that he was struggling to hold things together? Signs that one day, everything might fail?

No, she had to stay in the townhouse next door. She had to keep an eye on things.

But she couldn't let herself believe, not even for a minute, that there would ever be anything between her and Clay. She couldn't pretend.

Footsteps thudded down the stairs.

Clay appeared, wearing tan shorts and a navy polo. "I can't tell you how much I appreciate your watching them while I got cleaned up."

Time to get out of here. She didn't need to stick around, noticing the sheen of his damp hair and the way his arm muscles had filled out since high school.

She gave Lea a quick squeeze, then set her on the floor. "No problem." She walked over to Lark and touched her on the shoulder. "Bye, girls."

"Really, Kristen." Clay reached for her hand. "Thank you."

The scent of him fresh out of the shower hit her, and her heart twisted as memories came flooding back. Clay, his hair still wet, picking her up for school. The way she knew he raced out of the house to have a few minutes with her. The way he grinned at her as she climbed in his car. The way he drove one block, then stopped at the stop sign to kiss her—often until a car pulled up behind them and honked.

No. She couldn't go there. She backed away and gave her head a quick shake, as if she might jostle the thoughts out of her mind. The sense of smell had a strong connection to memories. She'd experienced it before in situations that had nothing to do with Clay. That was all these were—memories. The past. And she was moving forward.

"No problem. I'm glad the fire didn't damage your offices." She waved and slipped out the door.

Two seconds later, she was in her own apartment.

She ran upstairs, flopped down on her bed, and pulled a pillow to her chest, staring up at the ceiling of the room.

"I hope you can see this, Gwen," she whispered. "It's taking everything in me, but I'm keeping my promise.

Chapter Nine

Elvira waddled across the kitchen toward the back porch door, tags jingling. She turned and gave Lucas a soulful stare, accompanied by a soft whine.

"No problem, girl." Lucas shut his laptop. He'd far rather take her out for a late-morning walk than spend more of his Thursday updating his social media presence.

Sure, he enjoyed sending out a monthly newsletter to his readers with information about his writing. He didn't even mind taking care of the techy side of his author website. But he hated being on social media.

More specifically, he hated being on social media as Kendrick Larson, author of the Seven Moons sci-fi trilogy. He didn't mind posting as Lucas Stiner, talking about new barbecue rub recipes, but being online under his pen name felt like a lie. He wanted to make a real connection with his readers. But with every comment he posted as Kendrick Larson, he had to be careful so that no one would figure out that Kendrick Larson was actually Lucas Stiner, the guy who was eager to do a Jamaican jerk recipe on fifteen pounds of baby back ribs.

Although he was a decent writer and his readers seemed to love his books, he wasn't a huge success—yet. His "writing career" could be seen by some as a foolish waste of time. Jacqueline had certainly thought so.

One day, though, once he had more books out and more readers found him—uh, found Kendrick Larson—he'd be the success he dreamed of, a *New York Times* bestseller. Then, and only then, would he be willing to share his secret. Then people would come up to him at Whole Hog or at the grocery store or at Cassidy's Diner and tell him they'd read his new book and loved it.

But these days, letting that information out, taking the chance of having people laugh at him, wasn't an option. He had a deadline. He couldn't open himself up to that kind of negativity. If he was going to finish this book on time, anonymity was essential.

Lucas nodded to himself, grabbed Elvira's leash, and shoved it in his shorts pocket, just in case. Most likely, during the day in the backyard he wouldn't need it. Unless she was on the trail of a squirrel or rabbit or unsettled by someone new who'd moved in next door, the basset hound was about as low-key as a dog could get. He let her out the door onto the back patio and followed her into the grass.

It was a beautiful morning. Bright-blue sky, rich-green trees at the back of the yard, and an occasional breeze that made things comfortable despite the humidity. Sometimes Missouri served up a day in July that was absolutely perfect.

Completely the opposite of the planet where Captain Thad Stephens, the main character in Lucas's series, had just landed. Thad was far, far from Earth, somewhere in the Andromeda galaxy on an M-class planet, where the temperature was barely above freezing and the terrain was dry and rocky, lined with deep chasms.

Lucas frowned and paced back and forth through the grass, thinking about the next scene. So Thad had landed on the planet surface. Now what? Things were getting rather dull in the middle of book four.

What if... What if Thad wasn't alone? What if he'd been followed to the planet by his arch nemesis, Klodon, the Telegodian?

Lucas could picture the scene.

Klodon would appear from behind a boulder, his weapon aimed straight at Thad's chest.

Lucas squinted into the middle distance, focusing every sense on visualizing the scene. His body tensed as he imagined the alien before him.

What would Thad do?

Take cover.

Lucas's heart pounded as he darted behind the trunk of a tree. The oak wasn't quite the craggy outcrop he envisioned on the planet, but it was close enough.

Thad would reach for his communicator to signal for help, pull out his own weapon, and peek out from behind the outcrop of rust-colored rock. Then what?

Lucas crossed his arms, tapping one finger against his bicep as he thought.

He had written almost this same scene in book two. His readers would be bored if he wrote the same thing again.

What if... What if this time Klodon brought help? What if six other Telegodians appeared behind Thad?

Thad would hear the crunch of their boots against the rocky soil, dive over a chasm, and roll until he could take cover behind his shuttle craft.

Lucas dove, memorizing every motion and every feeling to get them down on paper later. The twist of Thad's head when the gravel crunched, the kick of adrenaline hitting his veins, the thud as his shoulder hit the ground once he'd cleared the chasm—uh, the basset hound—and the disorienting spin as he rolled behind the shuttle craft.

Which, most days here behind the townhouses, was Lucas's professional-quality backyard grill.

He stood, brushed the grass off his T-shirt, and looked over at Elvira. One would think she'd be disconcerted since he just dove over her, but she seemed completely absorbed with rolling on her back and wiggling in the grass.

"Come on, Elvira." He clapped his hands together and turned toward his back door. "I need to get this on the computer."

No more ridiculous posting on social media under his pen name. Nope, it was time to get some words on the page. This was going to be a good writing day.

Elvira trotted over beside him, then turned and gave a loud woof.

"Uh, hi." The voice hovered somewhere between amusement and alarm.

Lucas spun to his right.

The new neighbor. Little Miss Corporate Casual in khaki pants and a pink polo shirt. Her dark hair framed her face and fell, silky smooth, to her shoulders. Her lips were rosy and full in a way that, if he was writing in Thad's point of view, he would call "kissable."

And her big brown eyes were narrowed ever so slightly as if she had seen him dive over his dog and roll across the grass.

Why hadn't he stayed on Facebook?

Samantha set a glass jug of sun tea on her concrete back patio and tried not to let her mouth hang open as she stared at her new neighbor. What could she say to a grown man who was playing in the backyard with his dog as if he was nine years old?

"Um, hi." Lucas edged toward his back door. A flash of embarrassment shot through his gray eyes.

At least he recognized that his actions weren't normal. That probably meant he wasn't insane.

Sure, he looked good, with his T-shirt and shorts showing off long, tanned, muscular arms and legs. And she wasn't usually a fan of long hair on guys, but his blond hair, which fell past his shoulders, looked right. As did his beard. But still. "What were you doing?"

"Um, exercise." He nodded emphatically, as if to convince her. "Tae kwon do."

"Really?" She knew nothing about tae kwon do, but she didn't think it involved jumping over a dog. "You do this often?"

"First time." He glanced up and off to one side. "I was trying some moves I saw on the internet. I've, uh, got to go. I need to call the motorcycle shop to see if the repairs are done on my Suzuki." He looped a finger through Elvira's collar and hustled the dog inside, sliding the door shut behind him.

Inside. Exactly where she should be, spending her lunch hour on the last lesson of the class she'd found online about how to use the expense software. The sun tea didn't need her help to brew, and she didn't need to be standing out here, thinking about her next-door neighbor, no matter how good he looked. If she had the smallest flicker of interest in ever dating someone again, which was highly unlikely, it wouldn't be him.

The last thing she needed was some immature kid.

Who took foolish risks like riding a motorcycle.

And learned tae kwon do off the internet.

Chapter Ten

A *thump* sounded from outside Clay's patio door on Sunday evening.

He stepped past the twins, who were strapped into their high chairs, to check outside, and he caught a glimpse of Kristen as she disappeared around the edge of her townhouse. He still couldn't come to grips with the fact that she was living right next door to him. But Earl Ray was her cousin. Maybe he and Stacey had given her a discount. Still, it was weird, and Clay was hyper aware of having her so close by.

And now a large green flowerpot had been added to her patio.

Wow, that thing was big. It had to be plastic, or she never could have carried it. Even though he hadn't heard her, she must have been out there earlier. On the patio she'd lined up a trowel, a plastic cup, and three large yogurt tubs, each holding a good-sized tomato plant.

She returned, carrying a bag of potting soil over her shoulder.

Clay moved back from the door. "Ladies," he said. "Change of plans. You'll be dining alfresco this evening."

Before today, he'd never really thought about the fact that, unlike at some complexes, the back patios here had no partitions between them. Now he realized the beauty of the design.

He got out the food for the girls' dinner, little pieces of finger food, including some frozen peas that he popped in the microwave for 30 seconds. He stirred them and checked the temperature in three different parts of the bowl with his finger. Good, not too hot. Nothing the girls could burn their tongues on.

He opened the sliding glass door and, careful not to look toward Kristen, carried the food out to his patio table, then he brought Lark outside, high chair and all. He adjusted the patio table's umbrella so that the high chair was in the shade. Once Lark was happily situated, he went back inside, brought out Lea, put her chair beside her sister's, and slid one of his patio chairs into position facing them. Then casually he let his gaze drift over to Kristen.

Her blond hair shone in the evening sun, and she looked downright gorgeous in her navy shorts and red tank top.

"Oh, hi," he said, trying to sound nonchalant. "Isn't it kind of late in the season to be planting tomatoes?"

Kristen dug her fingernails into the top of the potting soil bag and ripped a large opening. "It is, but Aunt Patsy had these extra plants and said she was going to pitch them if no one took them. She swears I'll have ripe cherry tomatoes in less than a month."

"That's fast." And very fortuitous for him, since he'd been wanting to talk to Kristen. All he needed was a smooth transition to explain why he and the girls were out here when always before he'd fed them inside. "These back patios are one of the best features of this complex. It's restful out here, you know?"

"It is." Kristen seemed more focused on waving to Lark and Lea than on talking to him. "Hi, girls." She beamed at them.

"I thought the twins would enjoy some fresh air and"—a brainstorm hit, an even better reason for being outside today—"I've been letting them eat more real people food. Feed themselves and all. They seem to like it better than that goo in the jars, but not all of it gets to their mouths." Not by a long shot. "This way I don't have to clean up the floor."

"Still as efficient as ever, huh?" Kristen asked, her tone a shade cooler than he would have preferred.

So he was efficient. That was a good thing. Especially now that he had the twins to take care of. No matter, at least he and Kristen were out here at the same time. A little more small talk and maybe she'd warm up.

He set food on the girls' high chair trays so they could pick it up and feed themselves, giving them both a small sample of each type of food, some of which he'd—uh—efficiently cut up earlier. Peas, tiny chunks of cheese, and little bites of cantaloupe, which smelled pretty tasty, by the way. He tried one. "Mmmm, yummy." He pointed to the fruit as he took a seat in the patio chair.

Kristen lifted the bag of potting soil and awkwardly

poured some into her flowerpot.

"Here, let me help you." Clay got up and took the potting soil from her. "You direct it, and I'll hold the bag."

Stiffly, Kristen allowed him to take it. "I'm perfectly capable of handling it."

"I know you are," Clay said quickly. "But it's the least I can do after you helped me out the day of the fire."

Kristen acknowledged his comment with a twitch of her shoulders and focused on the potting soil that was rapidly filling the big flowerpot.

This wasn't going as he'd planned.

Lark let out an unhappy cry.

Lea, who had eaten all of her own cantaloupe, had reached over and started on her sister's.

Clay gave the bag one last shake, set it on the patio, and brushed off his hands, which were covered in dirt. "Can you watch them for a minute? I'll be right back. I need to wash up and serve seconds."

Kristen's mouth drew into a thin line, but she nodded.

As fast as he could, Clay dashed into his townhouse, leaving the door to the patio open. He cleaned his hands at the kitchen sink and returned to give a few more bites of each type of food to Lark and Lea.

Lea grabbed two pieces of cantaloupe, one in each hand, and shoved them both in her mouth, making one of her cheeks stick out like a chipmunk's.

Kristen giggled.

Clay's heart swelled. *Thank you, Lea, you little cutie.* "I think she likes cantaloupe, don't you?"

"I think she loves it." Kristen's eyes twinkled.

Apparently, her disapproval of him had eased, and

they could have exactly what he'd wanted—happy, casual conversation about the twins. The perfect lead-in. Because he wasn't a person who believed much in coincidence or signs, but somehow having Kristen move in next door seemed like it meant something. Like maybe he had a chance.

"Clay?" Kristen moved closer to him.

"Yes?" How to word this? He didn't know for sure when he could take her out, but surely he could find a teenage girl willing to baby-sit one evening.

Kristen's brow furrowed. "How come there hasn't been anything in the paper about Gwen's funeral? I know your parents might need to wait awhile until your dad is better, but shouldn't it be soon?"

The back of Clay's throat went raw.

Gwen.

He hadn't even thought about her today, and it had barely been a month since she passed away. "The doctors say it's going to be quite a while before Dad can move around easily. My folks decided it would be best to have a memorial service in the fall, sometime between Gwen's birthday in October and John's in November."

"Oh." Kristen glanced down, then looked up at him. "I'm sorry about your dad."

"Thanks.

"But he's supposed to recover fully?"

"According to the doctor's predictions, yes." Clay swallowed hard. "The information about the memorial service should be in the paper soon. Mom was waiting to hear back from some relative of John's to make sure the date would be good for him."

"Will you be sure to tell me?"

Pinpricks stabbed the base of Clay's throat. "Yeah, I'll tell you." Just what he'd expect from Kristen. No matter what had happened between them, she'd always been such a loyal friend to his sister. Even a few weeks ago, when she'd been so misguided with her idea about being the twins' guardian, she'd been trying to be a true friend to Gwen.

"I want to be there for the service. I...I..." Kristen spread her hands wide, fingers outstretched, as if grasping for a way to express her emotion, then let her hands fall. "I still can't believe she's gone. I actually sent her a text the other day, and then I realized..." She blinked, took a half-step back, and looked away.

"I know what you mean. Some days, I think about her almost every hour. Today I... I haven't. I've been caught up in other things." Some brother he was. Forgetting about Gwen as if she didn't even matter.

He ran a hand through his hair.

"I don't know why on earth they decided to go on that helicopter tour," he said. "Those things aren't regulated the same way as commercial flights."

"Do you know what happened?"

"No. I don't think we'll ever know. Probably pilot error." Clay's words sounded bitter, even to him.

"It could be that the pilot did everything right. Sometimes bad things happen and no one really is at fault."

"Yeah," Clay said. But he didn't believe it. Someone was to blame for his sister's being dead, and it wasn't just the pilot. If he'd been in Hawaii, as Gwen had asked...

A tiny piece of cheese flew down and hit his leg.

Lea waved another bite in the air, then launched it toward the ground.

"I guess the girls are done with dinner."

Kristen stared at him, nodded, and then knelt and arranged the dirt in her flowerpot.

Clay unstrapped Lark from her high chair, took off her bib, and brushed some crumbs off her shirt. "Would you keep an eye on Lea for a second?"

"Sure.

He carried Lark inside, wiped her hands with a washcloth, set her on the living room floor, and closed the baby gate to keep her in. Then he went back out for Lea. He gave the high chairs a quick brush, brought them in, and waved good night to Kristen.

Obviously, tonight was not the time to ask her out.

How could he have even selfishly considered it? It was too soon. It felt disrespectful to Gwen.

Kristen pressed the potting soil firmly around the last tomato plant, the one she was most optimistic about, the one with four blossoms and a tiny green tomato on it. She grabbed her big plastic cup of water and poured some on each of the three plants. Her gardening complete, she stood, brushed the dirt off her fingers, and studied the back door to Clay's townhouse.

Sometimes she got so wrapped up in thinking about how much she missed Gwen that she forgot that Clay had lost his sister and must be going through even more grief. The pain in his brown eyes when she brought up the funeral had been heart-wrenching.

He acted as if he felt guilty for not thinking about Gwen more. But a person couldn't grieve all the time. There was no way to control how to process grief, no right way to do it. He needed to be kinder to himself.

She let out a wry chuckle. A month ago she'd never have imagined that she, the president of the I-Hate-Clay-Norris Club, would ever feel sorry for him.

Was she nuts?

This was the guy who'd destroyed her self-esteem and made her feel unlovable for years. The reason for all the tears she'd shed on that simple white dress that still hung in the back of her closet, wrapped in a plastic garment bag. The reason she'd made one bad decision after another in relationships.

But none of that could erase the two and a half years Clay had been the center of her world. Every memory of those years seemed to be engraved in her heart. All the way back to that first day he stopped at her locker, early in her sophomore year. She'd thought he was there to pass on some message from Gwen, who was home with a cold.

"Do you want to sit with me at the game Friday night?"

A fluttery feeling had built in her chest. She must have misunderstood. "With you and Gwen?" Ugh, her voice wobbled.

"No-oo." He brushed a hand across her arm. "Just with me. As a date."

The fluttery feeling disappeared, squeezed out by the pounding of her heart. "S—sure," she mumbled.

"I'll pick you up at six thirty." He grinned at her and walked down the hall.

She slid her Algebra II book back in her locker and headed off to math class bringing nothing but her purse and her notebook for Sophomore English, a class she'd had two periods earlier. Clay Norris wanted to go out with her.

Unbelievable.

Over the next two months, though, the unbelievable became the norm. Clay taking her out every weekend, Clay walking her to class, Clay asking her to the Homecoming Dance.

After Homecoming, they were officially together, with no mention of dating other people. Gwen, who might have felt odd, having her best friend and brother dating, said they were made for each other. Kristen had felt so lucky, so sure it would last forever. Other couples fought and broke up over stupid, little things. She and Clay worked out little issues logically.

Until they hit an obstacle that wasn't little. Until his ambition to work with computers left no room for her.

But that had been more than two years later.

After all that time spent together, with that type of connection, was it any wonder she could read the grief in his eyes today? See the guilt when he mentioned forgetting about Gwen's death, even if only briefly?

She was a decent person. She cared about people who were grieving. Even Clay.

She picked up her gardening supplies. For a long moment she stood there, staring at the tomatoes. Was it more than that? Had she buried the truth the same way she'd buried the roots of those plants?

Did she still love him?

Was that why her heart twisted when she saw the pain

in his eyes?

No.

Maybe.

She didn't know.

She carried the yogurt tubs to the recycling container in her garage and put the potting soil bag in the trash.

Maybe her mixed-up feelings were an effect of losing Gwen.

She hung the trowel on a pegboard hook in the garage and watched it sway. Eventually, it would still. But would her mind? Somehow, she had to get some clarity and come to grips with her true emotions, but—

Oh, she knew what to do. She'd call Deirdre.

A moment later, after she went inside, she texted Deirdre. She was the perfect person to talk to. Calm, unbiased—because she lived in Chicago and had never met Clay—and the type of friend who told you the truth even if it wasn't what you really wanted to hear.

Crisis at work, Deirdre texted back. *I'll call tomorrow night.*

Not the answer Kristen wanted, but she sent back a thumbs-up emoticon.

She'd just have to wait.

Chapter Eleven

Samantha glared at the lifeless computer monitor on the desk in the smaller bedroom of her townhouse, the one she was using for a home office.

Earlier this morning the business next door to Norware had brought in electricians to run tests to make sure no further shorts would occur. Preventing another fire was certainly a good thing, but those tests, which all seemed to involve shutting off the electricity at the worst possible moment, made it impossible to work in the office. Not the best way to kick off a new week, especially not with only three weeks left until the new product launch. Clay needed her to send out emails while he went across town to meet with the insurance agent, so he suggested she work from home.

"I know it's a lot faster to cut and paste with two big windows open at once," he'd said, after he eventually accepted that no one could work at Norware today. "If you don't have a big monitor at your place, I'll carry yours out to your car and you can bring it back in tomorrow."

A reasonable plan. The monitor wasn't even that heavy. But here in townhouse number five, she had electrical issues of her own.

As in no power to the big monitor or the little lamp on her desk.

The only other possible work area she had, her kitchen table, was covered in her good dishes, the ones she'd unpacked last night but hadn't found a place to store.

Two minutes ago, she'd gone downstairs and checked the breaker for this bedroom. It seemed fine, but she'd flipped it off and on again, hoping to get the monitor to work.

No such luck.

Lucas broke open the cardboard box and pulled out three paperbacks, one copy of each of his first three books. He hadn't been expecting them until Thursday, but they were already here, three days early.

One by one, he examined them, running his fingers lightly over the covers, flipping through the pages, smelling the fresh ink, and stopping now and then to admire the tiny graphic of a cratered planet that he'd used to indicate a break between scenes when he laid out the interior himself.

They looked fantastic.

He'd been unsure about having the covers of the first three books redesigned. After all, he'd paid good money for the original covers. But the original designer had stopped accepting jobs and taken a demanding position as a graphic artist for some toy manufacturer. His new designer had convinced him that all the books in the series should match, and her initial ideas for redoing the first three covers had been so striking that Lucas had paid her to work up the final versions.

"Look, Elvira." He angled the books, one at a time, to where the basset hound could see. "Don't you think these new covers were worth every penny? Don't they make you want to read the books?"

Elvira blinked but gave no indication that she planned to start reading sci-fi.

He shrugged and stacked the books on his kitchen table.

Enough admiring. Time to get to work. He ran a hand through his hair, still wet from the shower, smoothed it out a bit, and pulled on his writing hat.

Dorky? Yeah, perhaps. It was more of a helmet than a hat—smoky gray, with a large red medallion front and center—and had been part of a cosplay costume from a convention he attended three years ago. But it wasn't as if anybody ever saw him wear it. Or knew that it helped him get into the mood of his fictional world.

He opened his laptop and dug through the notes on the table, ready to start Chapter 22.

The doorbell rang.

Was the delivery guy back?

Lucas pulled off the hat and tossed it on the table.

Someone pounded on the door, again and again.

Whoever it was, it wasn't the delivery guy. He always rang the bell and left. This sounded like an emergency.

Lucas hurried to the door and yanked it open.

"I'm sorry to bother you. I tried calling Stacey and Earl Ray, but neither one is answering." Samantha stood on his doorstep, her hair slightly messy, her blue skirt and white button-front shirt rumpled. "Would you have time to show me how the breaker box works in these townhouses? I thought I understood it, but even though the breaker for the front bedroom is on, I don't have power."

"Sure," he said.

She took a half-step forward, as if she thought he'd show her the breaker box in the little closet off his kitchen.

His muscles tensed. Not happening. Not with his scene notes and laptop and writing hat lying out in plain view. The last thing he needed was another woman telling him that his dreams were laughable.

"One second." He held up a finger to keep her on the porch, slid his feet into the tennis shoes he'd left by the couch last night, and snagged his keys from the coffee table.

"Let's see what's going on at your place," he said, as he joined her on his porch. "I'd hate to give you directions that wouldn't work."

"Thank you."

"Have you had this problem before? The guys who used to live next door never mentioned any issues with the breakers."

"Just my luck."

"I'm sure the two of us can figure it out." He shut his front door and locked it. Tension drained from his shoulders. Everything related to his writing was now safely out of sight.

Exactly the way he planned to keep it.

Normally, he was as brave as the next guy. Spelunking, scuba diving into fresh-water springs in the Ozarks, rock climbing on the bluffs along the Missouri River—none of those things gave him the slightest of qualms. In fact, he loved the adrenaline rush that came with a bit of danger.

But taking risks with the real identity of Kendrick Larson?

That scared him.

Because when Jacqueline had told him that his writing was a waste of time and that his dreams of being an author would never amount to anything, she'd come close to creating a self-fulfilling prophesy.

He'd almost never written again.

"Come in. I'll show you." Samantha led Lucas into her townhouse.

Thank goodness he was willing to help. Having a neighbor who was home during the day did have advantages. And he seemed like a decent enough guy, just young.

She walked into the utility closet off the kitchen and pointed to the list on the inside of the breaker box door. "See, it says 'Front Bedroom' beside number two. Even though that breaker's in the On position, there's no power to the big computer monitor or my desk lamp."

"Let me look." Lucas stepped into the utility closet behind her. "Yep, it's the same setup as mine."

She peeked behind her, over her shoulder at him. Before, when she was alone, she hadn't really noticed how small this closet was. "I don't see how that monitor and lamp could even draw enough power to flip a breaker. And I don't think my laptop was using any power. The battery was charged."

"Were you using any electricity in the bathroom? This breaker at the very bottom labeled 'Upstairs Bath' is flipped."

"Oh." Samantha peered down at it. "It's so dark down there, I didn't even notice it. I do have a curling iron and a flat iron plugged in." Which she should have shut off before she ran next door. Except apparently, they were already off because the breaker had flipped.

"A curling iron and a flat iron? Why do you want to straighten your hair *and* curl it?"

"Actually, they both can curl your hair, just different types of curls." She could explain further, but she really doubted he wanted to know. And how she did her hair, after it got so frazzled hauling her stuff home from the office, wasn't the problem. "That breaker for the bathroom shouldn't affect the bedroom. The bedroom is breaker number two." She turned to face Lucas, thinking she could squeeze past him, out into the kitchen. No such luck. He blocked the whole closet doorway.

"I don't think those labels are completely accurate." He reached past her and flipped the breaker for the bathroom to On. As he drew his arm back, it brushed against her.

A jolt of awareness shot through her. She scooted over slightly and bumped into part of the HVAC unit.

"Hey, careful there. That ductwork has sharp corners." He reached one hand behind her shoulder and pulled her slightly forward, closer to his chest.

Her heart rate picked up. Heat seem to radiate from his fingers through the fabric of her shirt, and some sort of electricity now hovered in the air, rooting her to the spot, a spot far too close to him. Close enough to notice how his hair, still slightly damp, was drying into waves. How the shadow of yesterday's stubble lined his neck below his beard. How his gray eyes had little starburst patterns around the pupils.

She blinked. What on earth was she doing? "I'll, um, I'll just dash upstairs." Her voice came out shaky.

He took a step back.

She slid past him and ran upstairs.

"Okay, the stuff in the bathroom is unplugged," she called down a minute later. Then she went into her study and sat down at her desk, her heart rate almost back to normal. It was time to act like a professional and get this fixed, so she could work on those emails. Not the time to think about the fact that Lucas had been so close to her that she could have reached up and—

"Try your monitor," he called.

She flipped it on, and the image from her laptop screen appeared. "It works!" she shouted.

"Sweet."

"The electrician who wired these places must be an idiot," she said as she came back down to the first floor.

"I imagine the builder did it himself." Lucas walked out of the kitchen. "You know, to save some money."

"But didn't the construction have to be inspected?" She stopped on the bottom stair.

"It's a small town." He shrugged. "Who knows? The inspector might have been the builder's brother-in-law."

"Yeah, I guess that might be how things work here." In fact, from what she remembered growing up, it sounded precisely like how things worked in Abundance.

"You know, just to be on the safe side, if I were you, I wouldn't leave your curling iron or flat iron plugged in when you're not in the bathroom." Lucas stopped, facing where she stood on the bottom stair, the height of the step making their heads almost level. "It kind of seems like a fire hazard."

"You're right." She nodded. "Thanks for your help. All this trouble because I wanted to curl my hair."

He tipped his head to one side. "You don't need to curl your hair. It looks great straight."

"Thanks." Her cheeks felt hot, and she glanced down. She hadn't been fishing for compliments.

"No, really. It's one of the first things I noticed about you. It's beautiful."

A rush of pleasure shot through her, and she looked up into his eyes.

That was a mistake.

The feeling of electricity surrounded her again, making the air thicker, the room warmer, her feet cemented in place. Her mouth went dry, and she swallowed.

Very slowly, almost as if he too was powerless against the strange phenomenon, Lucas raised one hand and ran it down the side of her hair, his fingers trailing over her shoulder and—

The air conditioning kicked on with a whir.

She jerked back and raised a hand to the edge of her collar, nervously twisting it. Good grief, what had almost happened? She edged past him, down the last step and into the living room. "Thanks again for fixing the breaker." She checked her watch. "Yikes. I was supposed to meet my cousin Abby for lunch three minutes ago."

He moved toward the entryway, but stopped, one hand on the doorknob. "Hey, would you like to go to dinner? Say Thursday night?"

"That would be great." Only the moment the words left her mouth, she realized it wouldn't.

"I'll pick you up at six." He waved and left.

She stared at the closed door. What on earth had happened back there on the stairs?

And what was she doing agreeing to have dinner with him?

That was a terrible idea.

Her response had slipped out before her brain even engaged.

But...

Her monitor was fixed

And there was certainly no shortage of electricity in her townhouse.

Chapter Twelve

Lark yanked the pacifier out of her mouth and flung it so hard that it flew out of the crib and bounced off the wall.

Then she started screaming again.

Her tone was slightly higher than Lea's, but volume-wise, the twins were equally matched. Both of them were loud. Really loud. And even in the dim glow of the night-light, their little faces were red.

Clay pressed both hands against his temples and moaned. "What am I going to do with you guys?" It was almost three in the morning. His Wednesday morning meetings started in five hours. He'd changed and fed the girls more than an hour ago, but they hadn't gone back to sleep, no matter what he'd tried.

He'd burped them. He'd walked with each of them, trying to do that easy swaying that sometimes soothed them. He'd sung them every *Hamilton* song he knew. He'd checked their temperatures. He'd pressed on their gums, trying to determine if they were getting new teeth. And he'd begged and pleaded with both of them to please, please go to sleep.

None of it had helped.

"Okay. Time for a new plan." He pulled out his phone and ran a search on the internet for reasons why babies cried.

He picked a source that seemed reputable and ran his finger down the suggestions the eminent pediatrician listed, mentally checking them off. He'd already addressed every idea the doctor suggested, except driving Lark and Lea around in a car, which had never seemed to help. He couldn't get both of them back out of the car and into their crib without waking at least one of them. Didn't this doctor have any good ideas?

Then he spotted a paragraph at the end.

"Sometimes, even when perfectly healthy, for no reason that can be ascertained, babies just cry."

"Some help you are, Dr. Bianco. Where did you get your degree?"

He scanned the italics at the bottom of the webpage. "So what? It's not like they know everything at Harvard Medical School. Or like you learned anything in your thirty years of practice." He shoved the phone back in the pocket of the shorts he slept in and turned to the twins. "There has to be a reason you guys are so unhappy. C'mon. We'll walk some more."

He picked up Lark, settling her on his shoulder, and began to walk around the twins' bedroom, jiggling her gently. This would be so much easier if he could carry both of them at once, but if one of them lunged away from him, he didn't have a spare hand to stop her. One at a time was the only safe choice. "You guys have got to go to sleep. I won't be worth much tomorrow at the office on less than four hours of sleep."

Round and round he walked, carrying first one girl, then the other, quietly singing every *Hamilton* song he remembered and making up lyrics for those he forgot.

After what seemed like hours, Lark's head sank onto his shoulder, one of her little hands clasping his T-shirt.

Clay's heart leapt. Finally, they were getting somewhere.

A moment later, Lea shifted in the crib and stopped crying.

The silence washed over him like a balm.

"See?" he whispered. "See how your sister has her head down? You can do that too, Lea. You can lie down and go to slee—"

Lea jerked and began screaming again.

Clay let out a long sigh. He laid Lark in the crib and picked up Lea, then trudged into his bedroom and checked the clock. *3:37* glowed in bright green numbers. Was he ever going to get to sleep? Tomorrow was going to be—

The doorbell rang.

Now what?

Kristen stood on Clay's small, concrete front porch in her bare feet. She pulled her purple terrycloth bathrobe tighter around her waist and retied the sash. Probably she was crazy to be doing this, but the girls had been crying for more than two hours. Thanks to the fact that there was only a single wall between their units, she certainly couldn't sleep, not with how loud they were wailing.

Plus, she was worried. Her niece Emma had never cried that long when Kristen watched her on overnights.

The door flew open. "Yes?" Clay spat out. He wore a T-shirt and running shorts and his hair stuck out on one side as if he might have been asleep.

In the faint light that shone from the fixture over the steps, she could see the tension in his jaw.

But now that there was no wall separating her from the girls, their cries from upstairs seemed even louder and more concerning. "Are they okay?"

Clay's nostrils flared. "Kristen, I—"

One of the twins gave a particularly high screech, cutting off his angry words.

His face crumpled. "Aw, I don't know. I've done everything I can think of, everything the baby website says to do." He looked up the stairs. "They're too exhausted to realize they need to sleep. And I can only try to calm one of them at a time."

"Let me try walking with one of them." Kristen stepped inside.

"Are you sure?"

She nodded. "Whichever one is fussier."

"That would be Lea. I almost had Lark asleep a few minutes ago." He led the way upstairs into the twins' nursery, then picked up a screaming girl in a yellow sleeper and held her toward Kristen. "Here." A note of guilt tinged his voice.

Kristen took Lea into her arms.

Clay reached out and gave the back of Lea's yellow

sleeper a small caress, then picked up Lark.

That tender gesture toward Lea—who had to be trying Clay's patience—squeezed uncomfortably at Kristen's chest. He was, in spite of what he'd done to her, a nice guy.

That was a good thing. The twins needed a kind, loving guardian. But somehow, it had been easier to think of Clay as a complete jerk, a man with no redeeming qualities. Seeing him as a brother grieving the loss of his sister, as an uncle doing his best with his nieces, as someone she'd once been in love with…was just confusing.

But she couldn't think about that now. She pulled Lea closer and rubbed lazy circles on her back, murmuring quietly, telling her how sweet she was and how much she was loved.

Gradually, so gradually that at first Kristen thought she was imagining it, Lea's cries grew softer and less frequent. After a few minutes, her little head drooped. A second later she sank against Kristen's chest, asleep.

Across the room, Clay swayed Lark back and forth in his arms.

Lark slid her thumb into her mouth and rested her head on his shoulder.

He slowed his motion, but didn't stop swaying. "They've done this before," he mouthed. "We have to wait."

Kristen nodded. She knew that much from taking care of Emma. Lark and Lea weren't fully asleep, just drifting off.

After a few minutes, Clay stood up taller.

Lark didn't move.

He angled his head toward the crib, eyebrows raised.

As gently and smoothly as she could, Kristen carried Lea toward it.

Clay settled Lark in the crib, then carefully took Lea from Kristen's arms and laid her next to her sister. He checked the baby monitor and crept into the hall.

Kristen gave one last glance around the room, taking in the diapers neatly stacked on the changing table shelf and the Winnie-the-Pooh mobile that hung over the crib, and then she followed him out.

Once they were in the hall, he pulled the door almost shut and turned to face her. "Thank you," he whispered.

"It's no big deal."

"It is." His voice grew a bit louder as he moved away from the door. "I stayed up reviewing resumes for a position we've got open at work. I'd barely gotten in bed when they woke up at one thirty."

"You have to be exhausted."

"Exhausted is my new normal these days." A note of stoic endurance rang in his words.

She pressed her lips together, thinking of that little pat he'd given Lea. Of how loving he'd been with the girls, of how hard he'd been trying to make things work.

"You're doing a great job with them. Really."

"Hardly." He walked down the stairs and toward the front door, then turned to face her. "If I was good at this, they wouldn't be up for hours, crying. But sometimes I just get one to sleep and the other one starts crying and... and tonight was especially bad." His shoulders sagged.

"That's probably normal for someone taking care of twins."

He rolled his eyes, and his lips twisted into a grim smile.

No matter what she might say, he was going to beat himself up about the twins' crying.

Without thinking, she hugged him.

Instantly, his arms wrapped around her and he pulled her close, squeezing as if she was a lifeline he was afraid he'd lose. "I can't thank you enough," he whispered in her ear.

Her senses overloaded with the familiar feeling of his arms around her, his lips close to her ear. He even smelled the same, as if he used the same soap and shampoo his mom had bought when they were in high school.

Heart aching, she blinked back tears and edged away. "You *are* doing a good job. They can't put it in words, but I bet the twins are still grieving the loss of their parents. You just need sleep. I promise, it will be better tomorrow."

He nodded.

She slipped out the door and went home.

Chapter Thirteen

Kristen stood in front of the bookcase in her living room Wednesday night, appraising her progress.

Almost two weeks after moving in, she'd gotten around to unpacking and arranging the first few boxes of her books. Nine more boxes to go, and then she could add a few small photos and mementos. There really wasn't room for much more, not with her extra-large library. One thing about being an editor was ending up with a lot of books that she had helped with. Plus, she had some favorite math texts she consulted from time to time and—

From across the room, her phone dinged with a text.

Are you free to chat? Call me.

It was Deirdre. Kristen quickly dialed her number.

"So, what's going on?"

"Oh, it's good to hear your voice." Kristen let out a sigh. "I need advice." Seeing Clay with the twins last night had only confused her more.

"This sounds serious. Fill me in, and then I've got some news."

"Oh? Do you want to go first?"

"No," Deirdre said. "You first."

"Okay." Kristen went upstairs to her bedroom and leaned back against the pillows near the headboard. "Do you remember the guy I told you I dated in high school?"

"Sure. Clay. You almost married him." The music that had been playing in the background on Deirdre's end of the line stopped. "And he's the guardian for your friend's babies, the ones you thought you were going to be taking care of."

"Yeah." Kristen shifted on the bed, then grabbed a pillow and went to sit on the floor of her closet, leaning back against the wall with the pillow behind her. Foolish maybe, but she felt a little less exposed. Cocooned. Safe.

"O—kay." Deirdre drew the word out, as she was wondering what Kristen might say next. "Keep talking."

A flutter of nerves ran through Kristen. Now that she was about to tell Deirdre that she had feelings for Clay, it seemed even more insane.

But she plunged in anyway.

Clay clicked on the baby monitor that sat on the lower shelf of the changing table. Then he turned on the night-light and checked on the girls in their crib.

They were bathed, their hair was washed, they were freshly diapered, and they'd been fed. He felt as if he'd finished an Olympic event. Bath time was fun with the girls, but it wore him out and he was already exhausted from last night.

He crept out of the room, pulling the door almost shut. Then he went into his bedroom, took off his now-soggy T-shirt, and walked into his closet to find a dry one.

"I moved in next door to him, thinking maybe I could keep an eye on the twins that way. You know, the helpful—but not nosy—neighbor."

Clay jerked his head through the neck hole of the T-shirt. That was Kristen's voice.

Coming through the return vent of the heating and air conditioning system. Which meant she must be in her closet too, since their houses were mirror images of each other. Who would she be talking to in her closet?

And seriously? She'd moved in next door to *spy* on him? Here he'd been thinking it was odd, but maybe somehow fate. Talk about an idiotic idea on his part, and talk about a sneaky woman. He glared at the vent.

Of course that didn't really excuse his eavesdropping, but it wasn't as if he'd tapped her phone.

Ah! That must be what he was hearing, though, since he didn't hear anyone reply. He could make out one half of a phone conversation, coming through the vent, which—in what had to be worst HVAC design ever—was in the walk-in closet.

He stood there, waiting beside his overflowing basket of laundry. Maybe it would be wise to listen for another minute or two to see what else she was up to.

"Oh, moving in next door wasn't hard. My cousin owns the townhouse complex."

Clay scowled at the vent. Lousy small-town connections.

There was a pause, probably Kristen listening to the person on the other end of the line. He should go downstairs and—

"So," she said, her voice trailing off. "I've run into Clay a time or two and… Listen, I know this might be the stupidest thing ever, but I'm starting to change my mind about him."

Clay froze, ears straining for what she'd say next.

But he didn't hear a thing.

Had she moved away from the vent on her side of the wall? Was the person on the other end of the phone still talking?

"No," Kristen said at last. "That's not what I mean. I think I'm starting to like him again, like I did in high school."

Clay's jaw dropped. Excitement bubbled through his veins, and he raised two fists in victory. Yes! This was perfect. He could ask her out like he'd wanted to and—

"Yeah," Kristen's voice now held a note of defeat. "I know it took me three years to get over him. I was there, remember?"

Clay's heart sank, and his fists fell open at his sides. Three years?

He ran a hand over his mouth. He'd been a jerk. Such a jerk. And such a fool. He'd dated other women. Beautiful, fun women. But even among all those engineers at school, no one else had a brain that worked so much like his.

"That's why I called, Deirdre." Kristen sounded confused. "I mean, what if I never really did get over him? What if I still love him? Or what if I could?"

Clay's heart beat faster. He walked right under the vent. Women were romantic, right? Surely this Deirdre person would encourage Kristen. Would tell her that, even if part of it was because she'd moved in next door, there was a reason their paths had crossed. Then Kristen would say "Yes, you're right. Clay and I were meant for each other."

But she didn't say that.

She didn't say anything.

He waited.

And waited.

And stared.

But he didn't hear another word.

Kristen tossed her pillow on her bed and went downstairs. Sitting in her closet was a ridiculous throwback to her childhood. Silly, no matter how nervous she felt about what Deirdre might say. She pushed the speaker button on her phone, set it on the kitchen counter, and opened the refrigerator.

"Wow. Do you think he likes you too?"

"Yeah, I do." Kristen pulled out a carton of peach yogurt. She knew Clay had been grateful last night for her help with the twins, but that hug had felt like more.

"How cool is that?" Deirdre chuckled. "What if that's the reason none of your relationships since have worked out? What if you were supposed to be with Clay?"

"Deirdre, I'm counting on you to be the sensible one here."

"I am being sensible. I never wanted to mention it, but

you always seemed like you were still hung up on him. You know how people say there's a fine line between love and hate? If you'd really been over him, you would have forgotten about him years ago."

Kristen ripped the foil off the top of the yogurt, scraped it clean with a spoon, and leaned back against the counter, squishing the foil into a tiny ball. "There is some logic in that, I guess." But the idea of getting involved again with Clay still felt risky. She couldn't ignore how he'd hurt her back in high school.

Of course, if she thought about it from the standpoint of what was best for the twins, a relationship between her and Clay was ideal. Look how she'd been able to help last night. And the girls were only crawling. She knew from watching Abby raise Emma that once Lark and Lea were running, things would get even more challenging.

But she wasn't going to risk getting hurt simply to make things better for Lark and Lea.

On the other hand, what if she and Clay really were supposed to be together?

"So, remember how I said I had news?" Deirdre said.

"Oh, yeah. What's going on?"

Deirdre hesitated.

Kristen tossed the foil in the trash. "Deirdre?"

"I don't really know how to tell you this, but you need to hear it." There was an odd note in Deirdre's voice.

Kristen sat down at the kitchen table, tightness building in her chest. "What?"

"Dylan and Amelia...got married over the weekend."

"Married?" Kristen's voice squeaked.

"Yeah."

A sick feeling rolled through Kristen's stomach. "I can't believe it. And—oh, man—I can't believe what I did. I mean, I always sort of felt responsible for Amelia, because she worked with me when she first started. When I saw them together at Tricia's wedding last month, I pulled her aside and warned her to be careful about dating Dylan."

"I remember."

"Guess I should have kept my mouth shut."

"You were pretty upset, and I think you'd had more than one glass of champagne."

"Another mistake. But it's been hard going to weddings lately. Truly, I was excited for Tricia. She's a wonderful person and a good friend. And I was thrilled for my sister Abby when I went to her wedding a few weeks ago. I don't begrudge them their happiness, but lately weddings make me feel...small."

"I know that feeling," Deirdre said. "It's like when a really deserving colleague gets promoted. You're happy for them, truly happy, and you don't begrudge them their promotion at all, but there's this tiny part of you that wonders what you're doing wrong."

"Exactly." Kristen tried to remember the details of the wedding reception but failed. "Do you think Dylan and Amelia were already engaged at that wedding?"

"No." Deirdre hesitated. "They started dating a couple of weeks before then."

Kristen did the math. "So Dylan, the guy who dated me for six months, the guy who said he couldn't marry me, marries Amelia after dating her for six weeks?" Her voice rose. "Six weeks?"

"I know."

"What about his wife?"

"He apparently divorced her quietly a couple of months ago. I heard that Amelia wouldn't go out with him until he did."

Kristen sucked in a breath that seemed to slice at her throat. No longer hungry, she got up, put the yogurt carton in a plastic bag, and stuck it back in the fridge.

"The whole office is in chaos," Deirdre said. "Rumor has it that when they come back from their honeymoon, she's going to be promoted to assistant director."

Kristen's mouth fell open. "No way. You've worked there for years. You know so much more than she does."

"I'm hoping it isn't true. If she's my boss, I'm looking for a new job."

"Good idea." Kristen pressed her lips together. Working in the same firm as Dylan had only led to disaster. Dating him was even worse.

But she'd done it.

Even though she'd known it was wrong. Even though it had been a new personal low, the bottom step on the never-ending staircase down, her most desperate attempt to feel loved—dating a married man.

In the end, when she couldn't take the guilt anymore and stopped seeing him, he'd made things miserable for her at Math and More Publishing. And now he'd married Amelia.

"I thought you should know. But hey," Deirdre added in a lighter tone. "It doesn't really matter. You work for a different publisher now. Besides, who needs Dylan if you're interested in Clay?"

"Hmm, maybe," Kristen said. But the news about Dylan and Amelia did matter. It reminded her of what she'd done and made her feel like she'd been rejected all over again.

"So, what are you going to do about Clay?"

"I don't know. I'll have to think."

About how stupid it would be.

About how it could never work out.

About how she'd get hurt again.

She changed the subject, chatted with Deirdre about different publishing houses that she might apply to work for, and then got off the phone and let out a long sigh.

The idea of her and Clay getting back together, of Clay really loving her, was a fantasy.

She needed to accept the truth. Some people just weren't lovable.

Like her.

Not ten years ago when Clay dumped her. Not when she'd dated all the other guys since. And, especially, not now. Not after she'd had a relationship with a married man.

Honestly, she'd never even told Gwen the whole truth about Dylan. Would she have wanted Kristen to be the twins' guardian if she'd known how bad her judgment was?

Probably not.

She didn't deserve to be loved. Not by Clay. Or by God. Oh, she knew God loved everybody, but wasn't it possible that he loved her less?

Because she didn't feel loved. At all.

Chapter Fourteen

"How long has this place been here?" Samantha looked around the Bluff View restaurant, taking in the sparkling table settings, the black tablecloths, and the stunning view of the Missouri River. She and Lucas had only driven half an hour, but there was nothing like the Bluff View in Abundance.

"A couple of years." Lucas gave his name to the hostess. "I thought you might not be familiar with it."

"I'm not, and I never would have expected a place like this in a little town like Hedgehog, Missouri."

Just like she never would have thought she'd enjoy the drive over here tonight with Lucas as much as she had. She couldn't remember the last time she'd laughed so much.

Certainly she wouldn't have expected him to arrive at her door promptly at six, wearing crisply creased tan pants, a dress shirt, and a tie. She'd expected shorts, a T-shirt, and flip-flops.

She'd even kept on her dress from work, thinking the contrast between it and his casual clothes might help her make her point when they talked. She was a mature adult, in her thirties, too old to date him, even if she wanted to.

But if she were younger, if she'd met him before Reg…

"Right this way," the hostess said. "We've got the table you requested."

He'd requested a specific table? Samantha followed the hostess to a table for two beside the windows. Sunlight glinted off the water, green fields spread out in all directions across the river, and here and there, at the water's edge, small clusters of trees could be seen. "This is breathtaking."

"I'm glad you like it." Lucas pulled out her chair and took a seat across from her. "I'm a big fan of the chef here. She's really innovative with her flavor combinations, and the menu changes every week, so it never gets dull."

The hostess set two menus on the table, filled their water glasses, and said she'd return with some bread.

Lucas pushed his hair behind his shoulders, picked up his menu, and gave Samantha an easy smile.

She smiled back, sure that after years of practice dealing with the social land mines sometimes laid by surgeons' wives, she appeared calm on the outside. Inside, though, not so much. This evening was unsettling. Since Monday, when she'd foolishly agreed to this date, she'd debated and debated whether or not to knock on his door and cancel. This morning she'd decided that it would be more polite to go to dinner, discuss how little they had in common, and kindly but firmly put their relationship into the Friend Zone.

She hadn't thought he'd take her to a restaurant that had quiet classical music playing and Audis and BMWs in the parking lot. She'd thought they'd go to the barbecue place where he worked. Whole Hog was practically an Abundance institution. She'd even planned out what she'd order—a brisket sandwich with sweet and tangy sauce, coleslaw, and fries.

She doubted this place even sold fries unless they called them "pommes frites."

She opened her menu, scanned it, and lowered it to the table. No fries. Even by Dallas standards, the offerings were impressive, the prices high. He'd clearly gotten the wrong idea. She should have canceled or said something as they drove past Whole Hog on their way out of town, but she'd been—well, she'd been enjoying talking with him and...

No matter. She needed to say something now.

"Lucas, I'm sorry. Dinner together as friends is great, but what happened the other day at my place..." She awkwardly gestured with one hand.

"You mean when I almost kissed you?" he said in a low voice.

Her pulse kicked up a notch.

His eyes gleamed, as if he could tell.

Her cheeks felt as if they were beet red. She ran a hand over the skirt of her dress and glanced around, but no one seemed to have noticed what he said or how she'd reacted. Diners at nearby tables continued their quiet conversations, and the wait staff was discreetly unseen. "Yeah that." She ran a hand over her collarbone. "That was a mistake." A big, big mistake.

"It did seem out of order," he said. "Dinner should have come first."

Samantha took a drink of ice water. She needed to pull herself together and act like the grownup here. "Not just out of order. Temporary insanity."

He didn't look as if he believed her.

"I mean it," she said firmly. "But it's not you. I'm not interested in dating anyone. In fact, I don't know if I'll be interested in dating anyone ever again."

He stared at her for a long moment, then leaned forward. "You're far too special to say you'll never date again," he said. "What happened?"

Samantha looked out the window at the river. Sad, wasn't it, how the way he'd said the word *beautiful* repeated in her mind? It had been so long since she'd felt beautiful.

But this was ridiculous. It needed to stop.

Maybe if she told him what happened in Dallas, he'd understand. She'd swallow her pride, bare her soul, and offer to split the check.

"I mean, it's fine if you'd don't want to talk about it. We don't know each other that well."

"No, I should explain."

Their waitress appeared with bread. She told them about the specials and suggested the bruschetta appetizer.

Lucas tipped his head to one side. "Do you want to try it? While we decide on our entrées?"

"Sure." Although by the time they finished the appetizer, she was fairly certain he'd be ready for the check. Once someone shared a certain level of personal pain, other people got uncomfortable.

"I'll get that right in." The waitress walked away.

Samantha picked up her silverware, tightly wrapped in a cloth napkin, toyed with it a moment, then laid it sideways in front of her, like a wall of cotton and stainless steel that might guard her from the oncoming pity.

She looked up at him. "You ready for this?"

His gray eyes held kindness and...something else. Steadiness, maybe. No pity though. At least not yet.

"Twelve years ago, right after I graduated, I married my college sweetheart, Reg. He went on to medical school and I worked in retail, supporting us. After he finished all his training, he took a position as part of an elite orthopedic surgical group and we moved back to Dallas, where we'd gone to college." There. That part sounded fine. "I stopped working, served on the hospital's auxiliary board, shopped, and went out to lunches with my best friend, Lena. And hosted all the right parties to help advance his career."

"Okay." Lucas took a drink of water and looked at her as if ready for more of the story.

"So, a couple of years ago, I was thinking...I was thinking we needed to see a specialist. We'd been trying to get pregnant and...and I couldn't." She reached for the edge of her dress, then forced herself to put her hand in her lap and not twist her collar. That was a bad habit, something she only did when she was uncomfortable. She was definitely uncomfortable. How had she wandered into the topic of infertility? This was not going at all as it should. "Anyway, I brought up the idea of a specialist with Reg, and that's when he told me he wanted a divorce."

"Wow," Lucas said softly. "You had no idea?"

"Not a clue." Samantha rotated the rolled-up silverware a hundred and eighty degrees, then twisted it back. "Actually, I must have been the most clueless woman in Texas, because it wasn't only that he wanted a divorce. He was leaving me to be with someone else—Lena."

"Man." Lucas shook his head from side to side. "What a total jerk. And your friend…" He said the word as if it tasted bad.

"I know." Samantha let go of the silverware and pushed her hair back from her face. "Not much of a friend."

"No. I'm sorry—"

She held up a hand to stop him. She wanted to get this out. "It gets worse." She drew in a breath. "I kept up my charity board commitments, and I was thinking about going back to school. But two months ago I learned that Lena's five-year-old daughter—my goddaughter—is Reg's."

Lucas's Adam's apple rose and fell. "So you moved back to Abundance to be around people you could trust."

"Yeah." He understood, without her even having to explain. Truly, after she learned that the affair had gone on for at least six years and that Reg and Lena had a child, the pain and embarrassment reached a level she couldn't bear. Every person she talked to, from the hairdresser she and Lena shared to the wife of the head of orthopedics at the hospital, made Samantha wonder. Did they know? Had they known for years? What were they saying about her? So yeah, moving back home had been a relief.

"I had no idea growing up here how lucky I was," she said. "I had a kind of security that I guess you can only feel if you've never been betrayed, if you've never doubted everyone around you."

"I think you were right to come home." His tone held kindness and supportiveness.

"Thanks. I do too. But there's no way I'm ready to date anyone, no matter"—she glanced down—"no matter what kind of chemistry I felt the other day."

Lucas sat back in his chair. "That makes sense."

Samantha let out a sigh. Thank goodness.

The waitress appeared, put a platter of bruschetta between them, and gave them each a small plate. Tiny balls of fresh mozzarella were still bubbling atop the bread, and Samantha could smell the fresh basil that was sprinkled over it.

She and Lucas each took a slice and were silent until the waitress left.

"You know, you're different from the women I usually date."

Samantha chuckled. "Older, right?" She took a bite of bruschetta.

"That's not what I mean." Lucas scooted closer to the table, his gaze earnest. "But I don't think you're that much older than I am. I'm twenty-seven."

She rolled her eyes. Not that much older. Ha. "I'm thirty-four."

"See, not that much older."

Maybe he meant it. He hadn't even blinked. Maybe it didn't seem like that many years to him.

It did to her.

"What I mean," he said, "is that you seem like even back in high school you went into relationships expecting something serious."

Didn't everyone? Maybe she was odd, wanting things to last. "You're right, but how do you know that?"

"The way you dress, kind of a vibe you give off. The exact opposite of what I usually look for in women."

Samantha set down her slice of bruschetta.

He held up a hand. "Wait, that sounds like I go around looking for one-night stands."

"That's precisely what it sounds like." Like he was the kind of man she'd never want to get involved with, if she ever did date again.

"That's not it. I just usually don't want anything serious."

"Why are you telling me this?" Even if he didn't sleep with all those women, it sounded like he had commitment issues.

"I don't know. I have this feeling in my gut that with you it would be different. And I tend to trust my instincts."

Samantha backed into the cushion of her chair.

"I know. You don't think you ever want to date again, but when the day comes that you do, I'm going to be here, waiting."

She stared at him. "I don't know what to say."

"You don't need to say anything. If that day never comes, it's okay. We'll be friends."

"But you'll date other people in the meantime, right?"

"I guess, if I meet someone incredible. But I've dated lots of women, and I've never had this knocked-in-the-head-with-a-post feeling like I do with you."

Samantha picked up her slice of bruschetta, then put it back down. This was nothing but talk. Incredibly flattering talk, but he'd change his mind. Probably in a couple of months she'd see him bringing some cute girl his own age back to his place, maybe even meet her when Lucas was fixing barbecue on his patio.

"For now, can we be friends?" He leaned toward her and held a hand out across the table, as if to shake on the deal.

"Yeah." She shook his hand.

It was warm but not sweaty. He didn't hold her fingers even a millisecond too long. It was a nice, simple, professional handshake.

That made her chest tingle.

"Really, you thought I'd take you to Whole Hog?" Lucas turned his truck onto a side street, nearing their townhouses. "That would make me pretty cheap, taking you to a place where they'd never bring me a check."

Samantha laughed. "I guess so. I hadn't thought of it that way. But I'd already planned what I'd order. The brisket sandwich."

"I knew you were a smart woman." He made a right turn, caught her gaze, and gave an approving nod. "Brisket is the pinnacle barbecue experience."

She laughed softly, as if she didn't quite believe there could be a pinnacle barbecue experience. Which, of course, there could.

"I guess barbecue's pretty important to you," she said.

Lucas pulled into his driveway. "Sometime when you're at Whole Hog, I'll show you the trophy I won in Kansas City." He parked outside his garage and turned to her. "Probably one of the proudest days of my life. People clapping and cheering and folks around town talking about it for the whole next week."

Her eyebrows raised. "You won a trophy?"

"Yep. First place." He glanced toward her unit. "C'mon, I know it's not a date, but I'll walk you to your door." Just as he'd refused to let her split the check.

"First place is impressive." She climbed out of the car.

"Yes, it is. I've found the perfect combination of ingredients for my dry rub. Stop by Whole Hog and I'll get you a plate of brisket that will make you a believer."

"I'll take you up on that." She walked toward her townhouse.

He followed, stopping at the edge of her porch as she unlocked her front door. "I know it sounds like no big deal, but barbecue is serious business to me. I've spent hours online, finding new recipes, and in the kitchen, of course, testing them out."

To be honest, sometimes he spent days totally focused on perfecting a single dish, making trip after trip to the grocery store, later dropping off ribs or brisket or pork with Clay or another friend because he'd made more than he could fit in his freezer. Sort of obsessive, but he got that way with his writing too.

She slid her keys in her purse and turned back to face him. "Maybe you should write a cookbook. You'd be famous."

He froze. How had a discussion of barbecue wandered into writing? "More likely people would think it was a joke."

"Are your recipes good?"

"Yeah."

"Then why would anyone laugh?"

"Maybe they'd laugh at the idea of me as a writer."

Samantha planted her hands on her hips. "I've spent the whole evening talking with you. You're funny and articulate. I'm sure your writing would be great, and everyone would be impressed."

Lucas stood taller. Was it any wonder he was attracted to this woman? "Thanks. Maybe one day I will write a book."

"A cookbook," She tapped a hand to her chest. "And, since it was my idea, you can dedicate it to me." She grinned.

"Yeah, a cookbook." Or a sci-fi novel.

"Thanks for dinner and for being so understanding." She gave a little wave.

"My pleasure," he said as she went inside.

He stepped over the grassy area between their porches and unlocked his own door.

He didn't really ever think he'd write a cookbook. He only had a handful of recipes that were topnotch.

But dedicate a book to her? Yeah, that was going to happen. One day.

After she got over her ex.

And after he won her heart.

Chapter Fifteen

"Okay, Mom, I'm opening the first box," Clay said loudly enough to be heard through his phone, which he'd set on the window ledge where the twins couldn't reach it.

When the three of them had arrived home after a long Friday, packages had been waiting by the door, packages whose delivery Mom had been tracking.

"I really hope they sent those little outfits with the bunnies on them," Mom said. "Gwen and I picked them out together, and I don't think the twins will fit into them much longer."

"Let's see what's in here." Clay opened the first package. "Here's a note from the couple who called you, the neighbors who had a key to Gwen's house. And"—he dug down to the bottom of the box—"lots of clothes."

"Do you see the matching outfits with the bunnies on them? They look a lot like the work of that artist Gwen loved."

"Huh?"

"You know, the artist who drew those sketches she bought for the girls' room. She posted them on Facebook."

"Mom, I don't know what those sketches look like."

"Then just look for bunnies on white outfits. Sleepers."

Clay dumped the box on the couch, but he didn't find what Mom described. He opened the second box, dumped it out and—"I got 'em." The minute he saw the rabbits, he knew. They looked just like something Gwen would love.

Lark and Lea could wear the sleepers tonight.

"You tell the girls that Gwen picked those clothes out," Mom said.

"I will." He'd already thought of it before she said it.

"Okay, talk to you later. Love you, Clay."

"Love you, Mom. Tell Dad I love him too." He hung up.

Then he looked through the rest of the things in the second box. He found more clothes and a soft, stuffed globe about six inches in diameter. When he squeezed it, a slightly tinny voice sang the lyrics of "He's Got the Whole World in His Hands."

Uh, no. Clay shoved it back in the box with the clothes. That voice would drive him crazy.

Finally, he opened the third box.

Inside, he found toys. Not toys like that globe thing, but toys that were fun.

He pulled a clear plastic tub out of the cardboard box and set it on his couch. "Excellent."

He popped open the lid and grinned at the pile of blocks. They were giant version of his childhood favorite, LEGO blocks, with pieces about two inches square so the girls couldn't choke on them. And some of them were not just blocks, but also rattles.

"Check this out, girls." He carried the tub over near where they sat on the living room floor and dumped it out with a loud clatter.

Lea's face tensed up as if she might cry.

"Don't be scared. These are fun." He found a block with a mirror on one side and held it up to her. "See? That's you."

She showed no interest in the mirror but grabbed the block and began to gnaw on it.

"Yeah, I guess they're good for that too. Hey, look." He built a small tower, naming the color of each block as he added it, like he'd read online to do.

Lark crawled over, reached for the tower, and toppled it.

Clay quickly rebuilt it.

Lark knocked it over again and giggled.

His chest grew light. How cool was that? They'd found a game.

Again and again, he built the little tower, sometimes getting it eight blocks high before Lark knocked it down. Before long, Lea joined in.

He tried making a separate tower for each girl, but they didn't seem to understand. No matter which of them knocked the blocks down, they both laughed, both loved it.

Almost as much as he did.

After a while, though, they seemed to lose interest.

Clay scooted them so that one was snuggled up against him on either side and sat for a moment. Truly, although work had been tiring, today was going well.

Maybe so well that he'd act on what he learned Wednesday night, when he overhead Kristen say that she liked him.

He'd almost called her first thing yesterday morning to ask her out.

But another part of the conversation had played in his mind and stopped him, the part where her voice had gotten so quiet, where she'd said it took her three years to get over their breakup.

Three years.

Every time he remembered it, it was as if some galactic alien reached inside his chest and dug its claws into his heart.

He'd blocked out their breakup by contributing to open-source computer code and drinking beer.

She'd spent three years getting over it.

He couldn't ask her out, not if there was a chance he'd hurt her again.

No, if he asked her out, he had to be sure that this time their relationship was forever.

Yet this was the same woman who'd said on the phone that she moved in next door to spy on him.

He glanced down at the twins. Her motives, at least, had been good. She'd wanted to be sure the girls were well taken care of.

Spying on him wasn't great, but was he any better? Listening in on her private conversation?

He should have gone downstairs as soon as he figured out what was going on.

Or yelled that he'd heard what she just said through the vent.

But telling her...didn't seem like the smartest choice. Really, her motivation for moving in next door, that brief conversation he'd overheard—none of it mattered.

What mattered was, if he was honest with himself, that since he'd broken up with Kristen, he'd measured every woman he'd dated against her.

Every one of them had come up short.

Not once had he felt the way he did ten years ago, that day they stood at the overlook at the top of the Hideaway Falls trail.

It had been April of their senior year at Abundance High. The day had been unseasonably warm, almost 80 degrees, and the sides of the river below the falls were a mix of spring-green leaves, snow-white dogwood, and purple redbuds. All of nature was young and full of hope, like he was.

Except probably not as nervous. Trees didn't get nervous.

But he was all nerves. In his pocket he had the thin, plain, gold band that had been his grandmother's, the band he'd found forgotten in the attic, the band that—since his grandparents had been married for fifty-one years—seemed forged in the deepest of love.

He wiped his sweaty palms on his shorts, reached in his pocket, and pulled out the ring.

Kristen's fingers shook as she covered her mouth.

Clay's pulse raced, faster and faster. "Will you"—his voice broke and he swallowed hard—"will you run away with me and get married? This summer, before we go to college? I know we've paid our dorm deposits, but surely we can get those back and get an apartment."

Her hand fell from her mouth, and her whole face lit. "Yes! Yes, I will!"

Carefully, he slid the ring on her finger. It was a bit big, but it didn't matter. Rings could be sized down, and she'd have to hide it anyway until after they eloped. Obstacles, like two sets of parents who had made comments about not getting too serious and the benefits of dating all through college, could be overcome. Nothing could stand in their way. He felt ready to run the country, rule the world, conquer the universe.

She'd said yes. His beautiful Kristen had said yes. They would be together forever.

She'd gazed at him, eyes shining.

Then she kissed him.

His heart beat so hard that it seemed it might burst right out of his chest.

The roar of the falls and the spray of the water fell away as if the river had stopped flowing. All that mattered was her.

He pulled her closer and kissed her again and again and again.

Until a family joined them on the platform above the falls, and one of the sons yelled "Ick, kissing!" at the top of his lungs.

Clay let out a low chuckle.

The memory was as real as if it had happened yesterday.

Was it all because Kristen had been his first love? Or because he'd been so young? "What do you think?" he asked the twins.

Lark and Lea offered no help.

160

Their mom, on the other hand, would have had an opinion.

That summer, after he'd broken up with Kristen, Gwen had burst into his room. "You're out of your mind," she shouted. "How could you be so stupid as to end things with Kristen?"

"Get out," he yelled. "It's none of your business!" And he might have included a few words his parents didn't approve of.

But no one had mentioned his language.

Mom must have said something to Gwen, because she never brought up the breakup again. At least, not for a long time, and not directly. For the rest of the summer, she'd given him space, mostly ignoring his moodiness. By Thanksgiving, things between them had seemed normal.

But Gwen's friendship with Kristen had never wavered. And every so often, even as recently as a year ago, Gwen brought up Kristen in conversation. Particularly if he happened to mention that he wasn't dating anyone.

If there was a chance for he and Kristen to get back together again, Gwen would have been thrilled.

She wouldn't want grief over her death and John's to stop him from asking Kristen out.

He had ten years of proof. Ten years of dating other women and finding them all wrong. Add in the attraction he'd felt being around Kristen these past few weeks, and it only reinforced what deep inside he'd known all along. He'd found the right woman ten years ago at Abundance High.

So, what was he waiting for?

He sent a text to Samantha, asking for Kristen's number. She replied almost immediately.

He added the contact to the address book on his phone, then hesitated, his finger hovering between Call and Message. Neither one seemed right.

"Time to look charming, ladies," he said.

Should he bother with the double stroller or just go next door? Granted, it was hard to hold both of the girls at the same time, especially if they were being wiggly, but this once, he could manage it.

He opened his front door, carefully picked up one of the girls in each arm, and rang Kristen's doorbell with his elbow.

Somewhere in the distance, a mower hummed, then footsteps neared.

Adrenaline shot through him.

The door opened and there she was. Her blond hair shone in the afternoon sun, and she wore a blue dress that looked like a long T-shirt, a dress that hugged her curves. She was even more beautiful than she'd been all those years ago at Hideaway Falls. No matter how much time passed, she was—and would always be—the woman for him. Why had it taken him so long to figure this out?

"Hi." Kristen smiled at the girls, said hello to each of them, then looked up at him. "Are they okay? Do you need help?"

No. He didn't need help with the girls. He needed her. In his life. Forever.

"They're fine. I wanted to see if you might be interested in doing something with the three of us on Saturday evening."

She glanced down as if studying her sandals. "I don't know, Clay."

What was going on? Two days ago she'd told her friend that she liked him. "Is it too last minute? Is Saturday a bad day?"

"No, it's just not a good idea."

His stomach sank.

But then he remembered.

Three years. Three years to get over the way he broke up with her after high school. Of course she'd be apprehensive.

He'd been young and stupid and said all the wrong things. He'd destroyed their relationship as carelessly as the twins destroyed the block towers. One swift blow and it was all over.

But he'd rebuilt the block towers. Somehow he had to find a way to rebuild things with Kristen.

Somehow he had to get her to say yes.

A large lump filled Kristen's throat as she stared at Clay, standing on her front porch. She couldn't do this, couldn't go out with him and set herself up for more misery.

"I was thinking maybe a picnic." He adjusted his grip on Lea, who was starting to wiggle. "I could pick up some fried chicken for us and bring some of the girls' favorites. You know, like cantaloupe."

Lea tipped her head and babbled as if she recognized the word. Lark gave Kristen's shoulder a light pat.

Kristen chewed her lower lip. She needed to word this carefully. Even if she didn't want to date Clay, she had an obligation to Gwen to stay in the twins' lives. She squinted and tried to move so that the afternoon sun wasn't directly in her eyes.

"Here." Clay scooted over so that he blocked the sun. "Listen, I know I hurt you in the past." His brown eyes shone with sincerity. "There's nothing I regret more. I'm hoping you can forgive me, because I'd like to make it up to you... and try again."

Try again. The words hit her like a physical force, reverberating through her chest like the *thunk* of a mallet on a kettle drum.

This was what for so many years she'd waited for, the words she'd longed to hear Clay say. She'd dreamed of this day, imagined how she'd make him suffer and then slowly—so he'd appreciate her this time—slowly allow him closer to her heart.

But all she felt was hollow. No excitement. No joy. No vindication.

That conversation with Deirdre, learning that Dylan married Amelia, had been more than she could take. It wasn't even really about Dylan. The man had his flaws, cheating on his wife at the top of the list. But rejection after rejection over the years had added up until Kristen finally realized the truth. No matter who she dated, it wouldn't end well.

Especially not with Clay. Look at the past, at how he'd hurt her. It would be utter lunacy to think he wouldn't do it again.

But he'd also asked her to forgive him. She had to, right? Refusing to forgive someone didn't solve anything. She knew that from church...and from her self-help book.

Her teenaged dream to make Clay suffer had been wrong.

But did that mean she needed to date him again?

No. Way.

"I thought," he said hesitatingly, "maybe we could go up to Hideaway Falls."

She drew in a sharp breath, and the emptiness of her chest suddenly filled with prickles, as if her lungs had been replaced with cactus. She hadn't been to the falls since high school, since the day they'd gotten engaged. Going back there with Clay would be gut-wrenching. She took a half-step back, shaking her head.

"Wait. Don't think about the past. Think about how we've gotten along these past few weeks. If we didn't know each other from back then, you'd go out with me, right?"

"Maybe." Once.

If *A Better You in Ninety Days* was right, the past didn't need to control the future. But eventually, whoever she dated, she'd have to be honest about Dylan. She didn't deserve a relationship with a good guy. Which, maybe, Clay actually was these days.

"If we'd never dated, I'd take you there, because it's the most beautiful place I know." His eyes held hers. "Really, Kristen, just one date."

He wasn't begging. Not quite. But his voice held a lot of emotion.

It felt—fine, she wasn't proud of it—but it felt incredible, having him act as if it mattered so much.

"I..."

Lark lurched toward her, arms outstretched.

Clay jerked up his arm holding Lark, raising his elbow to try to stop her from falling.

Kristen caught Lark and took her into her arms.

"See, even the twins want you to say yes." He tilted his head to one side.

Lark cooed and snuggled closer.

She did love the girls. But she didn't think she could survive another rejection, especially not from Clay. And rejection was certain. Even if he thought he wanted to date her now, he wouldn't once she told him about Dylan. "We've both made mistakes in the past, Clay. They do matter. I—"

"One date. One date focused on the future, not thinking about past mistakes."

That was what she wanted, right? Why she'd been reading that book?

"But..." She looked from Clay, to Lark, to Lea, who was drooling on Clay's shoulder.

He didn't even seem to mind. He was putting the twins first, not himself. He wasn't the same person as he'd been in high school. Maybe she wasn't the same person either. Not even the same person she'd been in Chicago.

Change was possible.

Mistakes could be left behind.

At least for a while.

"Okay." She rubbed a hand gently across Lark's back. "One date."

A smile slid across his face. "You won't regret it. I promise."

Chapter Sixteen

By six o'clock on Saturday evening, Hideaway Falls State Park was fairly deserted. Most visitors had gone home because the park didn't offer camping amenities.

Which was perfectly fine with Clay. He was more than happy to stand here on the platform overlooking the falls alone with Kristen and the twins. No need to share this view with anyone else.

Below the platform, water tumbled over the rocks, and droplets of spray sparkled as they fell to the frothy pool some fifteen feet below. Behind them and across the stream, the woods were a deep green. Three swallowtail butterflies danced in the air in front of the platform, and from somewhere in the woods, a bird called.

In the gravel riverbed, about three feet back from the edge of the falls, where the water was maybe eight inches deep, a path was worn through the green algae. That was where park visitors—although discouraged by the state—

waded across the river. He and Kristen had gone to the other side dozens of times as teenagers.

They wouldn't be doing any wading this evening though, not when each of them held one of the girls. Instead, he and Kristen stood well back from the rail and watched the water.

It was every bit as beautiful as Clay remembered.

Like Kristen.

With each minute they spent together, he grew more and more certain that she was the woman he was supposed to be with. Forever.

But first he had to get her to agree to a second date. Hopefully the picnic would help.

"Shall we head back?" She shifted Lark to her other hip. "Someone is getting kind of wiggly."

"Sure." He retrieved his sunglasses from Lea's fist. He'd hooked them over the neck edge of his T-shirt, but she had grabbed them and begun to gnaw on one of the earpieces. He slipped them in his shorts pocket. "Let's go have dinner."

He led the way down to the parking lot, grabbed a blanket from the car, and set Lea down in a spot where the grass looked soft. Then he spread the blanket under a big oak tree, set her on it, and carried over the cooler and opened it.

"You said you were just going to buy chicken," Kristen said. "That looks like a lot more work than driving through to get a bucket."

"I picked up dinner for us and the girls from Grace at Cassidy's Diner, including fried chicken."

"Cassidy's fried chicken?" Kristen's eyes sparkled as

she put Lark on the blanket and sat next to the girls. "It's the best."

The best was what he wanted tonight. In spite of the fact that he was scrambling to get things ready for the launch, still hadn't found the right candidate for the development position, and had the added hassle of dealing with insurance issues after the fire, tonight mattered. Kristen mattered. He just had to prove that to her.

He made one last trip to the car and pulled his surprise out from behind his back. "And…"

"You brought Oreos!" Kristen took the package from his hands.

"Double Stuf," he said, in case she hadn't noticed.

"You remembered." She gazed at the blue package with an expression that could only be interpreted as love.

Love of the Oreos, not him. But maybe a little would rub off.

"Of course I remembered." Hopefully he could get her to see that he remembered everything about her.

Maybe even prompt her to remember some good things about their time together, not just the way it ended.

They sat on the blanket and he opened the cooler, pulling out the containers of food that Grace had packed—fried chicken, potato salad, and coleslaw for him and Kristen. Easy-to-chew green beans, scrambled eggs, and cooked pasta for the girls. Plus a big tub of cut-up fruit for all of them. From the side of the cooler, he brought out four plastic plates that he'd wrapped in a towel and wedged in upright against the side. From the corner of the towel, he unbundled silverware. Real silverware, because he remembered a time when he and Kristen had been on a date and she'd cut her lip on the edge of a plastic spoon. That wasn't going to happen today.

If all went well, he'd be kissing those lips. He certainly didn't want them injured.

"This looks lovely, Clay."

"Thanks." He set plates in front of the girls, scooped out some clumps of scrambled eggs, and served them. "I know it's probably not as fancy as what you might get from some upscale deli in Chicago, but hopefully it will taste good." He handed Kristen a plate.

She took it, but made no move toward the food.

"Are you feeling okay?"

"Yeah." She smoothed a spot where the blanket was crumpled. "I was thinking about Chicago. Someone I know got married and…"

The sadness in her voice brought an uncomfortable lump into his throat. He'd seen pictures on social media of Kristen with other guys from time to time. Guys who he'd told himself she didn't really care about.

"Someone," he said, hoping he was wrong, "you had dated?"

"Yeah." She picked up the potato salad, toyed with the edge of the lid, and then removed it. "It's hard knowing he got married. Such a huge reminder of the mistakes I made." She dished out some potato salad, eyes focused on her plate.

"Hey." Clay tipped up her chin with one finger. "If he wasn't smart enough to marry you, that's his problem."

Her chin tightened and she edged back, moving her face away from his hand. "Really?" She put the lid back on the plastic container with a sharp *click*.

"Really." Couldn't she see how beautiful she was?

She grabbed another container from the cooler and put a few bites of cut-up green beans on each of the girls' plates. "We need to feed Lark and Lea and go home. I thought I could do this, but I can't, especially not listening to you tell me Dylan was stupid not to marry me." She wiped her fingers with a napkin and tossed it on top of the potato salad on her plate, as if she had no intention of eating. "After all, you were the original idiot on that count."

Kristen kept her eyes fixed on the twins, who were both mashing green beans partly into their mouths, partly onto their faces. How fast could they eat? The sooner they finished, the sooner she could help Clay pack up the car. Then he could drive them home and she could get away from him. At least far enough away to have a nice, solid wall between her townhouse and his.

"Don't." He grabbed her by both hands. "Don't think for a moment that I didn't want to marry you."

She pulled her hands away. "You could've fooled me."

"I was scared out of my mind."

"Scared? You never said anything about being scared. You said that when you went to orientation, they brought college seniors up on the stage and asked them to give advice to the incoming freshman engineering majors. You said they advised you to break up with your high school girlfriend." Her words rushed out. "But I wasn't just a high school 'girlfriend.' We were engaged." She glared at him. "I'd even bought a dress."

Clay recoiled as if she'd punched him. "You had?"

"Yes." She looked away.

It had been a plain white sundress that she bought with her baby-sitting money but to her it had been as important as one of those $5,000 gowns in a magazine. "It was probably foolish when we were planning to elope, but…I wanted to look beautiful for you on our wedding day." She'd loved him so much, spent so many hours dreaming of their wedding, been so ready to spend the rest of her life with him.

Clay leaned closer, eyes beseeching. "It's ten years too late, but would you be willing to listen to what was going through my immature brain and let me give you the apology I owe you?"

The heat in her chest cooled a couple of degrees. "All right." More apologizing from him wouldn't be that bad.

He reached into the cooler. "Just a second while I give the twins the rest of their dinner."

"All right." She helped, adding more green beans to their plates, and watched as Clay served cooked pieces of rotini.

He gestured toward a clear container of cut-up fruit in the cooler. "That's for later. Their dessert." Then he closed the cooler and ran a hand over the lid, tracing the grooved rim around the edge. Cicadas hummed, and Lark and Lea babbled, focused on each other, as if they were having their own conversation.

Clay raised his eyes and cleared his throat. "That day at college orientation, those seniors talked about how hard the classes in computer engineering were going to be. I'd just taken an online math placement test, and I'd bombed it."

She let out a sniff. "That's what you always said after every test all through high school. Every time, you got an A."

"This one was graded automatically, and I didn't get an A. I was going to be put back into the math class I had as a junior."

Clay Norris? Having to repeat a math class?

"After that I had three semesters of calculus, a semester of differential equations, and one of linear algebra ahead of me. I didn't even know what differential equations and linear algebra were."

Back then, she hadn't known what they were either. Although they'd been in the same grade, she'd been a level behind Clay in math all through high school, hadn't really figured out how cool the subject was, and certainly hadn't thought she'd get a degree in it. At the end of high school, she'd planned to major in anthropology.

"All I could see," he said, "when I pictured our life together, was my being so excited to be married to you that I'd never study. I pictured that I'd spend all my time with you"—he gave a sheepish shrug—"in bed."

Kristen couldn't help but smile. She'd kind of pictured married life the same way.

"Anyway, I didn't see any way I was going to pass those math classes. Marrying you and getting a job in computer science was one thing. Marrying you and flunking out, disappointing you and my parents and your parents…it almost made me sick at my stomach every time I thought about it."

"You never said anything about that." Her words came out harsher than she'd planned. "You should have," she said more gently.

"I know." He brushed a hand down her arm. "All I can say is that I was too young and stupid and proud to tell you how scared I was that I'd flunk out."

"I would have loved you anyway. And you aren't stupid. Not at all."

"I wasn't smart enough to handle this the right way after high school. I honestly thought that you'd be fine with waiting and that maybe, after we got through freshman year, it would be better. Maybe I'd find that the math classes weren't as bad as I thought and we could get married then."

Kristen's mouth fell open. "But—but—you didn't say that. You only said that we shouldn't get married."

Clay pressed his lips together and raised his eyebrows, as if unsure of how to proceed. "I, um, I did try to talk with you after that day, to explain things better. I even wrote you a letter and asked Gwen to give it to you."

A sick feeling tightened in Kristen's stomach. She'd refused to talk with him, again and again. After she'd pushed the letter back in Gwen's hands, then found it on her bed after Gwen left, she'd taken it out in the backyard and burned it, unread, in righteous indignation.

"I'm sorry." Kristen shook her head. "I didn't read the letter." And then halfway through freshman year she'd told her parents the college that she and Clay both had been attending was too big. She'd transferred, just so she wouldn't run into him on campus.

"I kind of figured you never read it. I thought that our relationship must not have meant as much to you as it did to me if you wouldn't even talk to me after we had a fight."

174

The words hit her like a meteor, sizzling into her chest and leaving an empty crater. He'd been scared. Scared of failing her, scared that she wouldn't love him.

The way she'd responded had confirmed his fears.

Yes, he'd handled things horribly. He should have explained everything, should have started with the fact that he loved her and still wanted to marry her. But because they'd never really fought before, because normally they were both so logical, the two of them didn't know how to have a fight and get through it. They didn't know how to handle it when their emotions were so high that logic didn't matter.

All this time she'd made him out to be the villain. If she hadn't been so hurt, if she hadn't taken his unopened letter out to the barbecue pit with a box of matches, if she'd acted more maturely...

"We could have been married for the past nine years." Her words came out wobbly.

Lark let out a cry and threw a green bean past them, into the grass.

"Yeah." He reached over to take Lark's plate and hand her a toy, then used a napkin to wipe green beans off the chin of Lea, who was still eating. "You know, I dated several women in college, and after I graduated. None of those relationships ever amounted to much. None of those women were you."

"Oh, Clay. I don't know what to say. I—"

"Say we can start over and give it another try. If we were meant to be with other people, we'd both already be married."

Her heart felt as if it had been split in two. With guilt

for how she'd reacted ten years ago. With longing for what they might have had. With the horrible weight of what she'd done.

She grabbed a paper napkin and used it to dry her eyes and wipe her nose. "I can't. I made mistakes in Chicago. Ones too big for you to forgive."

"Not possible."

"Really, Clay…"

"You didn't—surely you didn't—cheer for the Cubs?" He grinned. "I mean, I know you were living in Chicago."

"No." She shoved the used napkin in her pocket. "I did not cheer for the Cubs."

He gave an approving nod.

Trust Clay, a diehard St. Louis Cardinals fan from the Kansas City side of Missouri, to care about baseball.

"Did you murder someone?"

"No." She couldn't keep the frustration out of her voice. "Of course not."

"Then I don't care what you did, and I don't want to know. Can you forgive me for not communicating better and for giving up on us all those years ago?"

"Of course, but—"

"Then I forgive you for not reading my letter and for whatever you did in Chicago." He took her hands in his. "The past is over. All that matters is our future together."

A sensation of buoyancy teased the edges of her heart. "Are you sure?"

He squeezed her hands, his eyes never leaving hers. "I'm sure."

The buoyancy grew, spreading through her chest. "O—okay." The book she'd read was right. She should have believed it all along. She *could* leave the past behind. She *could* have a future with Clay. "I'm more than okay with it. We can give it another try."

"Yes!" He pulled her closer. Into his arms, into a circle of warmth and strength, into the place that was home.

He gazed at her, brown eyes shining. "Kristen Hamlin"—his voice grew husky—"I never stopped loving you."

"I never stopped loving you either," she whispered. She reached up to bury her fingers in his hair, pulling his face to where it was only inches from hers.

Heat flashed in his eyes, and, after a long moment, he kissed her.

A thousand tiny tingles exploded inside her. His kiss was exactly as she remembered, exactly what she'd yearned for...and more.

The rejections she'd suffered and the shame she'd felt over Dylan drained away, and joy and hope and wonder filled her.

Maybe, just maybe, she was lovable after all.

Her heart pounded and—

At the edge of her mind, she heard one of the twins fussing.

She ignored it. All those years, wasted. All that time they could have been kissing. All that time they could have been—

"Aaaaaaagh." The wail was too loud to ignore.

Clay pulled away. "What's wrong, Lea? Aren't you and Lark—wait a minute, where's Lark?"

Kristen blinked and looked around. "There."

While they had been kissing, Lark had crawled into the

grass, and she was now eating a stem of clover. The white head of the flower stuck out one side of her mouth as if she were a bunny.

"Lark!" Clay shouted. He scrambled over and pulled the clover from her mouth. "We don't eat clover."

"I guess we better feed them their dessert." Kristen chuckled.

Clay plopped Lark back on the blanket. "I'm on it." He doled out fresh fruit onto each of the girls' plates, cutting up the larger pieces.

"We probably should eat as well. I imagine you'll need to get them home so they can have their baths."

He pulled his phone from his back pocket and groaned. "We've stayed here so long that they'll probably conk out on the way home. I'll never get them to sleep tonight."

"Can't you move them to their crib while they're still asleep? I saw Abby do it with Emma when she was little."

"It doesn't work with Lark and Lea."

"Then we'd better eat fast and hope they stay awake until we get home." Kristen lifted the napkin off her plate and wadded it up. Then she served herself a piece of fried chicken and some coleslaw, and she handed the containers to Clay. "I can play with them while you drive."

"That might work." He took the food. "But there's one thing I want to do before we eat."

"What's that?"

"Will you go out with me on a real date, the beginning of our new relationship, next Saturday night?"

Her chest filled. "I will."

"Thank you." He glanced at the twins. "I'll ask someone at work for the name of a good baby-sitter. To make sure that next week both of the girls eat people food for dinner, not clover."

The next afternoon, at the monthly girls' get-together that Abby called Brownie Fest, Kristen leaned in and touched the soft, pudgy hand of the newborn baby in the carrier in the center of the table. The little girl curled her fingers around Kristen's finger, let out a faint, contented mew, and drifted off to sleep, her hand falling open beside her face.

She was so perfect, so darling, and so incredibly tiny compared to Lark and Lea.

Kristen scooted back in her chair and looked at her cousin Becky, who sat next to her at the picnic table on the screened porch of Abby's new house. "She's doing well?"

"Yes, indeed." Becky pushed back her dark hair and adjusted the light blanket that covered her baby's legs. "Miss Victoria Elise Williams is officially seven weeks old today and, according to her doctor's visit on Friday, eleven pounds and three ounces."

Kristen had seen Becky, a music teacher, proudly bow many times after one of her choirs' performances, but she'd never seen Becky's whole face glow like it did today.

"Well, little Miss Victoria is beautiful."

Samantha, who sat on the other side of Becky, murmured her agreement.

"She is." Tess nodded from across the table. "She makes me almost ready to have another one. It's hard to believe how big our Lettie is getting."

"They grow up so fast." Abby came into the porch, carrying a platter of peach shortcake that filled the air with a sweet, buttery aroma. "Just as you requested, Becky. A Brownie Fest dessert with no chocolate, in case it really is what's keeping little Victoria up at night."

"That smells wonderful." Becky moved the baby carrier to the floor, making room for the shortcake. "Who would have thought," she said in a dreamy voice, "that after years of not seeing Seth Williams, I'd end up married to him, with a baby no less?"

"Or that I'd come here to sell my great-aunt's house out at Sunset Lake and instead wind up living in it, married to Jack Hamlin, the guy I thought was such a jerk?" Tess added.

"Really, it is just like Pastor Corey said this morning in church." Abby served each of them a plate of shortcake. "God plans good things for us. He really does love every one of us more than we can comprehend."

"He does." Tess smoothed back a wisp of pale blond hair that had escaped her long braid.

Becky gave Victoria another loving gaze.

Even Samantha, who Kristen thought might find the topic of God's good plans a bit painful, given her divorce, nodded.

Kristen, not sure what to say, took a bite of shortcake. Abby had told her why Samantha's marriage ended, and now, as someone who'd dated a married man and helped ruin a marriage, Kristen felt awkward, sitting here with her.

Despite how amazing the picnic had been yesterday evening with Clay, despite the fact that she was beginning to think he might actually love her, she wasn't all that sure about God.

She'd said a quick prayer this morning, thanking God

for how things were going. But those moments didn't feel like her prayer time before Dylan. She still felt distance and a nagging doubt that her prayers might not be received.

The three other women sat in silence, eating their shortcake, with almost identical peaceful expressions on their faces. As if their lives were perfect, and they all felt God's presence every time they prayed.

She squirmed in her chair. Time to think about something else. "Speaking of men," she said, "I'm going out with Clay Norris on Saturday."

Four forks stopped in the air. Four faces turned toward her. And four sets of eyebrows drew together.

"Really?" Tess set her fork down with a *clank*. "Isn't he the guy who hurt you so badly when you were in high school?"

"Are you sure that's a good idea?" Abby peered at Kristen as if she'd spotted a rash.

"Yeah," Becky said. "I remember how hard that breakup was on you."

Samantha leaned closer. "Clay seems like a nice guy, but if it was me, I'd be careful. You don't want him to date you simply because he wants help with the twins."

Kristen gaped at Samantha. How could she say such a thing? "He's not dating me because of the twins!"

Abby raised both eyebrows and let out a sigh. "I know I'm usually the first to play matchmaker, but he could be."

"He's not, Abby. And I'm twenty-seven years old. I know how to run my own life." Kristen crossed her arms over her chest.

"Of course you do," Samantha said. "I could be totally wrong. I'll admit that, after my divorce, it's hard for me to see the best in any relationship." She shot Kristen an apologetic look.

Kristen tried to smile politely, then focused on her plate, slicing off a bite of peach with her fork. She'd thought everyone would be happy for her.

An awkward silence filled the air.

"Oooh, Samantha..." Tess wiggled her eyebrows. "Speaking of dating, I heard that you were at the Bluff View with Lucas Stiner on Thursday night."

Kristen looked up.

"You were?" Abby made an exaggerated turn toward Samantha. "Do tell more."

Samantha ran a fluttery hand over her hair. "We're just friends."

Abby continued to stare at her. Tess and Becky joined in, giving Samantha obvious, disbelieving looks.

"Besides, he's seven years younger than me. He lives like he's still in college."

"But he is awfully good-looking." Becky leaned back in her chair and eyed Samantha like a judge trying to determine if a defendant was lying.

"He's got that whole sexy surfer dude thing going on," Abby added.

Samantha's cheeks turned pink. "Didn't you get back from your honeymoon what, a couple of weeks ago?"

Abby laughed. "Even though I was on the beach a lot in Florida, I did not stare at the sun long enough to go blind."

"And he can cook," Tess added. "I adore my Jack, but he can't make anything more complicated than a frozen burrito. Think how nice it would be to marry a man who'd get up early, make you French toast, and serve it to you in bed."

"You can't let Reg affect your life forever." Abby nodded. "You and Lucas would get along well. Your personalities complement each other." She leaned in, as if waiting for the others to join her in some in-depth psychological discussion of personality types.

"Enough!" Samantha plunked her fork on her plate and put her hands on her hips. "No more discussion of Lucas Stiner serving me breakfast or doing anything else in my bed."

The women laughed. Even Kristen snickered.

"New topic," Samantha said. "Becky, what's going on with Victoria not sleeping?"

Becky let out a sigh and launched into the advice she'd gotten from her doctor, from Abby, and from some of her teacher friends about how to get her baby to sleep.

Kristen sat silent, eating her shortcake, thinking again about Clay.

All anyone here could talk about was how great of a couple Samantha and Lucas would be. They didn't have a thing in common except the fact that they lived next door to each other. What Samantha said was true—they were years apart in age.

How could they possibly be a perfect match when she and Clay, who had so much in common and were much closer in age, not be?

So they'd broken up ten years ago.

Look at Seth and Becky. They got back together.

Proof right there that the past did not have to control the future.

Chapter Seventeen

Having lots of extended family in Abundance came in so handy. Samantha hadn't had a bit of trouble finding a truck to borrow for her Saturday mission. Her cousin Hank, who worked at the hardware store downtown, had been happy to trade vehicles with her for the day. His big black truck was perfect for her plan to pick up patio furniture.

Not just any patio furniture. The most darling set that she'd found online. Too bad the delivery charge would have been more than the cost of the furniture, but she had the whole day. Driving to St. Louis to pick up the table and four chairs was no trouble at all, thanks to Hank.

Of course, the weather could have been more cooperative. It was pouring. But the furniture was going to sit outside anyway. A little rain on the way home wouldn't hurt it.

But first, before she picked it up, she needed lunch. She pulled through a drive-thru, thankful for the canopy over the pickup window, and then parked at the back of the lot to enjoy her sub sandwich.

While she ate, she pulled up the weather on her phone. It looked as if it was going to rain all day, but tomorrow looked nice. Maybe she'd text Lucas to see if he was free for lunch. They could even use her new patio furniture.

He'd come by three times over the past week, each time bringing her a new barbecue treat to try, saying she needed to learn to appreciate the finer nuances of dry rubs. As much as she protested last weekend at Abby's house, Lucas was growing on her. He wasn't pushing her to be more than friends, and he'd kept enough physical distance between them that she hadn't felt that electricity again. He was so humble—the complete opposite of Reg. Plus, he made her laugh and made her join him in being fully in the moment of whatever they were doing. And Abby was right. The man was awfully easy on the eyes.

Anyway, with all the food he'd brought her, she should cook something for him. Sunday lunch seemed perfect. Not a time of day that meant it was a date. Friends had lunch, right? And he didn't work on Sundays until five. She could fix something when she got up, like a quiche, so it could be ready quickly after she got home from church. Or was quiche too feminine a dish to serve a male friend for lunch?

She read a few recipes online and checked her email, nibbling on her sub.

Junk, junk, no, that totally looked like a scam, and—

What in the world?

She read the email, lowering her sandwich to the wrapper on her lap.

This couldn't be right.

Three of the biggest fans of Norware Games, part of the group who'd been sent the new game early for bug testing, said it wouldn't load.

She'd been the one who emailed them. Had she sent the wrong link?

Her stomach grew tighter as she grabbed her phone and dialed.

"Hey, Samantha. How are you?" Clay said. "The girls and I were just heading out to pick up our groceries. I'm getting good at this online ordering."

She explained about the emails.

"Tell me exactly what they say."

"Pretty much all the same thing. That they followed the link provided for download, but that nothing they do will launch the game."

"I thought we fixed that. You used the link I sent you, right?"

"Yes, and I cut and pasted it, so it should have been right. I didn't want to type it out because it was long."

"It's not your fault. What with the twins, I've been running on fumes too much of the time."

A loud wail could be heard in the background.

"Lea, please," Clay said away from the phone.

The crying continued, then abruptly stopped.

"Thank goodness I came to a stoplight," Clay said. "She'd dropped her toy, but I was able to reach back and give it to her."

"Good. One crisis resolved. But what do we do about the beta testers?"

"I've got to work on the file and send it out with an

apology." He let out an exasperated moan. "What a mess. I've got a sitter coming at five, but she made a point of saying that five was as early as she was free. There's no way I can fix this with the twins in tow."

"I wish I was in town," Samantha said. "But I'm in St. Louis doing some shopping."

The sound of Clay's horn came over the phone.

"Idiot driver," he said. "I swear, this store's parking lot is the most dangerous place to drive in Abundance. Hey, I'll call Kristen. I bet she'd be willing to watch the girls."

"I'm sure she would." Given the way Kristen's eyes had sparkled on Sunday when she talked about dating Clay, she'd probably be happy to help. Even if it did seem like precisely what Samantha had warned her about.

"Thanks for letting me know about the problem. I'll give her a call."

Samantha hung up and took another bite of her sandwich. She'd barely swallowed when Clay called back.

"Kristen's not answering. I left a message, asking if she could watch the twins. You don't, by any chance, know where she is?"

"No idea."

"Maybe if I called Marianne? No, she mentioned that she was going out of town. Um… I'm not sure who to call."

"I have an idea," Samantha said. "I'll call Kristen's mom, my Aunt Cara."

"You don't think she'd mind? I mean, after the way things ended with Kristen and me after high school…"

"I'll ask her as a favor to me, not you."

"I guess it's worth a shot. Thank you." Clay hung up.

Samantha dialed Cara, put the phone on speaker, and opened her potato chips while she waited for her to answer.

Maybe Clay was right, and it was weird to ask Aunt Cara, but she'd seen Cara post on Facebook last night that Uncle Will was out of town and she was bored. And somehow, maybe because Samantha was the first at the company to know about the problem with the file, it felt as if it was her fault. As if she should do something.

"Clay Norris?" The young kid from the grocery store leaned closer to Clay's window. Rain ran down the hood of his slicker and dripped into the car and onto Clay's arm.

Clay nodded and pulled his arm closer to his body.

"Whoops." The kid took a step back. "Sorry. Hey, we didn't have the diapers you wanted in the right size. I got you the brand my older sister buys for her kids. They're cheaper. Is that okay?"

"Sure." Clay signed the electronic pad the kid held out. It wasn't as if he had time to stop somewhere else to get the name brand. He needed to get to the office.

"Okay, I'll get you loaded up," the kid said.

Clay popped the trunk and drummed his fingers on the steering wheel as he watched the kid in the rearview mirror.

The phone rang, and he grabbed it. *Please, please let Mrs. Hamlin say yes.* He didn't see how he could focus on fixing the mess at Norware if he had to take care of the twins.

"You're good," Samantha said. "Head on over to my Aunt Cara and Uncle Will's house. They still live where they did when you were in high school."

Clay exhaled. Good thing he always carried a fully stocked diaper bag, even for short trips. "You're sure she doesn't mind?"

"I'm sure. She said she can't wait to spend time with Lark and Lea."

"Samantha, you're a lifesaver." It might be a little weird, seeing Mrs. Hamlin again, but he certainly trusted her with the girls, and he was in no position to be choosy. "Thank you."

In spite of the good news, his stomach still churned. He'd like to tell himself the problem with the game was a quick fix, simply a matter of uploading a different file, but he was 99 percent sure that wasn't it. And, if he was going to get feedback from the beta testers and get all the bugs worked out in time for launch, he needed to take care of the problem today.

He was going to have to cancel his dinner with Kristen, which was the very last thing he wanted to do.

This was not the way to show her he'd changed. Not the way to win her back.

But this *was* an emergency. Surely, if he explained, if he told her how sorry he was to have to postpone, she would understand.

He pulled out his phone and typed in a text.

Twins taken care of. Sorry but I have to cancel tonight. Work.
He hit Send.

Your mom is really nice to watch the girls. I'm bummed that I have to ask you to reschedule. I've been looking forward to our time together all week. Could we possibly do Monday night?

He'd get a sitter for Monday. Even if he had to beg.

"Sir, you're all ready to go." The kid was back.

Clay slid a tip out of his wallet.

"Really, you don't need to…"

"With all this rain? I insist."

Thunder rumbled through the sky and a crack of lighting struck somewhere close by.

Clay thrust the money at the kid and rolled up his window.

The kid sprinted toward the store, and Clay drove out of the parking lot.

Chapter Eighteen

"Pay me for watching the girls? Are you kidding?" Kristen's mom sounded insulted. "We had a blast." She batted away a moth that circled her porch light and led Clay into her living room, where Lark and Lea were playing on the floor.

"Thank you so much, Mrs. Hamlin."

"Cara, dear, remember?"

"Oh yeah." She'd told him to call her that this morning. Right after she assured him that she didn't hold the past against him. "Anyway, I certainly never intended for you to baby-sit for all that time for free." She'd kept the girls from after he got his groceries until past nine at night.

"I wouldn't dream of letting you pay me. Your little nieces are absolutely adorable and just as sweet as can be! I hope you don't mind, but I took some pictures of them. Would you mind terribly if I put a couple up on Facebook so your mom could see?"

His mom and Kristen's mom were friends on Facebook?

Weird, considering how long it had been since his parents had moved away from Abundance, but maybe that's why she'd been so nice about watching the girls.

"Sure. That's fine." He picked up the diaper bag, which Mrs.—uh, Cara—had all packed.

"Now you get these two home and in bed. I already gave them their baths, right after dinner. I didn't have sleepers, so I put clean diapers on them and put them back in their regular clothes."

"Wow, um, thanks." That wasn't what he'd expected, but maybe, with it being so late, it was for the best. Hopefully, since he didn't have far to drive tonight, they would stay awake until he got home.

It had been quite a day. Not at all the relaxing Saturday where he'd planned to get his act together for the following week, then have a great evening with Kristen.

He'd dashed home after dropping off the twins, thrown the cold stuff from the grocery store in the fridge, and raced to the office. The fix had taken hours.

But at last it was done.

Now if he could get the girls home before they fell asleep.

He carried them out to the car, strapped them in, and turned the stereo on to heavy metal as soon as he was out of the driveway. Maybe, maybe, he'd be able to keep them awake.

Late Saturday evening, Kristen let herself in her apartment

and dropped her duffel on the carpet with a thud. She let out a loud sigh, got a glass of water from the kitchen, and turned on the TV.

It was better to keep her mind busy than to hunt through her kitchen cabinets for chocolate frosting that she could eat straight out of the tub.

Especially because she knew she wouldn't find any.

Pizza delivered. Chinese food delivered. Why wasn't there a place that delivered chocolate frosting when a woman had a really bad day?

Oh, it had started out fine. She'd spent Friday night at Stacey and Earl Ray's, baby-sitting their son, George, while they went out of town so that Earl Ray could run a big auction.

Three-year-old George, though ornery as he could be, was really quite sweet. If someone could keep up with him. Honestly, George had to be the equivalent of two normal children. Even after one night, she had more appreciation for what Clay's life was like. This morning, as soon as it seemed polite, she'd even sent a text to Deanna, telling her that her earlier concerns had been foolish, that Clay was doing a good job with the twins. She'd felt a little guilty, thinking of her comments in the parking lot to Deanna, given what her job was.

But that was pretty much Kristen's last minute of peace. She had to make pancakes and let George eat them in front of the TV to even get a chance to take a shower.

After that, things went downhill.

First, she'd had to scrub syrup out of the carpet.

Then she'd checked her phone. In that short space of peace she'd had under the shower spray, Clay had called and asked her to watch the twins, texted to say he found someone else, and canceled their date for this evening with no explanation.

It had been all she could do to be a good sport with George until Stacey and Earl Ray returned—several hours after they'd said they'd be home, thanks to a problem with the auction, followed by a big wreck on the highway and a detour. At least, thanks to Clay canceling their date, she was available to stay and keep watching George.

Anyway, at last she was home. All she wanted to do was to curl up in a ball and eat chocolate frosting.

Or Oreos.

Or Peanut Butter M&Ms.

None of which she had in the house, and none of which would solve the problem.

The problem named Clay Norris.

Even her favorite TV show didn't distract her. She shut off the set, grabbed her phone, and opened her email, skimming down the list of messages as she hauled her duffel upstairs.

She should have known dating Clay would never work. He hadn't changed at all.

When she moved into this townhouse, she'd been worried that he would put his work first, that the twins didn't matter.

And what had he done today? Shoved the girls off onto a baby-sitter and canceled his plans with her. Everything he said on their picnic, about how much she meant to him, had been empty words.

She set her duffel on her bed, pulled out her dirty laundry, and looked back at her email. Hopefully, Kent, her boss at Fibonacci Publishing, had replied to the question she'd sent him yesterday about Chapter 6.

Phone in one hand, she tossed the dirty clothes in the laundry basket in her closet. She found not one, but two emails from Kent. The first was a reasonable answer to her question, something she could easily incorporate into the manuscript.

She read the second email and physically retreated from her phone, backing against the closet wall and then sinking to the floor. Her face grew hot and her stomach began churning.

A minute later, she forced her trembling fingers to dial Deirdre.

After four rings, Deirdre answered.

"Was Kent from Fibonacci Publishing in the office yesterday talking to Dylan?"

"Hi, I'm fine, thanks, and no," Deirdre said.

"Sorry. Are you sure?"

"Dylan wasn't in, but I did see your boss stop by. He met with Amelia."

"I was only trying to help her."

"What? I can't hear you," Deirdre said loudly.

Kristen swallowed. "I was only trying to help Amelia," she said, this time with more volume.

"Kristen? What happened?"

He'd made it. He'd gotten Lark and Lea home before they fell asleep, before he had to attempt the impossible car-to-crib transfer. Now they were both in their crib, out cold.

But he was beat. He set the baby monitor on his

nightstand and went into the closet to dig his pajamas, which he'd meant to wash today, out of the dirty clothes. Tomorrow he could deal with laundry and the semi-disaster that was now his home. Ever since those boxes had arrived from Gwen and John's friends, the place had been a mess. How did three boxes of toys and clothes push his townhouse from manageable clutter to the "Before" shot of a TV show about hoarding?

So much to do. How did single parents manage? Maybe he needed vitamins.

Wait a minute. What was that?

"You're not going to believe this."

He groaned. It was Kristen. Talking on her phone where he could hear her through the vent again.

This never happened with his previous neighbor. But that guy lived alone and was so shy, he probably never talked to anyone on the phone, at least not while standing in his closet.

Tomorrow, no matter what, Clay had to tell Kristen what was happening. But right now he was too tired. He pulled on his pajamas. Just a few more seconds and he could put his head on the pillow.

"I think Amelia badmouthed me to Kent. He's loved my work, told me he'd have books for me to edit for the next three years at least. But I just got an email from him saying the book I'm working on will be the last one Fibonacci needs me for."

Clay froze. Kristen had lost her job? Was that why she never texted him back?

"No, no contract. I was working month to month. And it's over. All because I tried to warn Amelia about what a slimy jerk Dylan is."

There was a pause. The other person probably talking.

"Yeah. Except with her. Her he marries after they date for six weeks. And now I think she's making sure no one says a word against her husband. So now I can't work at Fibonacci, and I can't work at Math and More. You know there aren't that many publishers who put out math textbooks."

Should. Not. Be. Eavesdropping.

He should walk out of the closet and close the door. But he didn't.

He just stood there, wanting the person on the other end of the phone to stop talking so Kristen would say more.

"That won't matter," Kristen said at last. "All that matters is that I dated my boss—my married boss—and then I added to that by warning Amelia about him. A warning that was totally worthless because, for her, he divorced his wife and proposed."

Clay stared up at the vent.

Kristen had dated her married boss?

Now he understood why she felt so guilty about her past. He'd said that unless she cheered for the Cubs or committed murder, it didn't matter.

Did it?

He wasn't sure.

Clearly she knew what she'd done was wrong and felt bad about it. And she was suffering the consequences.

It wasn't as if he'd lived a perfect life either, not when he was standing here listening in on her phone call.

He walked out of the closet and quietly closed the door. With a jerk, he grabbed his pillow, then his phone, and the baby monitor. He could sleep on the couch. He was not listening in anymore, and there was no way he was telling Kristen what he'd overheard. Tomorrow he would figure out a way to stop sound from coming through the vent. If nothing else, he could take off the vent cover and shove a bunched-up blanket in there.

Flopped on the couch, he tried to get comfortable and forget what he'd heard.

He needed to do exactly what he'd told her they should do when they were at Hideaway Falls, forget about the past and focus on today.

But she was right next door. Feeling miserable.

He couldn't call her up and say, "Hey, sorry, I overheard you lost your job."

But he could send a simple text to let her know he was thinking of her. He propped his phone on his chest, opened his texting app, and scrolled down to the message stream between him and Kristen and—

Blinked at the screen, as if somehow he might refocus and see things differently.

The message where he explained why he was canceling their date, where he asked about going out Monday and said how much he'd been looking forward to seeing her, had never been sent.

He'd been picking up the groceries and texting her and—

And then the kid came back, and he'd probably never hit Send.

Stupid. Stupid. Stupid.

He'd called her and asked to watch the twins and…

His stomach tight, he scrolled back to see the message

Kristen did receive:

Twins taken care of. Sorry but I have to cancel tonight. Work.

His pulse sped as understanding slammed into his brain.

He'd asked her to baby-sit, told her he found someone else, and canceled without explaining.

No wonder she'd never texted him back.

He sat straight up on the couch and dialed Kristen's number. He wouldn't mention her job, but he had to apologize and explain how he hadn't sent the whole message.

No answer.

He hung up.

Was she still talking to her friend?

Maybe. He'd wait five minutes and try again. He switched to the ESPN app and tried to distract himself with baseball scores.

Hopeless. After three minutes he tried calling again, but there was still no answer.

She couldn't have gone to sleep already, could she? It hadn't been that long since she'd been on the phone.

He dashed upstairs and shoved his feet into the tennis shoes that lay beside the foot of the bed. A quick check on the girls—who were perfectly fine—and he was out the front door, across the tiny strip of grass, and knocking on her door, with his own door cracked in case one of the girls cried.

He knocked softly at first, then louder.

But she didn't answer.

After a couple of seconds, he thought he heard the shower running.

Maybe she'd ignored his calls because she was too upset over losing her job to talk to him. Especially if she thought he didn't care.

All right. First thing tomorrow he was fixing this.

Chapter Nineteen

If there was one thing Clay knew, it was that apologizing to Kristen with flowers was not the way to go.

He would not let this misunderstanding drag on for a decade or a year or a week or even another day. Despite the work he needed to do today, he was straightening things out immediately.

But first he needed supplies.

He pulled his car into the lot for the strip mall that included Fletcher's Drugstore, the donut shop, and a nail salon. He parked, climbed out, and opened the trunk, ready to get out the double stroller. Surely he could buy one small item and be back home before Kristen even woke up for church. Living next door, he'd noticed that as regular as clockwork, she left at 8:45 each Sunday morning.

"Hey, Clay," Lucas called out the passenger-side window of his truck.

Clay hadn't even realized he'd pulled in right next to him. "Hi, Lucas. Can't talk. I've got to grab the girls and run into Fletcher's."

"A quick trip?"

"Yeah." He leaned in and unfastened Lea's car seat strap.

"Leave the girls. I'll watch them."

Clay refastened the strap, backed out of the vehicle, and turned to Lucas. "Really?"

"Sure. We already had Dad's birthday breakfast, but my mom's in the donut shop getting stuff to take to church to celebrate there. She says she likes to go in to see how they look, but she really goes in because they don't give samples in the drive-thru line. So I'll be here awhile. I can watch the girls."

Clay glanced at Lucas, then at Lark and Lea. "I guess I could leave the window open. It's not even hot yet."

Lucas climbed out. "I've got this."

"You'll text if there's a problem?"

"You know it. I'm not going to be out here changing diapers." Lucas chuckled. He leaned through the window into Clay's backseat and tickled the toes of each girl, then crouched down, popped up again and grinned at them.

Both girls giggled, apparently charmed.

"Thanks, buddy. Having you watch them would be great. Speed is of the essence."

Lucas angled his head toward the twins. "They're not sick, are they?"

"No. I need apology candy. I've got a woman seriously mad at me."

"Ah." Lucas's eyes relaxed. "Buy a card while you're

at it. That helps."

Clay gave a half-nod of acknowledgment and hurried toward the drug store. Did he need a card? Would it help? It wasn't as if Lucas was some guy who'd been married for thirty years, some valuable source of relationship advice. Clay knew Kristen. She had two favorite foods: Double Stuf Oreos and Peanut Butter M&Ms. He'd already used Oreos when they went on their picnic. M&Ms were the answer.

On the other hand, adding a card couldn't hurt.

Kristen found her flip-flops by her front door and slid them on.

Last night, she'd held it together after an exhausting day with three-year-old George, followed by that awful text from Clay and the email from her boss, telling her that she no longer had a job. She had not made a run to the store for emergency frosting or M&Ms or Oreos.

But when she woke up to the *ding* of a text from Deanna, explaining that she'd just gotten Kristen's message from yesterday because she'd been camping and saying how glad she was that things were working well with Clay and the twins, all the horrors of yesterday came crashing back.

Then, when the milk in her refrigerator, a gallon she bought two days ago that had a sell-by date a week away, smelled as if it had been in there for six months, it was the last straw.

Still in the shorts and T-shirt she'd slept in, she grabbed her car keys. Yeah, her hair was a disaster, but the kid at the drive-thru window would never notice.

Grateful that her townhouse had a door into her garage, which meant no one needed to see what she was wearing, she got in her car and backed onto the street, headed for the perfect Sunday morning comfort food.

Drive-thru donuts.

Ten minutes later she took her coffee and the waxed paper bag from the kid at the window who did not, in fact, gape at her hair. Opening the bag, she breathed in the sweet scent of the pastries.

She situated the coffee in the cup holder, grabbed a vanilla sprinkle donut, and carefully steered, one-handed, through the drive-thru exit. She pulled past the parking lot for the strip mall, made a right onto Beasley Street and—

Hold. On.

She could swear she'd seen Lark and Lea in the back seat of Clay's car in front of the drugstore. Her SUV was just tall enough to let her look down into his low-to-the-ground hybrid and notice their little feet wiggling.

And they'd been alone.

She tossed the rest of the uneaten donut in the bag, made a left turn across traffic into McDonald's, worked her way through the crowd of cars in the lot, and turned around.

Surely Clay would never leave the girls alone when he went into a store. It was illegal. It was crazy. It was *dangerous.*

She went back down Beasley and turned into the strip mall lot.

His car was gone.

Now what?

She checked both directions in the lot.

No Clay. No Lark. No Lea.

The base of her throat grew tight as one ugly scenario after another flashed through her mind. Panic rose in her chest.

Okay, first things first. She'd go home, put on real clothes, and call him. If something had happened, she couldn't help in her pajamas.

She put the car in gear and gunned it.

Five minutes later she neared her townhouse.

Clay's car was in his driveway. One girl sat in the double stroller beside the car while he lifted the other girl out of the back seat. They looked as happy as could be. All the horrible things she'd imagined, and the girls were just fine. And—

Oh! Her hair! Kristen ducked down in her seat, sped by, and turned down the next cross street. There was no way she was driving into her garage, where Clay might come over to talk to her, with her hair like this, wearing her pajamas, and with donut frosting all over her face.

Instead, she drove a couple of blocks, parked, and took a long drink of her coffee. Okay, she knew she'd been driving around, but it was not as hot as it should be. Still, it was coffee. She pulled out her half-eaten donut.

Once she finished it, she wiped the goo from her hands and texted Deirdre to tell her what she'd seen. She needed to get dressed, then have a serious conversation with Clay. He couldn't leave the twins in the car when he went shopping, no matter what had been going on at his work yesterday.

But this was not about yesterday. Not about the fact

that he'd blown her off and crushed her dreams yet again. This was about the twins. How could he possibly leave them in his car all by themselves? Was he even more thoughtless and irresponsible than she'd imagined?

She took another drink of coffee, hoping Deirdre would call right back. Maybe if she talked to Deirdre long enough, she'd be able to handle the situation sanely.

Without screaming.

Chapter Twenty

This does sound like something my office should investigate. I'll look into it.

Huh? Kristen stared at her phone.

Then, as realization hit her brain, the drive-thru cup slipped through her fingers.

She shrieked and scrambled for the cup, spilling more coffee in the process. Frantic, she put the nearly empty cup in the cup holder and blotted the coffee off her leg with her napkin, and—when the napkin wasn't enough—with a sweatshirt she snagged from the back seat.

After she'd wiped up all the coffee she could, she examined her leg. No second-degree burns or anything. Her skin didn't even feel hot. Apparently she should be more grateful the next time she was served lukewarm coffee.

But where was her phone?

She searched through her car and found the phone

wedged between the front passenger seat and the door. She pulled it out of the narrow space and opened the texting app.

Her stomach twisted and her mouth went dry.

There it was, in clear letters at the top of the screen. Proof that she was an idiot.

She hadn't sent her text about Clay leaving the babies in the car alone to her friend Deirdre.

She'd sent it to Deanna. Who was a social worker.

Who was now planning to investigate Clay.

All because Kristen hadn't been paying attention.

A month ago, she would have been thrilled to see a thorough investigation, proof that Clay was a bad parent, a reason for the girls to be out of his care and hopefully placed with her.

But now…

Oh, she was mad at Clay for breaking their date.

Mad that it probably meant they'd never have the future she'd started dreaming of again.

She was flustered by what she'd seen. Or thought she'd seen.

But *she* knew there had to be another explanation. She knew Clay loved the girls and would never leave them alone. Never ever.

Deep down, she was just still mad and hurt and wanting to vent more to Deirdre.

And deep, deep down, way under everything else, was the truth.

She wanted a reason to talk to him. A reason to have a conversation where he'd explain what she'd seen in a way that assured her he'd been a good guardian. A conversation where—oh, she was so small and selfish—he'd apologize again and again and again. Maybe even getting down on his knees to grovel for canceling their date and making her doubt him.

A way to let him win her trust. Again.

The last thing she wanted was to make him the target of an investigation by social services.

Quickly, she dialed the phone.

"Deanna, Kristen Hamlin here." She kept her voice light. "Please ignore that text I sent. The twins are home and they look fine, and like I said earlier, I've seen Clay with the girls and he's doing a really good job."

"Kristen, I have to investigate."

"No, really—"

"My boss will insist. Don't worry, though. I'll just stop by tomorrow evening and see how everything is going. Believe me, when you're in my job, you get a feeling really quickly whether things are right in a home."

"But—"

"You'd be surprised how often people report things, then try to walk it back because the custodial parent threatens them."

"Nobody threatened me. I meant to text someone else."

"I'm sorry. This is my job, you know. The state has to take the welfare of children seriously."

"Yeah, it does." The donuts twisted in Kristen's stomach. "I understand." She hung up, then numbly set the phone in the console.

Clay was going to hate her.

But she had to tell him.

Now.

She flipped down her visor, looked at herself in the vanity mirror, and rubbed the donut glaze off her cheek. Then she ran a hand down the front of her T-shirt. Inappropriate, since it was wet with coffee. She pulled on the slightly soggy sweatshirt, got a brush out of her purse, and did the best she could with her hair.

And she put the car in Drive.

Clay licked the flap of the greeting card and sealed it while surveying the toys that littered his living room floor. After he talked to Kristen, he had some major tidying to do. How had he gotten so far behind in just one day of dealing with a work disaster? Except for what he'd shoved in the fridge, he'd never even put away the stuff from the grocery store yesterday.

He'd deal with it all after he talked to Kristen. Once it was a little later, he could knock on her door and—

Wait. That was her car, turning at the end of the road.

He pressed Play on a toy piano that normally kept the girls entertained for a few minutes with music and flashing lights, then checked the baby gates that led into the kitchen and up the stairs. Both were secure. The twins could hang out in the living room for five minutes—if he was lucky and Kristen would talk with him that long—and he could apologize.

He grabbed the card and candy and walked toward her vehicle as she pulled in the drive.

The second she turned off the engine, he opened her car door. "Kristen, I'm so sorry about last night. I thought

I'd sent another text, explaining what was going on, but I never hit Send. I didn't mean to cancel on you so abruptly. I'm hoping I can take you out to make up for it." He thrust the candy and card at her.

Then studied her more closely.

She looked... well... not at her finest. She'd apparently spilled something all over her clothes, her hair was flat on one side and stuck out over her ear on the other, and she seemed a little pale.

She glanced at the card and candy, and an odd look passed over her face, as if instead of offering M&Ms he was handing her a helping of deep-fried rattlesnake. Her movements jerky, she took the card and candy and set them awkwardly on the passenger seat of her car.

"Let me move out of the way." He backed away from her door.

She got out cautiously. "You...you had a texting problem?" Her voice sounded oddly thin.

"Yeah. I thought I hit Send on another message to you, but I didn't. I hated having to cancel our date last night."

"I've done that." She leaned back against her car, twisting her hands together in front of her. "Not sent a message when I meant to. I can certainly, uh, understand that sometimes texting doesn't work right."

"You can?"

"Sure."

She didn't sound sure.

"Really, Kristen, I'm so sorry. I—"

She held up a hand, silencing him. "I...I had a texting problem of my own that I need to tell you about."

"Okay." He frowned. Maybe she'd been getting a

bunch of texts last night and turned her phone on silent and that's why she didn't return his calls.

She let out a shaky breath. "A few minutes ago I, uh, I thought I was texting my friend Deirdre and actually sent the message to the last person I'd gotten a text from. You see, I was at the donut place this morning and I saw the girls in your car, alone…"

"They weren't alone." Did she think he'd leave Lark and Lea in the car all by themselves? "Lucas was standing right outside the car, watching them the whole time."

A visible shudder ran through her body, and she shrank against the side of her car. "I didn't see anybody watching them."

"He was playing peekaboo with them. Maybe he was hiding when you drove by. Anyway, I ran into the drugstore to get the M&Ms for you," he said. "And the card." He pointed to where they sat, abandoned on the passenger seat of her car.

Kristen ran a hand over her mouth. "I… I didn't know that."

Hold on. What she'd said a moment ago suddenly clicked. "You texted someone that I left the girls in the car unattended? Call them. Tell them you were wrong."

She rubbed her fingers back and forth against her lower lip. "I did. I told her I must have been mistaken. But Deanna says she can't ignore my text."

"Who's Deanna?"

"She's…" Kristen's voice was so low that Clay could barely hear it. "She's a neighbor of mine, a caseworker with social services. She says she has to investigate. She'll be stopping by your house tomorrow night."

Clay felt his eyes bug out. "Investigate, as in make sure I'm a fit guardian?"

Kristen went a shade paler. "I'd texted her yesterday to tell her what a great job you were doing, and she replied this morning. I'd been texting a lot with Deirdre and I thought I was sending her the message about the twins in the car. And I tried to talk Deanna out of it, but she said her boss will insist." Her voice broke off. "If endangerment is reported—"

"Endangerment?" Clay's breath was coming out in heaves. "Can you call her back? Tell her you didn't see Lucas?"

Kristen backed up a step and rubbed a hand against her leg. "I still think she'd come by."

He felt hot, then cold, then like he might throw up. What if he was wrong to leave the girls in his car with Lucas watching? What if he didn't meet the caseworker's expectations when she visited tomorrow? What if the state took Lark and Lea away?

No. That couldn't happen. He simply had to be the best guardian on the planet. By tomorrow night. This woman was coming over and— "I've got to clean."

"Let me help." Kristen stepped closer.

He shoved out a hand, stopping inches from her chest. "No way. I can only imagine why you're communicating with someone from social services." He whirled around toward his front door.

Kristen ran along beside him. "Really, I can help you."

"Your help is the last thing I need." He stalked into his townhouse and slammed the door.

Four hours later, Clay's kitchen was clean. He'd put away all the groceries from yesterday. He'd done the stack of dishes in the sink. He'd taken everything out of the fridge and scrubbed every shelf. He'd scoured the floor on his hands and knees. He'd even placed a new order at the grocery store, which he was picking up in two hours, so he'd have tons of formula and baby food and diapers and wipes on hand.

He walked into the living room and his shoulders sagged.

The room looked as if a bomb had gone off, dispersing baby toys into all corners and crevices of the room. He climbed the stairs. In his bedroom the pile of laundry spilled out of the basket and pooled around it, three feet deep. A similar pile sat in the girls' room. Despite the fancy device he'd purchased, the smell of dirty diapers hung in the air. It probably didn't help that when he'd emptied the fancy diaper gizmo two days ago, he'd shoved the plastic-wrapped used diapers in the bathroom trashcan.

And the girls were fussy, fussier than they'd ever been during the day, except on the airplane. It was as if they knew how stressed he was and felt compelled to join his panic.

Half of the time when he should have been cleaning the kitchen, he'd been trying to make first one, then the other, of them happy.

In desperation he'd tried everything from television to the toy piano to even that squishy globe that played music.

Big mistake there.

The twins loved it. So much that it kept them happy for half an hour.

During which he'd had to listen to "He's Got the Whole World in His Hands" again and again and again until he wanted to rip open the miniature planet and smash the recording device with a hammer.

Seriously, if God had everything in his hands, if he was in charge, why would he let Gwen die, and why would he let the current situation get as bad as it was?

Clay ran his hands through his hair, sank onto the edge of the couch, and blinked back tears.

How was he going to get his place—and Lark and Lea—looking and acting perfect by tomorrow night? How could he possibly lose them?

Sweat broke out on his brow just thinking about it.

And yet, it might happen.

Because of Kristen.

Chapter Twenty-One

"Banana fudge cheesecake." Lucas wiggled the handles of the plastic bag. "The best dessert we serve at Whole Hog, and I happened to bring home two slices, in case you might want to try it."

Samantha stepped back from her front door and waved him inside. "I could be convinced to eat cheesecake."

It wouldn't take any convincing at all. She loved cheesecake. And, thanks to the world's pokiest service at the place with the patio furniture, she'd been too tired to grocery shop when she got back yesterday and had scrapped her plans to invite Lucas over for lunch today. Which had been, well, kind of disappointing.

More disappointing than she'd expected.

Lucas walked in. "Have you seen the moon tonight?"

"No. I've been unpacking my winter clothes. I just put the last sweater away about five minutes ago."

"Perfect timing, then." Lucas moved closer, close

enough that—unlike the past few times he'd been in her apartment—he blew right through the boundaries of the Friend Zone. He ran one finger down her cheek, stopping under her chin. "You, my beautiful neighbor, work too hard."

Samantha's pulse pounded. Did he feel the heat pouring off her face? Did he know how flustered he made her, simply by touching her skin? Did he—? She glanced at his eyes.

They twinkled.

He knew.

"Let's go sit on your porch on that new furniture I saw that you got and eat dessert."

She edged back, putting space between them. Sitting in the moonlight did not sound like something friends did. She should remind him that she wasn't ready to date. But...

"I'll get some plates." She hurried to the kitchen.

Was she out of her mind? They should eat inside, at her kitchen table.

Only that was close to the utility closet, which made her think about the day he'd helped fix her breaker. About how close their bodies had been in that small space. About how later that same day he'd almost kissed her.

That flustered feeling returned and her cheeks grew hot again.

Lucas followed her into the kitchen. "You're going to love this cheesecake."

She busied herself pouring two glasses of iced tea, hoping her face wasn't red.

He didn't seem to notice, but went to her patio door,

opened it, and peeked out. "The view is even better from back here!" He carried out the bag of cheesecake, came in to grab the tea glasses, and disappeared outside.

For a moment she stood there, looking back and forth from the door to the cabinet where she stored her dessert plates. Did she want to do this? Did she want Lucas to move out of the Friend Zone? Into the Dating Zone?

The Kissing Zone?

If she was honest, kissing him sounded even better than cheesecake.

But what about trusting him?

Deep inside, around the edges of her heart, nasty little pinpricks stung when she thought about that.

But maybe...maybe she could test things out tonight to see how it felt.

Quickly, she pulled out plates, forks, and napkins, and—before she could overthink it—went out to her little back patio.

"Wow." She sat in one of the chairs and tipped her head back, staring up at the sky.

The moon was full and huge, filling the backyard with as much light as a streetlight. Shimmering with promise.

"See what I mean?" Lucas said. "It's too great to miss."

"Yeah." Somehow it felt as if he wasn't talking about the moon. It felt as if he was talking about her life, about what she was missing.

She swallowed. When she thought about it logically, maybe *she* was missing out, living in fear of getting hurt. What if a relationship with Lucas would be wonderful?

He lifted the container of cheesecake out of the plastic

bag, plated the slices, and set one in front of her. "Try this."

She cut off a bite, making sure to get plenty of fudge topping, and popped it in her mouth. The banana and chocolate flavors were a perfect combination, and the graham cracker crust provided crunch in contrast to the creamy filling. "This is amazing." It was way better than she'd expected. Better, in fact, than a certain chain that served a lot of cheesecake.

"Glad you like it. It's my favorite."

"You've got good taste."

"I do." His words rolled lazily off his tongue. "I know when I find something special."

There was an intimate note in his voice that wrapped around her heart. She looked over at him.

He smiled at her, relaxed and steady. Kind. Honest. Uncomplicated. Everything Reg hadn't been.

Just because Reg had been a horrible husband, it didn't mean every other guy on the planet was a jerk. How much power was she giving her ex-husband if their divorce made her afraid to date again? The last thing Dr. Reginald Wyler needed was more power to inflate his ego. It was already the size of the Goodyear Blimp.

Statistically, the male population had to include some good guys, guys women could trust, right?

But she felt so fragile. So afraid.

Did she want to live like that?

If she did, she was letting Reg ruin not only the past several years of her life, but the future as well. So, no, she didn't want that, didn't want it at all. In fact, starting right now, she wasn't giving him that power anymore.

A fluttery feeling gathered in her chest, a feeling that

might have been courage. She laid down her fork and reached over toward Lucas's left hand, which was resting on the edge of the table. She placed her fingers over his and gave his hand a squeeze. "I know when I find something special too."

His eyes widened. "You'll go out with me, on a real date?"

Her chest fluttered again, from nerves this time, not courage, but she wasn't letting fear stop her. "I will."

His smile deepened. Then he turned her hand over and kissed the inside of her wrist.

Her chest, which had been fluttery before, felt electrified.

He looked up at her, his eyebrows raised.

Now was the time to say no. No, I don't want this. No, I can't date you. No, I'm afraid.

But she didn't say a word.

His eyes held hers for a long moment, and then slowly—excruciatingly slowly—he kissed his way up the inside of her arm, his lips warm and tender, his long hair and beard brushing against her skin.

Then he stopped and pulled away.

Why was he—

Oh. He was drawing his chair closer to hers.

Its metal legs made a scraping sound against the concrete, a sound that she'd never given much thought, a sound that now made her shiver.

He looked back at her face, as if he'd noticed the tremor that ran through her. He held her gaze and slid one hand behind her back, gliding his fingers over the fabric of her tank top.

"One kiss?" His voice was as smooth as the cheesecake.

She swallowed hard. "Uh, technically, you've already kissed me."

"Those were just pre-kisses. They don't really count."

Her breathing grew deeper, and her pulse pounded. "One kiss."

He pulled her closer and kissed her shoulder.

And her neck.

At last…at long, long last…her lips.

Warmth filled her whole body, and she slid her arms around him, moving toward his gentle strength.

And her heart, which had hunkered down like a tender perennial struggling through winter, opened in the sun.

Samantha gave her hair one last fluff and studied herself in her bathroom mirror.

Did she look like a woman who'd been kissed the night before?

Granted, after that one kiss on her lips, Lucas had finished his cheesecake and gone home.

But that one kiss… What a kiss. Was it any wonder she had such a sparkle in her eyes?

It wasn't just physical attraction she felt for him. She enjoyed talking and laughing with him. When she was with him, she felt braver and happier and more like herself. And Lucas would never lie to her the way Reg had. He was straight-forward. Decent. Honest.

She never had fixed a meal for him as she'd planned. Maybe she should. Something simple, casual, not a big deal.

She let out a long sigh and rolled her eyes. She'd almost avoided getting involved with him because she thought he was too young, and which of them was currently acting like a teenager? It was time to stop mooning about and get to work.

She unplugged her curling iron, ran down the stairs, and grabbed the letter she needed to mail.

As she headed to the mailbox, Lucas appeared in the early morning sunshine, walking Elvira.

"Good morning," she called.

He turned to face her. "Hey, beautiful, how are you?"

"Great." Really, really great. Better than she'd been in, well…years.

He switched Elvira's leash to the other hand. "I meant to tell you last night. I'm heading out of town today."

"Oh." She'd miss him. Even on days she didn't see him, she liked knowing he was next door. Now she'd have to delay her plan to cook for him again. "Where are you going?"

"Uh, to a cabin that a friend of mine owns down in the Ozarks."

"A guys' fishing trip?"

"No. No fishing." His smile was gone, his face tense. "I just need a few days away."

Her muscles tightened. Her pulse kicked up. The hope that had blossomed inside her heart instantly shriveled.

Because although his words sounded fine, his tone didn't. It had that faint coating of untruth that she'd heard in Reg's voice time and time again. That note she'd told herself repeatedly she was imagining.

Look how well that turned out.

She held up her letter, forced her lips to smile, and tried to keep her voice light. "Be right back. I'm going to drop this in the mailbox." She hurried across the road.

She should have known that getting over Reg would take years of healing, if it was possible at all. She wasn't in any way ready for a relationship. All it took was that odd note in Lucas's voice to send her mind bolting down paths to paranoia.

To start her wondering what kind of man kisses a woman so sweetly and tenderly and then needs a few days away. To make her wonder exactly what he needed to get away from. To even make her wonder if he was leaving to see some other woman.

"Sorry, but I've got to grab my lunch and get to work," she said, as she came back across the road. She bent down and petted Elvira's head, as if nothing was wrong. "I hope you have a great trip."

Then, before he could do more than mumble goodbye, she scurried back inside. She grabbed her things, went through the door from the hall into her garage, and—with him still standing in the grass—drove away with her best ladies-auxiliary-board smile firmly in place.

At least until she turned onto the next street.

There, she pulled over and parked under a large maple tree. She turned off the engine and sat, motionless, veins throbbing with adrenaline.

Okay, it was obvious that she was being paranoid, that she should talk to him and ask more about his plans.

But it was just as obvious that kind, honest, uncomplicated Lucas was hiding something. No matter what explanation he gave, she wouldn't be able to believe it.

All the pain and anger she'd felt in Dallas were back, as if a switch had been flipped, flooding her mind and body with the bitterness and brokenness of betrayal.

She'd thought she'd moved past this.

Wrong.

Wrong.

Wrong.

She couldn't handle a relationship. She wasn't ready.

If she ever *was* ready for a new relationship, it wouldn't be with another man with secrets.

Lucas was lost.

Totally, completely, these-directions-are-worthless lost.

"Feel free to navigate, Elvira."

Elvira, sitting on the passenger seat of his truck, gnawed on her rawhide bone.

Lucas reread the Post-it with his scribbled notes and studied the so-called road ahead. It wasn't much more than a deeply rutted dirt path with a few pieces of gravel sprinkled here and there for effect. Not that all the roads around Abundance were four-lane interstate. Down here in the Ozarks, though, the back roads seemed narrower, hemmed in by intensely green trees whose branches knit together overhead, almost blocking out the sun. The hum of the insects seemed louder, loud enough that he could hear all those bugs over the AC, through his rolled-up windows.

The trip, which had seemed like such a good idea, may have been a mistake.

Yes, he was grateful his buddy at Whole Hog had been

willing to lend him his cabin. Yes, he understood that except on the hill by the canoe rental place, there was no cell signal out here. But Lucas had been driving for forty-five minutes and he had no idea where he was or how to find that canoe rental place. If he couldn't find that, there was no way he'd find the "little road a half mile past it, right after the big stump" that was supposed to take him the last three miles to the cabin.

In theory, the plan had been perfect. He'd taken off Monday, Tuesday, and Wednesday from Whole Hog, plenty of time to drive down here, smooth out the rough places in his manuscript, and get it turned into his editor first thing Thursday morning. He'd tossed some clothes and a toothbrush in a duffel bag, and packed up his computer, his printer, two reams of paper and his favorite red pens. He'd brought provisions: leftover barbecued brisket, chips, peanut butter, bread, apples, and a case of Red Bull. And he'd thrown in dog food and Milk-Bone treats for Elvira.

The idea was to be where he could focus, away from the internet, family, friends, and his distracting next-door neighbor.

Absolutely nothing to keep him from completing his work on time.

But none of that was going to help if he spent the next three days lost.

Frankly, none of it was going to help if he kept stewing about Samantha.

Even though he'd texted her, "Hey," and, a few minutes later, "Heading out," before he left Abundance, she hadn't replied.

Why did he have to bring up his trip to the Ozarks earlier this morning without first thinking it through?

Was he a moron?

No. He was a coward. A coward with a deadline.

He wanted to tell her the truth about why he was leaving town. After she'd mailed her letter, he'd had an urge to explain everything—the books he'd written, the pen name, the deadline.

When she told him to have a great trip, she'd sounded as if what she actually wanted was for him to wander down to the river behind the cabin, fall in, and drown.

But had he told her? No.

Total coward.

He could call her right now, before he lost cell service.

He eyed the phone, tucked into the console between his seat and Elvira's.

He'd known Samantha less than a month. Was he really ready to tell her that he was Kendrick Larson?

Sure, she'd made that nice comment about him writing a cookbook. But, seriously, recipes weren't creative writing. The creative part about a cookbook wasn't the words. It was the recipes. Plus, look at all those celebrity chefs. People thought chefs were cool.

They thought science fiction writers were weird.

Besides, he was on deadline. His book was due to the editor in three days. No pushing the date back. No excuses. If he didn't get the manuscript delivered, he'd have to give up his slot in the editor's queue. His book would get edited in the next available slot, a slot which, knowing how much his editor was in demand, was probably eight months away.

With all he had to get done, he didn't have the time or emotional energy to deal with his insecurities about writing. If Samantha said anything that wasn't downright glowing, his mind would twist her words into snark and play them again and again every time he opened his computer.

The only way to get his book finished was to stay in a bubble where there was nothing but him and the story, no negativity.

It could be that everything with Samantha was fine. She might have sounded stressed because of work or a toothache or uncomfortable shoes—something his mom said was a real problem with women's fashion.

Plus, they'd never even been on a real date. He didn't need to tell her what he was doing every minute of the day. He was his own man. A guy who never wanted to be bored, never wanted to be tied down. He was independent.

Or as independent as a guy could be when he was totally lost.

He rounded a huge curve, and the road dipped, then rose again.

There—now that he'd reached the top of the hill, he could see it. A small wooden building with a big, hand-painted sign that said *Bubba and Lou's Canoe Rentals*. A rickety-looking trailer sat in the side lot with six canoes strapped on. A row of brightly colored life vests hung over the porch rail. And in the window, a smaller sign, painted by the same hand, proclaimed that the establishment sold *Ice, Night Crawlers, and Beer*.

He pulled into the dirt parking lot and dug his phone out of his pocket.

Yep, two bars.

But not a single message from Samantha.

Should he try to call her? Or send another text?

Nope.

He had a cabin to find and a manuscript to finish.

Chapter Twenty-Two

"Well, Clay..." Deanna, the social worker, leaned back against his living room wall and scribbled on her clipboard. Her dark-brown hair fell forward, hiding what she wrote.

Clay hugged the twins, one sitting on either side of him on the couch, tightly against him.

She had to think he was doing all right, had to let him keep the girls. Sure, he'd looked it up online, and he knew this was what was called a family assessment, knew that the state couldn't take Lark and Lea away without a court order, but if this visit didn't go well...

"You're doing an amazing job with your nieces." Deanna smiled at him. "If only every child who lost her parents was as lucky."

His breath came out in jerks and his eyes blurred. He pressed a kiss onto Lark's head, then Lea's.

"I'm so sorry to stop by unannounced on a Monday evening and put you through this. I hope you understand, though, that the state has to investigate anytime there's a report of a child in danger."

"I understand." His voice came out shaky, and he cleared his throat.

"You keep right on doing exactly what you're doing. The girls are getting along wonderfully." She smiled at each of the twins and headed toward the front door. "Here's my card so you'll have my number if you want that information I mentioned."

Clay set the girls on the floor, then followed her to the doorway, said goodbye, and watched her leave.

She got in her sensible sedan and gave a quick wave. As if nothing had happened.

As if he hadn't just aged ten years.

He kept a polite expression in place and waved back as she drove away into the warm evening. Back inside, he took out her card and dutifully typed her number into his phone, just in case.

Then his shoulders drooped, his muscles—clenched for the past half hour—turned to Jell-O, and a numbness replaced the buzzing litany of fears that had filled his head since his conversation with Kristen.

Those fears had echoed in his mind while he stayed up until one in the morning, cleaning and organizing everything in his townhouse. They'd repeated in his head as he worked eight hours today, then came home and fed the twins. And they'd gotten nearly deafening after dinner, as he watched the clock, telling the girls again and again how much he loved them, and expecting a visit from social services at any minute.

All because of Kristen Hamlin.

He'd been a fool, thinking the two of them should get back together.

No way. He'd never date someone so heartless and underhanded and mean.

He turned back to the living room, where the girls were playing with the giant Lego blocks. "No one is ever, ever taking you guys away from me. I couldn't bear it."

Then he picked up Lea, carried her up the stairs, and put her in the crib so that he could go get Lark.

"Bath time," he said to Lark once he'd scooped her up. "After that, you two have to go to sleep quickly. Don't even think about that routine where you have me come in every few minutes for an hour and a half."

Lark looked up at him, all innocent eyes.

"Really, you two have to sleep tonight." He put her in the crib. "With that mess I created on Saturday and spending all day Sunday cleaning, I am so behind I can't even believe it."

Lea babbled something, and Lark replied.

"I'm serious. If Uncle Clay is going to keep his company afloat, he's got to get stuff done." He walked toward the bathroom to fill the tub. "But first, it's time to play with the duckies."

Just after eight on Tuesday morning, Samantha brushed the grass clippings off her shoes onto the mat and knocked on the door to Clay's apartment.

He opened the door. "Hey, thanks for coming over. I've got the flash drive in the kitchen."

She followed him inside, where Lark and Lea sat in

their high chairs, eating Cheerios and banana slices. One girl—she wasn't sure which—had a pink sippy cup and bib. The other had a purple sippy cup and bib.

"Hi, Lark. Hi, Lea." She waved at them.

"Uh, this is Lark." Clay touched the shoulder of the girl with the purple bib. "That's Lea." The one in pink.

Samantha looked from one girl to the other. Absolutely identical. "How do you tell them apart?"

"At first, I couldn't. Before I brought them back from Hawaii, I wrote their names on the bottoms of their feet in Sharpie."

Samantha glanced over at the girls. Four bare, clean little feet stuck out at the bottom of the high chairs.

"Now that I know them, they act differently. And Lark's got darker hair."

Samantha nodded, as if she saw what he meant, but both girls had the exact same amount of hair in the exact same color.

"Anyway, I'll be in later," he said. "After I drop the girls off and meet with the building owner about the fire." He shuffled some papers on his kitchen table. "Again, thanks for coming over to get the flash drive. It's in this pile somewhere."

"No problem."

Clay looked horrible. His eyes were bloodshot, his skin was pale, and he had dark shadows under each eye.

She wasn't going to tell him that, and she understood that the launch day for Caribbean Treasure was getting closer all the time, but his business was never going to survive if he kept pushing himself so hard. She knew his plans hadn't included twin baby girls, but they were part of his life. He had to adjust. In a healthy way. "Did you sleep at all last night?"

"A little." He shrugged. "I got behind on work Saturday and yesterday I had to spend the whole day cleaning."

Now that he mentioned it, his townhouse was clean. Really clean. So clean that it made her feel as if she needed to mop her kitchen floor tonight.

"I'll be fine. Lots of coffee." He motioned toward a large travel mug on the counter. "Tonight I'll go to bed when the twins do."

After fishing the flash drive out of the pile, she slid it into the pocket of her dress pants, and they started toward the front door.

An odd sound came from the back of the townhouse.

"What was—" Clay dashed toward the kitchen. "Oh, no!"

"Clay?" She took two steps toward the kitchen.

He met her in the hall and held out a warning hand. "Leave. Fast. Before you get it too." His skin, which had merely been pale before, now had a tinge of greenish gray.

"They're sick?"

"Lea is. And all of a sudden I don't feel so good."

"Can I do anything to help?"

"Just leave. Wash your hands. Maybe Lysol the flash drive."

Samantha nodded and scurried out the door.

Once outside, she took deep breaths of fresh air. Each grassy lungful would hopefully clean out any germs she'd inhaled. Then she hurried back to her townhouse, washed her hands twice, wiped the flash drive down with a Clorox wipe, and got in her car.

She now had a stop she needed to make before work, because a woman learned a lot about medicine when her husband went through residency. Half an hour later, she left a bag with Gatorade and Pedialyte on Clay's front porch and texted him to look for them.

Then she headed to Norware.

The marketing team was at a meeting out of town. Clay was out sick. So it would only be her, Gareth, Heidi, and Glen, getting ready for the launch.

She couldn't do much, but at least she'd be there to answer the phones.

Chapter Twenty-Three

Clay lugged the laundry basket down the stairs. The stacked washer-dryer combo in the corner of the kitchen was small, but he wasn't sure he'd have survived the past twenty-four hours without it.

He moved the wet load to the dryer, shoved another load in the washer, and added soap and liquid disinfectant. If he had to guess, he'd say this raised the score for the flu to five crib sheets, eight little outfits, two of his shirts, two pairs of his shorts, and the living room carpet.

At last, though, as the sun came up this Wednesday morning, the vomiting and diarrhea seemed to have stopped for both him and the twins.

Today Norware would have to survive again without him. He had to sleep.

He pushed Start on the washer and dragged himself upstairs to look in on the twins. Both were asleep.

Then he stumbled toward his bedroom, ripped the

sheets off his bed, and stepped under the shower.

Ten minutes later, free from the germy grunge, he pulled on clean clothes and collapsed onto the bare mattress.

Her world had collapsed so fast.

Kristen watched the rain pour down outside and pushed the last bite of her TV dinner of spaghetti and meat sauce back and forth in the little plastic dish, not really hungry.

A week ago she'd been looking forward to a special date with Clay, and she'd been sure her work with Fibonacci Publishing would continue for years to come. She'd even gotten past the shock of Dylan and Amelia's marriage and—though she felt bad for his first wife—had reached a place where she hoped the new marriage would make both Dylan and Amelia happy.

Then she'd learned that Amelia had gotten her fired from Fibonacci.

Next, she'd accidentally texted Deanna and made Clay furious with her.

Oh, the past couple of days she'd tried to move forward and fix things.

She'd sent Clay several texts, but he'd ignored them.

She'd stopped by her dad's newspaper this afternoon, hoping perhaps he needed an extra hand in the newsroom. Her experience was with editing textbooks, and she really didn't want to be a reporter and go out and interview people, but she needed a job. Maybe she could learn AP style and be a copy editor for the newspaper.

Instead of getting a job offer, she'd heard that *The Abundance News* was struggling, about to switch from publishing five days a week to two.

No job. And unless she got a chance to apologize, no hope with Clay.

She pushed her flip-flops around under her chair with her bare feet and took a bite of her spaghetti.

Which had grown cold.

Outside, lightning flashed in the distance and thunder rumbled, almost drowning out the faint *ding* of her phone.

It was a text from Samantha, asking her to call if she was home.

Kristen dialed her cousin. "Hey, Samantha, I'm home."

"Great. Listen, can you peek out on Clay's porch and be sure he took in that bag of Gatorade and Pedialyte I left there yesterday? I was running late this morning and forgot to look when I drove to work, and I haven't heard from him all day."

"Pedialyte?"

"Yeah. The twins got a stomach virus yesterday morning. I know from when my ex was doing his residency that they'll need Pedialyte. I'd check Clay's porch myself, but I'm on my way straight from the office to have dinner with Jack and Tess."

A jolt of worry shot through Kristen. The twins were so little. She couldn't even imagine the poor things with a stomach virus. "I'll go check right now." She hung up, slid her feet into her flip-flops, and dashed to the door. No wonder Clay hadn't replied to her texts. He'd been taking care of the twins when they were sick.

But not giving them Pedialyte.

The package was still on his porch, the plastic bag half blown off in the storm.

She knocked on his door.

No answer. But his car was right there in the drive, where it had been when she went to see Dad at the newspaper. She should have realized something was wrong if Clay was home during a weekday afternoon.

She banged harder on the door and rang the doorbell. *Don't ignore me, Clay Norris, just because you're still mad.* If Samantha said the twins needed this stuff—Kristen pulled the bottle out and scanned the label—to prevent dehydration, then it was important.

The door jerked open and the smell of bleach wafted out.

"Clay, Samantha brought this over yesterday. She says if your girls have a stomach virus, they need it." Kristen held the bottle toward him.

"What?" He squinted, as if he'd just woken up and even the stormy, gray day was too bright. "Kristen, the girls and I were sick all last night. What we need is sleep."

He did look pale and exhausted. But the poor girls were probably even worse. "What about dehydration? Maybe you should wake them up and give them some of this stuff to drink."

"When I left the hospital in Hawaii, my mom told me never to never wake a sleeping baby."

"Can we go check on them? Please?"

"What is this, Kristen, part of your—" his voice raised in pitch and came out in a singsong tone—"'helpful, but not nosy, neighbor' routine?"

For a second, she stood there, mind spinning. She'd heard...no, wait, she'd *said* that very thing. On the phone. To Deirdre. Not to Clay. "How did you hear that?"

His chin jutted out. "Through the HVAC vent. I know all about why you moved in next door to me. I even know you've been fired."

Heat poured through her body. "You've been eavesdropping on me? Spying?"

"Isn't that the very same reason you moved in next door to me?"

Her stomach tightened. "I—I—" There was more to it than that. She'd done it for Gwen. But now wasn't the time to try to get that point through the concrete of his skull. "I'm going to check on the girls." She slipped past him and raced up the stairs toward their room.

Lark and Lea lay curled together, looking pale and fragile.

"Lark." Kristen brushed a fingertip across the little girl's cheek. "Sweetie, wake up."

Lark lay there, motionless.

Carefully, Kristen lifted her from the crib and patted her on the back.

She stayed asleep, and she looked...wrong.

Adrenaline shot through Kristen's veins. "Clay," she screamed. "Get in here!"

Heavy footsteps raced closer.

He burst into the room and looked at Lark, then picked up the other baby. "Lea, wake up. Lea!" He shook her arm and squeezed one of her feet.

Lea let out a tiny groan, but hung limp.

"Lea!" he shouted.

There was no response. At all.

Clay's face went white.

"Kristen." His voice came out raspy. "We've got to get them to the ER."

Clay shoved his car into gear, then sped toward the hospital, struggling to see through the rain and the flapping windshield wipers.

In the back seat, Lark and Lea lay in their car seats, little heads drooping.

Kristen, squeezed in between them, held sippy cups full of Pedialyte to their lips.

How could he have slept without checking on the girls?

He could have set an alarm to wake him after a few hours. He could have called his mom or Marianne Quigley and to ask if there was anything he should worry about with a stomach bug. He could have called the doctor's office. He could have Googled it. He could have asked Kristen or Samantha or even Lucas to come over and check on the girls. Had he done any of that?

No.

As soon as Lark and Lea were no longer vomiting or having diarrhea, he'd just left them in their crib, taken a shower, and gone to bed.

He glanced back at them in the rearview mirror.

Tiny. Helpless.

His hands trembled, and he gripped the steering wheel tighter and whipped the car around the next corner.

The sound system of his car beeped, signaling an incoming text on his phone.

He read the screen on the dash.

A message from Deanna.

His stomach clenched. No matter how good he'd made things seem two days ago when Deanna stopped by, he wasn't qualified to be the twins' guardian. One virus and that was obvious.

But how did she know? He shot a glance at Kristen. "You didn't tell her the twins are sick, did you?"

Kristen glared at him. "Are you out of your mind? When would I have done that?"

"Oh, right." Maybe Deanna was following up. Or letting him know that the incident report had been closed. He punched a button on his steering wheel so his phone would read the text aloud.

The electronic voice came over the car's speakers. "Clay. I hope it's okay to text you. I wanted to warn you that I've had a horrible stomach virus the past two days. I might have been contagious when I visited you and your nieces. I hope you all stay well."

For a second, his mind felt numb, then blood rushed in and he heard his own heartbeat, pounding in his head.

"This is your fault!" he snarled at Kristen. "If you'd kept your nose out of my business, that social worker never would have come to my house and the girls never would have been exposed."

He turned onto the street that led to the hospital, quickly gaining on the car ahead of him. "You move in next door, acting like you're perfect. Even when you dated your boss—who was married. And now the twins are sick because you interfered." He jerked the car into the ER entrance and into a parking spot. "If anything happens to them, it's your fault."

Kristen opened the back passenger-side door. "But—but—" she mumbled as she wriggled her way out of the car.

"Stop," Clay yelled.

"But we need to get the girls inside." She unbuckled Lark.

He grabbed the double stroller from his trunk, put Lea inside, then strode around to the other side of the vehicle. "Now give me Lark."

Her movements stiff, Kristen held the little girl and the sippy cup toward him.

He tossed the cup in the storage compartment at the bottom of the stroller, strapped Lark in, and popped open an umbrella. "Now leave us alone."

He couldn't run. He didn't want to jostle the girls in the stroller, and it was awkward, pushing with one hand and holding the umbrella over the girls with the other, but he walked as fast as humanly possible to the ER door.

Getting his nieces to help. Getting them away from the cause of all their problems.

Getting them away from Kristen Hamlin.

Chapter Twenty-Four

Kristen stood motionless by Clay's car as the rain poured down, soaking her hair and matting her clothes to her body.

He hurried through the parking lot with the stroller, then disappeared into the double doors of the emergency room just as a huge bolt of lightning shot across the darkened sky. A rumble of thunder followed.

Numbly, she walked under the covered portico, where only ambulances were allowed to drive. She slumped against a brick pillar, eyes never leaving the door where Clay had gone in.

Bit by bit, the numbness faded from her body. Her throat felt thick and her stomach burned.

Clay was right. All of this was her fault. Those poor little girls would be happy and healthy and doing perfectly fine if she hadn't gotten involved in their lives. If she hadn't blabbed to Deanna.

She'd thought she was doing what Gwen wanted. But Gwen would never have wanted this.

So what should she do now? Go home?

That was what Clay would want. In fact, he probably wanted her to pack and move out of the townhouse. Or, better yet, out of town. She couldn't blame him. All her efforts to help the twins had been, at best, unneeded. Clay had been doing fine.

Without her help.

That book she'd read while trying to improve things in her life had been useless. She hadn't changed at all, hadn't left the past behind. She was still the same person she'd been in high school. Still the person who'd had an affair with a married man. Still the person who, at her very core, was unlovable.

No wonder Clay wanted nothing to do with her.

She lowered herself to sit on the concrete—still dry under the canopy—and leaned back against the brick pillar. Her head fell to her knees, and she closed her eyes.

God? I know I've messed up. Again and again and again. But please don't let anything happen to Lark and Lea. Please let them be okay. And please, if there's any way, forgive me for what I've done.

"Amen," she said aloud.

For a long moment, she sat there, waiting.

The rain didn't stop, and the clouds didn't part, letting down rays of sunshine. She didn't feel instantly washed and pure and holy, but she did feel a tiny bit better. And she did know what to do.

She stood up, squared her shoulders, and moved to the edge of the canopy. Then she dashed through the rain to the ER doors where she'd seen Clay go inside.

The woman at the desk sat up taller. "Do you need to be seen?"

Kristen shook her head. "I came with a friend." She must look pretty bad, soaked to the skin. Even if she texted him and begged, though, Clay would never allow her to wait with him and the twins in an examining room.

But eventually, the twins would be treated and sent home. Or they would be admitted. If they went home, Clay would have to take them to his car, going right past her. If they were admitted, the hospital had visiting hours. She could walk into their room.

One way or another, she was going to see the twins.

And if the worst, the very worst, happened, and the twins didn't make it—she squeezed her eyes shut to keep from crying—she would be there for Clay.

Clay's heart pounded as he watched the nurse examine Lark and Lea, then call for help.

A doctor rushed in, her shoes silent on the tile floor.

"I think they're both severely dehydrated," the nurse said. "Their diapers are dry. Sounds like they've had that stomach virus." She angled her head toward Clay.

He nodded. "We all got sick yesterday morning."

The doctor examined Lark, then Lea, pinching the skin on the side of their stomachs, looking in their mouths, and running a hand over their heads.

"Start IVs on both of them, this one first." She touched Lark's arm. "I'll get someone in here to help you."

The nurse rushed away.

The doctor drew back the curtain. "Maureen, I need you in Room Nine."

Another nurse rushed in.

"Chelsea went for IV bags. I want both these girls started on saline drips. Stat."

The first nurse returned, opened a drawer, and pulled out tubing and needles.

Clay's throat ached. The needles looked so big.

But even when the nurse inserted the needles, the girls barely responded.

All those times he'd been so frustrated when they cried. All those times he'd begged them to be quiet. What he wouldn't give to hear them screaming their lungs out.

Five minutes later, the IVs were in, tiny blood pressure cuffs were strapped on each of their left arms, and wires were taped to their chests, connecting each girl to a heart monitor.

The monitors beeped, four jagged green lines ran across each screen, and numbers displayed by the lines changed every second or so. But Clay didn't know what any of them meant. Heart rate—yeah, he knew what that was of course—but he didn't know what the girls' heart rates should be.

"What happens now?" Clay said, barely above a whisper.

"We're going to do some tests." The doctor opened the curtain to leave. "And give the IV fluids time to kick in."

The nurse named Maureen ran a gentle hand over Lea's face, brushing back a wisp of hair. She adjusted Lark's blood pressure cuff, then glanced at Clay. "I'll be right back."

"Will they be okay?"

"Dehydration can be very serious in infants, but we're doing everything we can." She checked the IV drip and stepped outside the curtain.

Pinpricks jabbed at the back of his eyes.

She didn't answer his question.

Which meant she didn't know.

Clay positioned his chair to where he could see both girls and clenched his hands together, knuckles white. Every issue at work boiled down to one of three answers: more thinking, more time, or more money. None of those would help. He couldn't fix this, no matter what he did. Even the medical staff didn't know if they could fix this.

Then, for some reason, that annoying, squishy globe came to mind. The line where it said "the little bitty babies in God's hands," played in his head.

He blew out a long breath and twisted his hands together. He didn't talk to God very often, and he wasn't sure it was okay to pray with his eyes open, but he was going to try. Hopefully God would understand.

"God, help them be all right. Let me have another chance to do better taking care of them." He swallowed hard. "Please."

He leaned forward slightly, gripped the front edge of his chair with both hands, and stared at his nieces amid all those wires and tubes.

If only, if only, he'd never met Kristen Hamlin.

Time dragged on, minute by minute. One hour, then another. He filled out paperwork that the woman from the desk brought back. The medical team checked for meningitis and did X-rays to look for infection in the girls' lungs. Mostly, Clay just sat, watching Lark and Lea, holding their little hands. Once, he thought he saw Lea move, but he wasn't sure. Maybe he'd imagined it. He shifted his position on the hard, plastic chair and peered at her more intensely.

Outside, beyond the curtains that separated him from the rest of the ER, the wheels of a gurney rolled by, accompanied by a set of feet in white tennis shoes.

"Don't worry, ma'am, we'll take care of you," said a woman who sounded like she was from the Deep South.

More footsteps neared. "I'm here, Marianne," a man said. "By the time I got parked, they'd taken you back. It took me a while to find you."

"I'm glad you're here," a different woman said. Her voice sounded like someone from here in Abundance, sounded like…

Clay jerked his head and stared at the curtain. That was Marianne Quigley's voice.

"We'll run a number of tests," said the woman with the southern accent. "But I expect you've got this stomach virus that's going around. You wouldn't be the first person to pass out from it."

"One of the kids from my day-care center had it. His mom called right before I got dizzy," Marianne said.

A hollow feeling filled Clay's chest as his mouth dropped open and the gurney moved away.

One of the kids at Lark's and Lea's day care had the stomach bug.

Sure, he and the twins might have gotten the illness from Deanna.

More likely, they got it at day care. Especially if the

other children drooled as much as the twins. It also made more sense, now that he thought about it, because people didn't get usually sick immediately after they were exposed to a virus.

He'd blamed their illness on Kristen.

Kristen, who pounded on his door and woke him up. Who insisted on checking on the girls. Who was the whole reason he brought them to the hospital.

And what had he done? He'd yelled at her that it was her fault and left her outside in the pouring rain. She was probably worried sick.

His stomach burned. He was not only a total failure as a guardian, he was a horrible human being.

He reached for his phone and pulled it from his pocket, eyes still on the girls.

He gave each of them one last steady gaze, glanced down at the phone, and as quickly as he could, tapped out a text to Kristen.

Kristen's phone dinged, and she pulled it from her purse.

A text from Clay.

I'm sorry I said it was all your fault. It's not.

She sucked in a sharp breath and texted back.

Are the girls okay? I'm in the waiting room. Can I do anything?

A second later, a reply came through.

Girls getting IV fluids. No change yet. Hold on.

Hold on? What was going on? Was the doctor talking to Clay? Was something happening with one of the girls?

She squeezed her phone tighter and tighter, peering at the screen as if she might make a text appear, but Clay didn't send another message.

A moment later, a man in scrubs came out of the emergency room into the lobby. "Is there a Kristen Hamlin here?"

She leapt up. "Right here."

"Can you come with me?"

She hurried to his side and walked with him past the nurses' station through what seemed like a maze. At last he stopped and pulled back the pale-blue curtain to the area marked Room 9.

Inside, the twins lay side by side on the ER bed, and tubes and wires stuck out from under the blanket that covered their bodies.

Her throat went raw.

Clay rose from a plastic chair.

Tears welled in her eyes as she moved toward him. "Are they going to be all right?"

"I don't know." He pulled her into his arms. "I can't lose them, Kristen. I can't. I love them."

"I know you do, Clay." She held him close, tears streaming down her cheeks. "I love them too. I've been praying for them and—"

One of the girls let out a small sound.

Kristen and Clay spun toward the bed.

Lark moved one arm.

And Lea shifted her head.

Kristen gasped.

"Nurse," Clay yelled. "They're moving!"

The curtain slid back, and two women hurried in, both in scrubs.

"Let's take a look," the younger woman said.

Kristen saw "M.D." on her nametag.

At a pace that seemed painfully slow, the doctor examined Lark, peering at her mouth and her eyes, and pinching the skin on the side of her tummy. "Yes. This little girl seems to be doing much better."

Kristen gripped Clay's arm, squeezing tightly.

He turned to her, his eyes filled with hope.

The doctor turned to Lea.

Step by step, she went through the same checks. At last she faced Clay. "This little one is doing better too." She wrapped her stethoscope around her neck. "I'd like to keep them overnight for observation, but I expect a full recovery for both of your nieces."

Clay's breath whooshed out, and Kristen's shoulders drooped.

"Thank you, thank you so much." Clay shook the doctor's hand.

Kristen stood beside him and nodded. "We're so grateful to you, to everyone here."

"Dehydration can be risky in infants. Another hour or two could have been dangerous. It's a good thing you brought them in when you did." She pulled the curtain open, walked through, and closed it behind her.

Clay leaned down and cupped the twins' faces with his hands. "You're going to make it, girls. You're going to be just fine, thanks to Kristen."

Kristen's breath caught. "Clay, they might never have even gotten sick if it hadn't been for me." She'd caused the whole problem. She certainly shouldn't be thanked.

"No." He turned to her. "I think they got exposed to the virus at day care. It wasn't your fault. If you hadn't come by this evening and insisted on checking on them..."

For a second Kristen felt as if her heart had stopped, then her words tumbled out. "They got it at day care?"

"I learned that a little boy there had it. I guess we could have gotten the virus from Deanna, but I bet a drooling kid is a much more likely scenario."

Kristen's legs went weak, and she sat back down. "Oh, Clay." It wasn't her fault. She wasn't the reason the twins got sick.

"I'm so sorry." He sat beside her. "When I overheard you through the vent, I should have told you. When I was scared because the girls were sick, I shouldn't have jumped to conclusions. I shouldn't have yelled at you. Is there any way you can forgive me?"

She gulped in a ragged breath. "Of course, I forgive you. Anyone would have been terrified. And after Deanna's call, it did seem like it was my fault."

"But it *wasn't*." He pulled her into his arms and held her tightly. "You saved them."

"Actually," she said, "I think God saved them."

"Yeah, you're right." He ran a hand over her still-damp hair. "But you helped."

Then, right there, with the monitors beeping, he pulled her onto his lap and kissed her.

Warmth filled her heart, and she wrapped her arms around him and kissed him back.

And she kept on kissing him, right up until the curtain slid back, an orderly walked in, and the nurses at the desk clapped and cheered.

Kristen felt her cheeks grow red. She scooted over into her own chair and gave the nurses an awkward wave.

Clay just grinned.

Chapter Twenty-Five

By seven thirty Thursday morning, Lucas was packed and ready to go.

More than ready.

His manuscript was done. He'd smoothed the language, reworked some sticky plot issues, and added more internal monologue until he was happy with the story and fairly certain his editor would be as well.

It was time to leave the shack his buddy called a fishing cabin.

The place had four walls and a roof. The electricity worked. And the bed had been...adequate.

But it had been three days since Lucas had talked to anyone besides Elvira, three days since he'd taken a shower with more than a trickle of water pressure. And, after repairing a tear in the window screen with duct tape from his glove box, he'd killed seventeen mosquitoes in the cabin and slept each night coated in a thick layer of DEET.

He couldn't wait for central air conditioning, for Wi-Fi, and for fancy, overpriced coffee.

And though it might mean he was a little farther gone on Samantha than he'd admit out loud, he couldn't wait to talk to her.

He'd known she was special, but until he was away for a few days and had time to think about her, he hadn't realized how special. She was more serious than some of the women he'd dated, and yes, older, but she was also a woman that made a guy think, well…long term.

He locked the cabin—not that anyone in their right mind would break in—and mulled that idea around in his head. *Long term.* That was certainly an unfamiliar phrase in his dating vocabulary.

But in his gut, he knew it was what he wanted. He'd been kidding himself to think that he'd ever want to move on to someone else.

Not when she was the most fascinating woman he'd ever met.

He might have messed things up with her before leaving Abundance, but he could fix that. He *would* fix that, because he wanted her in his life.

"C'mon, Elvira." He opened the passenger door for her, and she leapt up. Even she knew it was time to get back to civilization.

He tossed his duffel in the back of his truck and started the engine.

A few minutes later he pulled into the rutted, gravel lot at Bubba and Lou's.

Sure enough, he had a cell signal again. His phone gave off a series of beeps as he hopped out of his car. Finally.

What he wouldn't give for conversation with a live person and a venti vanilla latte. He'd be happy if they simply had fresh, hot coffee. Ecstatic if they had real cream.

He rolled down a window for Elvira. Then he strode past the spot where the canoe trailer had been parked and walked across the wooden porch to the door of the small shop.

Locked.

Without even a *Be Back Soon* sign.

So much for conversation.

Or coffee.

He got back in his truck, rubbed Elvira's ears, and pulled out his phone. He'd continue his hunt for coffee on the way back, but he had to deal with first things first. He had to get his manuscript emailed to his editor. A few quick taps on his phone to set up a Wi-Fi hotspot, a moment to log in on his laptop, and he was able to send the email he'd already composed, manuscript attached.

Now, to check those phone messages. Maybe there was one from Samantha.

Yes! She'd texted him on Monday afternoon. He'd known she'd get over her little annoyance about his trip out of town. The two of them had something special, something that could last.

Probably, if things got serious between them, this episode would be something they laughed about in the future. Because the more he thought about it—he reached down to scratch a mosquito bite on his ankle—the more he could see something serious working out.

He opened her message and scanned it, then read it again.

Lucas, I'm going to be super busy with the new product launch at Norware. Why don't we think about that real date in a month or two?

His stomach grew hard and a dull ache formed around his heart. He was no dummy. He recognized a brush-off when he saw one. If she were interested in him, she wouldn't suggest waiting a month to go on a date.

What a mess. He'd found a woman he truly connected with, truly enjoyed. She was smart and beautiful and funny and absolutely perfect for him, and she was dumping him.

Was this some sort of cosmic payback for all the women he'd eased away from after only dating a few weeks?

No. This was totally connected to the other day, and it was his fault. At least partly his fault. He should have told Samantha the truth about his writing.

But it was also her fault. She was way overreacting. What they had could be special. They'd had one awkward conversation, and she was bailing?

Ridiculous.

This wasn't over.

And they weren't going to be discussing their relationship by text.

Samantha leaned forward with her elbows on her desk at Norware Games, hands holding her temples.

Why did Clay need the website updated today of all days? Why couldn't it wait until Friday, until tomorrow?

Today Clay was at the hospital until the twins were discharged. Everyone else—everyone who'd been in that meeting late Monday with Clay—was home sick with the stomach virus. She was lucky she'd been at her desk manning the phones, instead of attending the meeting, sharing germs and the giant chocolate chip cookie that Julie C. had made. Lucky she'd said no when Julie offered her some of the cookie afterward.

Sure, she'd avoided getting sick, but now she was on her own, the only person in the whole office. There was no one she could ask about the website software.

She should have told Clay the truth about how clueless she was regarding the software they used at Norware. Every night at home, she'd been going through training videos she found online. She'd gotten good with the calendar program and almost finished the tutorials about the expense software, but she hadn't learned how to use the website.

"Three changes," he'd said. "They won't take but five minutes."

She could call him back and tell him she couldn't do it. She could confess that it had taken her twenty minutes to figure out how to sign into the program and find the page that needed updating. But that would mean admitting how unqualified she was for this job.

She wasn't ready to do that.

It was time for one more try.

She squared her shoulders and reread the notes she'd taken when she talked with Clay. Then she scanned through the directions she'd found online and typed the changes in again.

And—

She clenched her hands into fists and let out a scream.

The changes were gone. Just like the other two times she'd tried. Why didn't they save? Why—?

A blur of a figure passed by the window, and Lucas burst in the front door. "Are you okay?"

She jerked her head up. She hadn't known anyone else was around, much less close enough to hear her scream, and Lucas was the last person she wanted to see. "No, I'm not okay. I'm having a computer problem."

"It's almost twelve. It might be easier after a break and something to eat. How about we go to lunch?" His normal, easy-going grin was gone. "We need to talk."

He was mad. Or hurt. Which, in her experience with men, was often the same thing. She'd thought her text was so well worded. She'd hoped any idea of the two of them dating would fizzle out. They could be neighbors, plain and simple.

No such luck, but she couldn't deal with him now. "I'm not taking a lunch. With Clay at the hospital—"

"Clay's at the hospital?" Concern replaced the irritated edge in Lucas's voice.

"He and the twins caught the stomach virus, and the girls got dehydrated."

Lucas stepped closer to her desk. "Are they okay?"

"They're fine, being discharged this morning. But with Clay gone and everyone else home sick with that virus, he needs me to update the website, and I haven't been able to get it to work."

"What do you think about a break? For a quick snack?" Lucas said. "I came here as soon as I got back in town—I mean, as soon as I'd taken a real shower."

She glanced down, searching for the right words.

"Really, I can't go." She looked straight at him. "Listen, I don't know what was going on with your trip to the Ozarks, but I had this weird feeling that you were lying to me. Probably paranoid, I know." She spread her hands awkwardly in the air. "But clearly I'm not over Reg, not ready to trust anyone and date again."

"Samantha, I—"

"Please, just leave." She gestured to the door. "I have to figure out this website stuff."

For a second he stood there, chest rising and falling, mouth tight.

And then, thankfully, he left.

Lucas strode toward his car, breathing hard. The woman was infuriating. He was not her ex-husband, the cheating scum. But that didn't seem to matter. She hadn't even given him a chance to explain.

He grimaced. He knew all too well that he'd had plenty of time to explain about his writing. He could have told her what he'd be doing in the Ozarks that night eating cheesecake or the next morning when he was in the yard with Elvira.

No, he hadn't actually lied, but he'd been less than forthcoming. He'd known she was uncomfortable, known he should have told her. But he hadn't.

He'd been too scared.

That was not who he was.

Not who he wanted to be. He wanted to be Thad Stephens. Honorable. Ready for adventure. Courageous.

One hand on the door handle of his truck, he stopped.

With a nod of his head, he spun around, headed back toward Norware, and walked in the front door. "Show me the problem."

"Lucas!" she jerked back.

Maybe he should have come in the building a little more quietly.

"I didn't mean to scare you, but I can update a website."

"Really?" Her face scrunched up. "Do you do the website for Whole Hog?"

"No, but… For now, just tell me what's wrong."

She studied him then gave a half-shrug. "I can't get the changes to save, no matter how many times I try."

"Did you hit the blue button that says Update?"

"What blue button? I made the changes. I saw them on the dashboard thingy. But when I check the live page, they're not there."

"I think I know what you're doing wrong. Let me show you."

"Okaaaay." She looked at him as if he might crash the whole system.

That wasn't going to happen. He wasn't an imbecile. Except for maybe how he'd handled things with her. "Do you mind?" He gestured toward her chair.

"I guess not." She got up. "But don't do anything without telling me first. I don't want you to make it worse than it is." She gave an awkward laugh.

"Are your changes in here? The way you want them?"

"No. Hold on." She leaned over him, her hair falling against his arm, the sweet floral scent of her perfume filling his system.

She typed, then scrolled up and down, checking the page. "Now it's ready."

"So, we hit Preview…" He moved the mouse to hover over the Preview button, but remembered her paranoia. "Is it okay if I do that?"

"Yes, but I hit Preview. Every time."

He clicked the mouse and a new screen opened up, showing the changes she'd made. "Does this look okay?"

"Yes," she said in an exasperated tone. "I've done this again and again. When you go back to the live page, it won't be there."

"That's the tricky part. Watch." With a quick move of the mouse, and without asking her permission, he clicked back to the previous screen, scrolled over slightly, and hit the Update button.

Samantha let out a gasp. "I never noticed that button."

He opened a new window, a live window, showing her the changes in place. "See? All fixed."

She leaned down, staring at the screen. "That's all I needed to do? Click that stupid button? I was going round and round and making the changes and not saving them?"

"Yep. Been there. Done that. Got all freaked out that it wasn't working and missed the obvious."

"Oh, my goodness, you really did know how to fix it. Thank you!"

He might not be Clay Norris, computer genius, but he did know a thing or two. "Now, can I show you something else?"

"All right."

He typed quickly, then jerked his head toward the screen.

She read aloud, "Sci-fi thrillers from Kendrick Larson. See what readers are talking about." She sounded confused.

"That's me." He touched the screen. "That's my pen name, and that's my website, which I have to update from time to time." He glanced up at her.

She looked at the website, then at him, then at the website again. "You're an author?

"Yeah." He drew in a deep breath. Moment of truth here. How would she respond?

Her eyes narrowed. "So, working at Whole Hog is what, just something you tell people like me?"

"No. You know my love of barbecue is real. I work at Whole Hog in the evenings. Then I come home and write. I wanted to tell you but…"

"This is why you went away? What made me feel as if you were lying?"

He sat up taller in the chair, back rigid. This wasn't going at all as he'd hoped. "I wasn't lying. I said I had to go out of town. I just didn't say that it was because I had to finish a book. But I didn't mean to hurt you. I wasn't ready to tell you yet. I haven't told anyone except my parents."

Her forehead furrowed. "Why not?"

He turned his chair to face her. "When I told the girl I dated for most of college, Jacqueline, about my writing, she made so much fun of me that I didn't write for two years. Two. Years. I couldn't miss my deadline this week, and I certainly couldn't miss it by two years."

Samantha's eyes grew wide. "You had a serious girlfriend?"

"Yeah."

"And she made fun of you?"

Lucas shifted his weight in the chair. "Yeah," he mumbled.

Her lips grew thin.

He didn't know what to say. Did he mention that Jacqueline hadn't been the brightest bulb on the Christmas tree? No, that sounded petty. Did he tell Samantha how much his writing had improved since college? Mention how many five-star reviews he'd received? Or did he keep sitting here, feeling as if she was judging him? Aaargh, this was horrible. He had to say something.

Suddenly, her face relaxed, and her lips parted in an expression that was half smile, half wonder. "You know, we're doing the same thing."

"What do you mean?"

"We're both being afraid. I'm afraid of being lied to. You're afraid of being laughed at."

He felt as if he'd been kicked in the gut. It was bad enough knowing he was a wimp. It was a thousand times worse knowing that she knew it too. He was no Thad Stephens, starship captain. He was more of a frantic salamander, darting under the leaves. But—

He pushed his shoulders back. "What's your email?"

She told him.

He typed it in. Connected to his backup storage in the cloud, and sent her a copy of his manuscript. "There. I'm not hiding who I am anymore, not being afraid. You can read the book I just sent to my editor this morning. It's part of a series, but it will make sense by itself."

"Really? How cool is that?" Her smile spread across

her face. "But what I was trying to say was that I'm not laughing at you. I'm proud of you."

He froze. "You are?"

"Yeah, I am."

His chest swelled, and he stood, facing her. *Proud of him.* She was proud of him.

"I should have talked to you. I shouldn't have let the anger I still feel toward Reg affect how I treated you," she said. "I can't wait to read your book."

"You may not like it. Most of my readers are men, and the stories are pretty violent."

"I'll like it."

Maybe she would, especially since he'd added that new character that was supposed to appeal to women and—

"Oh." He ran a hand across his mouth.

"What?"

"One of the characters…" He moved his weight from one foot to the other. "You have to know, I created her a long time before you moved in next door. That's why I was kind of freaked out when I met you."

She tilted her head to one side. "Why?"

"She looks like you. She even acts like you sometimes, the way you twist up your collar."

"Oh, yeah, I do that. That's weird that she does too." She angled her head to one side. "Is she an ax murderer or a prostitute or something?"

"No, she's the sexy heroine. The character I dreamed up to be the strong balance to my hero."

"The sexy heroine?" Samantha's arms fell to her sides, and a grin spread across her face.

Lucas stepped closer to her. "Yep." That grin was a

good sign. Maybe all this soul-baring had been worth it. "The stunning, sexy heroine, who my hero thinks about all the time. The woman who's so brave that he tries to be braver and stronger so he can be worthy of her."

Samantha's mouth pursed up. "That doesn't sound like me." She backed away slightly. "Remember? I'm the person who ran away from everything she knew so she could go to her hometown and hide."

"Are you kidding?" Lucas took her face in his hands and tipped her chin up so he could look in her eyes. "You suffered the worst possible betrayal and didn't let it break you. Yeah, you moved home, but you took a risk starting over here as an adult. You got a new job. You're creating a new life for yourself. You are very, very brave." He ran his thumb over her cheek. "Every bit the heroine."

"Oh," she whispered. Tension fell from her face and her shoulders lifted.

"The woman," he said, "I'd like to date."

"I'd...I'd like that too."

He slid his arms around her waist and kissed her.

She let out a soft moan and moved nearer, erasing the distance between them.

Electricity shot through every nerve ending in his body.

And all thoughts of Captain Thad Stephens and Lexi Ballard slipped from his mind.

This was not sci-fi hundreds of years in the future.

This was real.

This was now.

This was much, much better.

Chapter Twenty-Six

Clay peeked in the twins' room.

Their crib was empty, and the late-afternoon sun streamed through the window.

He spun and hurried toward the stairs. Kristen never should have let him sleep so long. What if the twins had needed him? What if they'd shown more signs of dehydration and she hadn't noticed? What if—

"Hey, there," Kristen called from the kitchen. "I'm glad you got some sleep."

"Are they okay? Have they been drinking enough?" He rushed into the kitchen and saw Lark and Lea sitting in their high chairs.

Lark was examining a Cheerio. Lea was playing with her sippy cup. Although they appeared alert and happy, neither girl was drinking.

"They're fine," Kristen said. "See how perky they look? They took a good nap and had some formula earlier.

I just brought them in and gave them each a few Cheerios to eat while I got their dinner ready."

"How much did they drink?" Clay grabbed a notepad and pen out of a kitchen drawer. "I'm going to start logging their fluid consumption in ounces."

"You don't need to do that. Remember what the nurse said? All you need to do is make sure they look healthy and have a normal number of wet diapers every day."

Clay held Lark's sippy cup toward her, but she ignored it. "More data would be better. It doesn't seem as if they're drinking enough."

"Clay, look at me."

He looked. She didn't even appear tired, though neither of them had slept a lot, staying with the girls all night in the hospital. Then she'd insisted he nap once they got home.

"You're going overboard here," she said. "Lots of parents probably do, after a scare. But you can't micromanage every little detail of their lives. You can't control everything."

"I'm not micromanaging."

"You are."

"No, I'm not. Even if I was, it's my responsibility to take care of them. I can't believe I let them get dehydrated. It's not happening again. I owe it to Gwen to make sure nothing bad happens to them."

Kristen leaned back against the kitchen counter, her face scrunched up. "Why?"

"Why what?"

"Why do you owe the impossible—making sure her kids never get sick—to Gwen? I mean, I know you miss her. I do too. But you're sacrificing a lot to take care of her kids and, even though I didn't want to believe it at first, you're doing a great job."

"Thanks. It means a lot to me to have you say that." He took a step toward the hall, hoping she would follow. "It was really nice of you to watch the twins so I could nap, but I should let you go home and get some rest…"

She didn't move. "I'm sure I'll go to bed early tonight. But you're ignoring my question. Why are you acting as if you have to make up for Gwen's death, as if it was your fault?"

He glanced toward the front door. This was not a conversation he wanted to have, but that didn't seem to matter to Kristen. The woman was stubborn. No, he knew her better than that. She was beyond stubborn.

She moved closer to him. "How could Gwen's death possibly be on you? You weren't even there. You—"

"Don't you see?" The words burst out. "I should have been. If I'd been there, I'd have told them not to take that helicopter tour. I knew they were dangerous. I had a friend in college whose dad had been a helicopter pilot in the military. One time, we all went out to dinner, and he told us those tours are regulated differently than normal flights."

"Clay." Kristen's tone was warmer, edged with a note of pity. "You can't really believe that."

"Of course I believe it. The guy knew what he was talking about."

"No. I mean you can't really believe that you could have convinced Gwen not to go on the tour."

"I could have if I'd been there. Only I had to work. But

there must have been some way I could have taken the time off. Told Blake and Brynn that giving two weeks' notice wasn't enough. Or delayed the launch of Caribbean Treasure."

"Clay," Kristen said firmly. "Stop." She leaned toward him, hands planted on her hips. "Do you even remember your sister? A helicopter tour is exactly the type of thing she would have latched onto and thought was a grand adventure. Nothing you could have said would have changed her mind."

The air solidified in Clay's lungs. "She—she..." His brain seemed to churn its way down the logic in Kristen's words, but get hung up on one line of code. Most of what she said made sense. Gwen probably did see some helicopter tour brochure and get all gung-ho. She would have ignored anything he or anyone else said to try to dissuade her. John and Mom and Dad would have followed along, all caught up in her excitement. She had that energy that got people on board with whatever crazy scheme she came up with. Surely though, somehow, he could have...

"She would have gone, no matter what you did. You aren't responsible for her death. And you aren't responsible for the twins' getting that stomach virus. Things happen. What you're saying, it's...it's almost like an issue of pride. You can't control everything. You're not God."

Clay leaned back against the wall behind him. His legs, his chest, his stomach... everything felt empty. Numb and tingly. After a second, he let out a long breath. It wasn't his fault. He wasn't in charge. God was. "You're...you're right."

"Yeah," Kristen said gently. "You don't owe Gwen anything. You don't need to take care of the girls out of some sense of duty. Or to atone for anything or—" She stopped, gave an odd twitch, and looked away.

"What?"

"Nothing." She jerked her shoulders, like a wet dog shaking off the last bit of water. "Anyway, you don't need to feel guilty, and you don't need to obsess over every ounce of fluid that the girls drink."

He checked again. The level of formula in the girls' sippy cups hadn't changed. Not even a quarter of an inch. "But they're not drinking."

Kristen turned and studied the twins a moment.

Lark gurgled at her.

Kristen picked up Lark's cup. "Wow," she said, in an overly dramatic voice. "This formula you have, Lark, is the best there is. I bet it's way, way better than Lea's." Kristen gave an exaggerated glance toward Lea and carried the cup over closer to Lea's high chair. "Sure, Lea, you can have it. After all, Lark doesn't want it."

She handed Lark's cup to Lea.

Lea, who already had her own cup in one hand, grabbed Lark's cup with the other and began guzzling from it.

Lark's face grew red and her lower lip jutted out.

"Oh, you're left out, aren't you, Lark?" Kristen said. "I can fix that." She snagged Lea's sippy cup right out of her hand and gave it to Lark.

Lark gave a happy squeal, took the cup, and tipped it high.

Kristen turned to Clay, chin raised, eyes sparkling.

"Really," she said, with a note of triumph in her voice, "I don't think you have a problem here."

Kristen looked from one twin to the other. Both of them had taken a big drink. Her plan had worked perfectly.

She quickly peeked at Clay. Any time he wanted to admit that she was amazing with the girls and that he needed to listen to good sense, she was ready to hear it.

"What's going on with you?" His tone didn't sound nearly as impressed as she'd expected.

"I'm getting the girls to drink, like you wanted."

"I mean, what was that look when you were talking about me taking care of the girls to atone for something?"

Her heart stuttered, but she kept her expression neutral. "I don't know what you're talking about." She tugged her T-shirt squarely into position and ran her hands down her shorts. "But you were right earlier. I should go home and get some rest."

"Not so fast." Clay picked up both sippy cups and set them on the counter. "Girls, dinner is going to be a bit delayed." He removed Lea from her high chair and carried her into the living room. Then he returned for Lark, gave Kristen a pointed gaze, and led the way in. He set Lark on the carpet next to her sister and gestured Kristen to the couch. "Sit."

Not happening. She edged toward the door. "Really, I—"

"You can't make me talk about stuff and then clam up about what's bothering you. It's hypocritical."

"I'm not hypocritical." Except she was. That was the

very word that had echoed through her mind when she'd accused Clay of trying to make up for something by taking care of the twins. Because that was one reason she'd felt such a need to become their guardian. To atone for her sins. Sins that she certainly didn't want to discuss.

"Prove it. Tell me what's going on. Is this about you going out with some guy who was married?"

Her lungs grew tight, and she crossed her arms. "Throwing something in my face that you heard while eavesdropping is out of line."

"It might be, but I don't care. The guy should have told you upfront that he was married. You're an ethical person. It probably never crossed your mind because you don't think that way."

The back of her throat pinched. He thought she was ethical. Thought all her problems had been caused because she was naïve. If only that were the case. If only she was worthy of his respect. Of his love. Of God's love.

"Really, Clay, I don't want to talk about this. I'm exhausted, and my mistakes are my own business." She glanced at Lark and Lea. Shouldn't they be fussy? Needing Clay's attention?

The twins happily babbled to each other, seeming perfectly content to let the adults continue their conversation.

"Kristen, we need to be honest with each other if we're going to get involved again. I want that, don't you?"

"Yeah." More than he could possibly know. "But you won't want to be involved with me if you know the whole story."

"Try me." Clay stepped closer. "You're giving up on

our relationship before you even talk to me. You're making assumptions."

It wasn't an assumption. It was a logical conclusion.

"Don't you think you should give me a chance? What if I don't think it's a big deal?"

"You will." Shame and guilt and regret twisted together inside her. Why had she been so stupid? How had she done something so despicable?

"Kristen?" Clay stroked her arm.

She pulled it away and reached for the doorknob.

"I know I was an idiot when I let our relationship end after high school. But I was a *teenager.* You don't have that excuse."

Pain stabbed into her chest. "You know what, Clay? You don't really know me. You knew me in high school, before I'd had my heart broken again and again and again. Before you and the next guy and the guy after that dumped me. Before my self-worth eroded into nothing."

His eyes widened.

"Oh, I'm not blaming you. Lots of women go through breakups and bounce back, no problem. But I didn't. Each time it happened, I thought less and less of myself. I'd start dating someone else and think that I had value again, but when they eventually broke up with me, I was even worse off than before. So when Dylan asked me out, when I had just started working at Math and More and didn't know he was married, I said yes."

"Why would I hold it against you if you didn't know he was married?" Clay spread out his hands, palms up, as if the answer might fall from above.

She pressed a fist to her mouth, then continued.

"Because I kept seeing him for four months after I found out, after I wanted to end things. But I never ended things. Why would I? I clung to each guy I dated as proof of my self-worth. Why would I ever give that up?"

Clay's hands fell to his sides.

Just as she'd expected, all his arguments were gone.

"Did he break up with you too?" Clay asked.

"No. When I learned that he had kids and that he had skipped doing something with them to be with me, the guilt was too much. I finally stopped seeing him. When he made things really awkward at work, I got a job freelancing for another publisher. It didn't pay as much, so I moved back to Abundance, where the cost of living was cheaper."

"Can we…?" Clay gestured to the couch.

She shrugged, walked over, and sat down.

Lark grabbed a stuffed star out of Lea's hands and chomped down on one point of it.

Clay took the star from her, gave it back to Lea, and handed Lark a plastic cup and teapot. She cried for a second, but then discovered how much noise she could make when she banged the two toys together.

Clay shrugged and sat close to Kristen on the couch, facing her. "It's loud, but it's probably the best we can hope for."

She nodded, eyes down, studying the mesh of his tennis shoes. She could feel his gaze on her, his disappointment, his judgment.

Nothing less than she deserved.

The edges of her eyes prickled, and she squeezed them shut, pressing her tongue against the roof of her mouth to keep from crying. "Go ahead. Whatever you want to say, get it over with, and let me leave."

He grabbed her hands, pulled them together, and wrapped his own hands around them. "Kristen, you are an amazing woman. Even if none of the men you dated could see that, you are valuable."

She glanced up at him for a fraction of a second, then looked back down. He didn't sound as if he hated her, but there was probably a "but" coming. *But I could never date someone like you. But I don't think I can respect you. But*—she winced—*you're not the role model I want for Lark and Lea.*

"I'm so sorry, Kristen."

Here it comes.

"I handled things all wrong when I was eighteen. I can't tell you how awful I feel that I made you think the problem was you. It wasn't. You were wonderful."

She looked up. Wonderful?

"You still are." He leaned closer and squeezed her hands. "Don't you see that?"

"You don't—you don't hate me?"

"No." Clay shook his head and let out a soft chuckle. "I'm sorry you've had so many relationships that left you feeling bad about yourself. But—" he hesitated. "Okay, maybe I'm not really sorry. If one of those relationships had gone perfectly, you'd probably be married. But I don't hate you. I love you." He held her gaze, and his eyes shone.

A fizzy tingle burst inside Kristen's chest and ran down her arms. "Oh, Clay, I love you too."

"Do you believe me, really believe me? That you're wonderful, no matter what I think or any other guy thinks? That it's because of who you are, because of the way you were made?"

The tingle grew inside her, warming her heart. How she was made...

By God.

Her value came from God.

Was it all that simple, like some Sunday school answer from when she was in youth group? That God made her and loved her and that was what made her special?

Yes.

The answer rang in her mind, strong and clear, as if it came from someone bigger, all-powerful, and all-knowing.

Not like her wishy-washy mental arguments. Not like all the times she'd tried to convince herself to live in the present and forget about the past. All she needed to do was believe, really deep down believe, that as God's creation she had value. Could she believe that?

Maybe.

"But Clay, about what I did in Chicago—"

"I understand."

"You can't want a relationship with me."

He slid an arm around her waist. "Kristen, I do. You messed up. We all make mistakes, but then we move on."

"But I still feel so bad about it."

For a long moment, he looked at her, his head tipped to one side. Then his eyes narrowed, as if he'd just figured out a puzzle. "You know, I don't make it over to the Abundance Community Church as often as I should, and I guess I *was* kind of acting as if I thought I was God, but I wonder...do you need to ask God to forgive you?"

"I've done that." She sighed. "Again and again and again. I still feel terrible."

"Yeah, but you didn't seem very quick to accept that I

was ready to move on. Have you accepted that God is?"

A sick feeling rolled through her stomach, and she shook her head, tears running down her cheeks.

How did he manage to see the things she couldn't? Was it because he knew her so well?

He was right. The answer to her problems wasn't in that self-help book she'd read. The answer was with God. She'd been asking him again and again to forgive her and, even when she felt better after praying, assuming that it wasn't enough. She'd accepted God's forgiveness in her mind, but not in her heart. Just as she hadn't really accepted that she had value simply because God made her. She'd made it all about her earning his love and forgiveness. All about…her. Then she, in what had to be her most hypocritical move ever, had said that Clay's problem stemmed from pride. All while, because of her own pride, she'd been rejecting the sacrifice Jesus made for her sins, throwing it back at God as if it wasn't enough.

Her throat grew tight, and right there on the couch beside Clay, she clasped her hands together and bowed her head.

God, I'm sorry, so sorry. Thank you for forgiving my sins and for creating me and giving me worth. Thank you for loving me even when my pride gets in the way. And thank you for saving Lark and Lea and for bringing Clay back into my life. Amen.

She looked up and blinked.

And Clay pulled her into his arms and held her close.

Chapter Twenty-Seven

Lucas pulled up beside Samantha's car in the Whole Hog Barbecue lot but didn't get out of his truck.

A few seconds later she rapped on his window.

Slowly, he opened his door. "I can't believe I'm doing this."

"C'mon, the article is awesome." She held the day's copy of *The Abundance News* toward him. "Most people in town will have gotten their copy. Announcing your big secret to Abundance in the local paper is a perfect start."

"Then why do I feel sick to my stomach?"

"That's just nerves—and the fact that you won't turn your phone on. If you did, you'd probably be getting all sorts of texts and phone messages from people telling you how proud they are of you."

He shot her a dirty look and climbed out of his truck. He never should have let her talk him into going in early to share a slice of cheesecake. All he wanted to do was work his shift in the kitchen, where no one would see him.

"You'll see, it will be fine. We'll go in, have a piece of cheesecake, and you can work your Friday evening shift. Tomorrow you can announce your real identity on social media and add your real name where you tell about yourself on your website."

"Maybe." Lucas tossed the newspaper in his truck and slammed the door. Any other woman would have let him handle things in less of a rush, one small step toward publicity at a time. Not Samantha. She'd consulted the marketing team at Norware and come up with a splashy plan for announcing to the world that he was Kendrick Larson.

He glanced toward the tinted windows of the restaurant. At least three in the afternoon wasn't a busy time. Maybe he'd get lucky and the place would be empty.

"You'll feel better after some cheesecake."

"I doubt it." Most likely, he'd feel more nauseous.

With a long sigh, he walked beside her as she approached the main door of Whole Hog. It would be so much easier to slip in the back. He could tell everyone he came in early to check on the dry rub situation, and— "I can bring cheesecake home, Samantha. We can eat it later tonight. Not, uh, not spoil your dinner."

She turned to face him, lowered her chin, and raised her eyebrows.

Okay, she wasn't buying it.

He pulled open the door, held it for her, and followed her in. The woman was way too excited about this and—

He froze.

Hanging from the ceiling, right over the hostess station,

was a huge sign. In large handwritten letters, it read "Home of Abundance's Best-Selling Author, Lucas Stiner/Kendrick Larson." Behind the hostess station, on the shelf that normally held barbecue awards, paperback copies of all his books sat, front cover out, displayed for everyone to see. The books looked worn, as if someone had read them more than once.

"Lucas!" The cry came up in unison from everyone in the room—two waitresses, eight diners, and Clint, the high school kid who worked after school as a busboy.

"You should have told us!" Jordan, the owner, said as he rushed out of the kitchen. "I can't believe we've had a celebrity working right here and we never even realized it."

Lucas brushed the comment aside. "I'm not a cele—"

"You are, man. I love your books," Clint said. "When Jordan showed us the newspaper, I couldn't believe it. I told everybody I had all your books, and Jordan sent me home to get them so we could display them."

"Do you have copies you can sell? And autograph?" A female customer walked over. "I'd like to get your books for my nephew. He loves science fiction."

"Who doesn't?" a man called out from the table in the far corner. "Can we order them as e-books online?"

A jolt of adrenaline shot through Lucas. "You sure can," he hollered back. They wanted his books. People he knew wanted to read his books. Or already had! "But I don't have copies to sign."

"A book signing...that's an excellent idea," Jordan said, his round face shining. "You could have it here one weeknight. We'll order in a bunch of copies, and I bet people will come in droves." His eyes gleamed. "Books and Barbecue. I can see it now on the website."

Lucas looked from Jordan to Clint to the customer in the back, amazement hollowing out his chest.

Samantha elbowed him in the ribs. "Told you so. Turn your phone on."

Should he?

She elbowed him again.

He pulled it out, turned the power back on, and slid it back in his pocket.

Clint stood before him, paperbacks and a pen in hand. "Speaking of autographs, would you?"

"I'd be happy to." Even though he wasn't sure what to write. After a second he signed his pen name and put his real name underneath in parentheses.

"Awesome," Clint said.

In that moment, Lucas's phone came alive in his pocket. Buzz after buzz after buzz vibrated through it. He pulled it out and scanned the text messages.

Whoa, dude. Way to keep a secret.

I'm so proud of you.

Wow! You're a published author!

Just ordered a copy of all your books online.

And the best one of all—

I can't believe it! My favorite author is YOU!!

"I guess you were right," he said under his breath to Samantha.

"Imagine that." Laughter colored her voice. "You're buying the cheesecake. You're going to earn enough royalties from this crowd alone to afford it."

"One minute," Samantha called, as she hurried down the stairs of her townhouse. She squinted through the peephole, then unlocked the door and pulled it wide.

"For you." Lucas thrust a plastic bag into her hands.

"What's this?" She opened the bag and peered in.

"A whole banana fudge cheesecake. When Jordan learned that you were the reason I finally told people about my writing, he insisted I bring it." Lucas strolled into her townhouse. "We were swamped tonight. I had to go out in the dining room and sign autographs every half hour."

"You did?"

"Yep. I still can't believe that people I actually know have read my books and liked them."

"I'm not surprised at all. If your first three books are as good as the new one—"

"You started reading it?" Excitement rang in his voice.

"Started? I read the whole thing! I opened the computer file you emailed me as soon as I came home from Whole Hog. I didn't stop reading until I finished. I even ate dinner in front of my computer."

"You liked it?"

"I loved it."

Lucas beamed. Then he tipped his head to one side. "Even the part about the sexy heroine, Lexi Ballard?"

"Oh, yeah. I was so proud of her when she killed that creepy alien and freed Thad. You're going to write another book with her in it, right?"

"Probably."

"You have to. You can't just have that one kiss at the end of the book and that's it."

"So, you think they belong together?"

"Of course." How could he write about these characters and not understand?

He pursed his lips and rolled his eyes upward, as if giving the matter deep thought.

"Lucas, they're perfect for each other. They need each other."

"Weeellll...I guess I can see that." He slid his arms around her waist. "The thing is, Thad Stephens is based on me, and—even though I didn't plan it that way—Lexi Ballard is totally you. I probably need to do some research before I write the next book." He pulled her closer.

"Research?"

"You know," he said, lowering his face toward hers, "spending lots of time with you."

If he put it that way, research sounded like a very smart idea.

"Like in order to describe the experience properly on the page, I'd need to kiss you about, um, five thousand times."

"Five thousand?" Happiness bubbled inside her. "That sounds pretty good."

"Are you sure?" The teasing note left his voice. "All those kisses would require...a long-term relationship."

A zing of adrenaline shot through her. Lucas wanted a long-term relationship? The man who never wanted to date anyone for very long?

"Because I think Thad wants something serious," he said. "I think he's falling in love with Lexi."

Samantha's heart faltered. "He is?" If Thad was Lucas, and Lexi was her...

"He is," Lucas said, his voice husky.

A shiver shot down her arms, and her heart soared.

She'd thought, when she moved here, that the last thing she wanted was romance. Thought she might never even date again. Thought love was out of the question. And definitely thought it would be crazy to date a guy, seven years younger, who was passionate about barbecue and had a dog that barked at all hours.

She couldn't have been more wrong. That man had erased all her fears about being betrayed again.

"That's a really interesting story line. About Thad falling in love with Lexi. Because"—she buried her fingers in the hair at the nape of Lucas' neck—"she's falling in love with him too."

A grin spread across his face. "Now that sounds like a book I need to write. After I do this."

And then he kissed her.

Chapter Twenty-Eight

At ten a.m. on September 1, Clay pulled up the gaming sales site on his office computer, ran a search for "Hidden Pirate Treasure: Caribbean," and watched it appear on the screen.

There it was, available for sale!

The past few days had been hectic, but the launch was live. At least things hadn't been as crazy as that time three weeks ago when Lark and Lea were in the hospital. With Kristen helping more with the twins, with the girls getting into more of a routine, he'd been doing better.

He'd even had time to think about what Kristen had said, about believing he was God, believing he was in control. She was right.

Logically, he knew he wasn't God, but it had been easy while running his own business to think that it was all on his shoulders and that if success came, it was all due to his efforts. He hired the staff, he made the final decisions, he was in charge.

But that wasn't the whole truth.

So when he'd hired a new head of development last week, he had—for the first time ever—prayed about a work decision. In the end, he'd picked the guy who had a little less experience and a slightly less impressive resume, but it felt right. Clay hadn't stewed over the choice for days. He'd prayed, flipped through the resumes one more time, and just known.

That five-minute prayer had helped.

Maybe it was time for another one. He closed his door, sat down at his desk, and bowed his head.

God, the new game is out there for sale.

It's a big deal. If it goes well, Norware's on pretty good footing.

If not, we'll really be struggling, and it will be my fault. You know I never had any training in how to run a business when I was getting my engineering degree. I've done the best I could, but what if it's not enough?

He stopped. He was doing it again, thinking he had all the control.

Okay, God. Scratch that earlier prayer.

If it be your will, let this game be a success.

If not, I will trust—at least I'll try really hard to trust—that you're in control and that you've got different plans for me and my staff.

Uh...amen.

He looked up. Somehow the weight on his shoulders eased. And, in an instant, things shifted in his mind. He still wanted to work hard, wanted to do his best, wanted Caribbean Treasure to be a hit, but if it bombed, it wasn't the end of the world.

He turned his head slowly from side to side, seeing his office with new eyes. The memo the head of marketing had sent with ideas they needed to discuss. The sticky note on the bottom of his monitor, reminding him of a meeting tomorrow with his new head of development. The white board where, months ago, he'd brainstormed a new game that he'd never had time to pursue.

Suddenly, the old excitement about creating computer games bubbled up inside him. Norware, which had felt like such a responsibility, now felt like a business filled with possibility. A business that, even if Caribbean Treasure never sold a single copy, he could make a success.

With God's help.

And, with God's help, hopefully one more piece of his life would fall into place tomorrow.

Kristen waved goodbye to the guy from the delivery service who had picked up her last project for Fibonacci Publishing.

The delivery van pulled away from the curb just as Clay drove into his driveway.

She dashed over to meet him.

"Hey." He opened his car door and climbed out. "You look happy."

"I am. I have news!" She leaned into the back seat from the passenger side, said hello to the twins, and unbuckled Lea.

The little girl came to Kristen eagerly and reached for one of her dangling earrings.

"Oops." Kristen unhooked her earrings and tucked them in her shirt pocket.

Clay unstrapped Lark, took her out of the car, and grabbed the diaper bag. "What's up?"

"About fifteen minutes ago, I was packaging up my last project to send back to Fibonacci and feeling really down, thinking that as of tomorrow I'm officially unemployed." Kristen followed him onto his porch step. "Then I got a voicemail with a job offer! I must not have heard my phone ring when I was upstairs printing the mailing label. I tried to call back, but they're on the east coast and they must have called me right before they went home."

Clay stopped, his hand frozen on the doorknob. "The east coast?"

"Yeah, the company's in North Carolina, near the Research Triangle area."

"But you haven't accepted yet?" He opened the door, set Lark on the carpet, and turned to face Kristen.

"No, but it sounds like a great job and—"

He held up one finger. "Hold on." He went through the baby gate at the base of the steps, then raced to the second floor, feet pounding on the stairs.

Lea stretched a hand toward Kristen's pocket, smart enough at eleven months to know right where the shiny earrings were hidden.

Kristen gently moved her hand away and, when Lea reached back immediately, set her down on the floor by her sister.

Within seconds, and without a single wobble, both Lark and Lea pulled up to standing at the edge of the couch. Kristen was no expert, but she'd guess they were going to be walking any day now.

Clay dashed back down the stairs, took her hand, and led her to the other end of the couch. "I messed things up before. I'm not doing it again. I'm not losing you."

"Clay—"

"Wait, let me finish." He slid to the floor, kneeling before her. "Please don't move to North Carolina. Stay here in Abundance with Lark and Lea and me."

Her mouth fell open. Oh, she wanted to marry him. She'd wanted it for more than ten years. But she didn't want him proposing simply because he thought she was moving. "Clay, the job—"

"Please don't take that job—"

"The job," she said, speaking over him, "is online. I'd be helping develop content for math software for home schoolers, and I'd be working remotely. You don't need to propose to get me to stay here."

"You're right. I need to propose because I love you. The job offer only sped this up by one day. Remember I asked if we could go out to dinner tomorrow? I planned to ask you then."

"You did?"

"I did." He dug into his pants pocket and pulled out a small white box with the tiniest white bow Kristen had ever seen, a bow that was somewhat squished. He made a futile attempt to fluff the bow and held the box toward her. "Kristen Hamlin, will you marry me?"

She sucked in a gulp of air and stretched an unsteady hand toward the box, then unwrapped it. Inside, in a black velvet case, was a ring with a large, sparkling diamond.

She stared at the ring, then gazed into his eyes. This

man, this wonderful man whom she'd loved in high school, whom she'd never gotten over, who loved her in spite of all her mistakes, wanted to marry her.

"Would we...?" She shouldn't ask this. It was silly. But part of her had always thought that back in high school, if he really had planned to marry her, he would have told people. "Would we be keeping our engagement a secret?"

"No way. If you say yes, I'll tell everyone I know, post on every social media site out there, possibly even buy billboard space."

Tears sprung to her eyes and streamed down her face. "Oh, Clay. Yes, I'll marry you. I'll marry you tomorrow if you want."

"How about we wait long enough to plan the biggest church wedding Abundance has ever seen? So that everyone can know you're mine."

She nodded, unable to speak.

"Correct that." He angled his head toward the twins, who were now playing on the carpet. "So everyone can know you're *ours*. I admit they're a handful, but—"

"You know I love them just as much as I love you. It will be my privilege to help you raise them, and my privilege to be your wife."

He pulled her into his lap and took her face in his hands.

"My beautiful Kristen." He brushed her hair aside with one hand, then ran his fingers down her cheek. "I never stopped loving you. And I never will."

Her heart full, Kristen raised her face to his.

Their lips met, sealing their promise.

Clay's phone buzzed.

He ignored it. He buried his fingers deeper into Kristen's hair and kept kissing her and—

It buzzed again.

Kristen pulled away.

"I'll shut it off." But as he pulled the phone from his pocket, he saw the text on the screen from Samantha.

Check order stats NOW!!!!!!!!!!!!!!!!!!!!!!!!

"Hmm." He held the phone toward Kristen.

"That's an awful lot of exclamation points. Maybe you should look first, then kiss me again."

He chuckled. "I guess I'd better. Otherwise, she may come over and pound on the door."

"You check your sales." Kristen stood up. "I'll give the girls something to eat."

"Okay." He'd, um, sort of forgotten about the twins. "There's cheese cut up in the fridge and some cooked potatoes. And I was going to give them some slices of banana."

"I can do that." Kristen picked up Lea, told Lark she'd be right back to get her, and went into the kitchen.

Clay pulled up the sales app on his phone. He'd checked earlier, right after he left the office, and seen a trickle of sales, but the marketing team had planned the ad blitz to start at 5 p.m. Eastern. Plus, sometimes there was a delay between when a sale was made and when it showed on the website.

After a second, the sales screen opened. Four hundred or so, from what he could tell. Not bad. Not quite what he'd been hoping for, but maybe people didn't think pirates were as cool as he did. And, he reminded himself, God was in charge, not him. There might be a plan here that he wasn't privy to.

Kristen came back in and took Lark into the kitchen.

Clay looked again at his phone. Wait a minute. The graph was so little. Maybe…

He spread his fingers across the screen, enlarging the Y axis of the sales graph.

Adrenaline surged through him. "Kristen," he croaked.

"What?" she called from the kitchen.

He sank deeper into the couch. "I can't believe it."

"What?" She rushed back in the living room. "Are you okay?"

He held up his phone. "Those marks on the graph aren't for a hundred units. They're for a thousand units. We've sold almost four thousand units in the first two hours."

"That's good?"

"At $29 per unit?" He tossed his phone on the couch, stood, and flung out his arms. "That's more than $100,000 in sales. Today. It's way beyond our wildest projections."

"More than"—her voice grew higher with each syllable—"$100,000?"

"My worries about Norware Games are over!" he shouted. He pulled her into his arms and spun her around and around.

"Clay, stop." Her words came out with a laugh. "You're making me dizzy."

He put her down. "Where are the twins?"

"Strapped in their high chairs."

"Are they happy?"

"They were both quite busy smashing little pieces of banana into their high chair trays," she said. "They seemed to think it was lots of fun."

"Perfect. Then neither of them will be eating any clover." He drew her closer. "And I can kiss you."

He did. Again and again and again.

He missed his sister Gwen. He always would. But he had the sweetest nieces in the world. He had success beyond his dreams, success that would allow his business to thrive. And he had the love of the most wonderful woman in the world.

God had blessed him more than he could have ever imagined.

Epilogue

Almost four months later

"Aunt Kristen!" Emma raced toward her, crossing the Sunday school classroom in a blur of red satin.

Kristen bent over, hugged Emma, and kissed her cheek. "Hey, cutie pie."

"Will you bring me seashells from your honeymoon too?"

"Clay and I aren't going to the beach, Emma, but I promise to bring you a present."

"Yay!" Emma skipped, then twirled. "I love it when people get married."

Abby walked over, chuckling. "Let's see how your flowers go with your dress." She lifted Kristen's bouquet out of a box on a table.

Kristen took the bouquet, a mass of red roses interspersed here and there with single snow-white stephanotis blossoms. She walked to the standing mirror Abby had brought from home and held the flowers at her waist.

"You look amazing," Deirdre said. "There's so much contrast in the bouquet, and the red of the roses just pops against your ivory gown."

"With us standing beside you in our red dresses," Becky added, "it's going to be beautiful."

"The perfect Christmas wedding," Samantha added.

Kristen looked from Abby, her matron of honor, to her bridesmaids. Each of them shone with her own special beauty. Abby, her dear, sweet sister, with her wide smile. Deirdre, with her ebony skin and dark hair. Becky, dark eyes gleaming, looking far too rested to be the mother of a baby who was six months old. And Samantha, with her big brown eyes and glossy brown hair.

Their full-length dresses were a bright Christmas-red and had satin skirts, lace bodices, and tiny lace cap sleeves. Their bouquets were the reverse of hers, each a mass of white roses with tiny red carnations interspersed.

Emma, who was practically a professional flower girl, having been in Abby's wedding six months ago, wore a similar dress but with a fuller skirt and a higher neckline.

"Oh, Kristen," Mom said.

"Doesn't she look lovely, Aunt Cara?" Becky said.

Mom walked closer, looking lovely in a dark-green silk suit that brought out the green in her eyes. She brought her fingers over her mouth. "Lovely doesn't begin to cover it. You look like a princess."

"Thanks, Mom." Kristen hugged her, then glanced in the mirror at her delicate ivory dress. Slender straps came down from her shoulders to a lace bodice with a sweetheart neckline, then the lace billowed out at the waist over a full skirt. Her blond curls flowed over her shoulders, covered by a simple veil attached to a band of white roses.

Together, the dress, the hairstyle, the veil, and the bouquet looked even better than she had imagined. She truly felt, down to the marrow of her bones, like Mom had said, like a princess.

"Have you seen the church?" Mom said. "It looks wonderful."

"Yes, I peeked in." She turned to her bridesmaids. "You all did a great job. I love the white candles and the strings of fairy lights, and those big clear vases of red Christmas ornaments are perfect in the windows."

The perfect wedding, the wedding she'd dreamed of.

Even though years ago she'd been thrilled at the idea of eloping with Clay, Kristen had secretly dreamed of a big wedding. It hadn't been easy to pull it off in four months, but she'd had lots of help.

This wedding was definitely big. More than five hundred people had RSVP'd.

Every step she and Clay had taken along the way to tell everyone they knew had made her feel more loved. Again and again he'd shown her how certain he was that he wanted to marry her. How sure he was they belonged together. And how very much he loved her.

The pain she'd felt after their breakup had faded to a hazy memory, replaced by trust in this man, in their future together, and in the knowledge—especially after the time they'd both spent these past few months in Bible study—that their union would be blessed by God. In less than an hour, she would be Mrs. Clay Norris.

She couldn't be more ready.

"Knock, knock?" A voice called from outside the doorway. "It's Fern. May the girls and I come in?"

Becky hurried to the door and let in Clay's mother, who was pushing Lark and Lea in the double stroller.

Although Clay's dad still had another month of physical therapy to go, he and Fern had been able to visit Abundance in November, and Fern had recovered fully from her injuries in the helicopter wreck. Even more exciting, she was responding well to a new medication for her MS. "Don't the girls look darling?" She unstrapped Lark and handed her to Mom, then took Lea into her own arms.

The girls did. Each of the twins wore a tiny red satin dress, the same fabric as the bridesmaid's skirts. They had red satin headbands that encircled their head and featured tiny red bows, and they wore little white anklets and tiny black patent leather Mary Janes.

"Kris-Kris!" Lark exclaimed.

"Hello darling one," Kristen said. "And hello to you too, Lea." She kissed the twins' foreheads. "You both look beautiful. And you do as well, Fern. That dark-green chiffon dress is fabulous," she said, giving her future mother-in-law a hug. "And I love those new highlights you got in your hair."

Fern brushed the compliments aside with her hand, but her blue eyes twinkled.

"Thank you so much for getting the girls ready," Kristen said. "Clay actually flinched when I mentioned headbands."

"My pleasure." Fern blinked back tears. "I can't tell you how happy I am that you two are getting married. I knew ten years ago you were perfect for each other. I wanted to tell him that, but my husband told me I'd do more harm than good. The boy does have a stubborn streak."

Kristen grinned. "We both do."

"In a woman, we call that 'inner strength,' dear." Fern chuckled. "You'll probably both need it to raise two girls at once." She gazed at each of the twins, then bit her lip. "I miss Gwen every day," she said, voice full of emotion, "but I can't think of anyone I'd rather have bringing up her girls."

A bittersweet ache washed through Kristen, and she raised a hand to her chest. "Thank you. Thank you so much. I will do my very, very best."

"I know."

Kristen squeezed Fern's arm and blinked furiously, wishing with her whole heart that Gwen could be here today to share her joy. Still, it almost felt as if her friend was here in spirit, watching over her brother and her girls.

When Gwen and John had both died, when Kristen had believed she would be the twins' guardian, she'd thought it was an honor but also an obligation. Now it wasn't an obligation at all. It was the greatest gift she could have ever received.

"Don't cry!" Abby dashed from across the room with a tissue. "Blot. Don't mess up that makeup."

"Okay." Kristen took the tissue and carefully dried her eyes. "All good?"

Abby nodded.

A loud knock sounded at the door.

Samantha opened it slightly, then pulled it wide. "C'mon in, Uncle Will. Take a look at the bride-to-be."

Dad walked in and rested one hand on Kristen's arm, his lips pressed together and eyes shining. "My baby girl. First your sister and now you." He hugged Kristen close, then slid his arm around Mom's waist, gazing down at her with love. "It seems like only yesterday I was marrying your mother right here in this very church."

"We just pray that you and Clay will be as happy as we've been." Mom tipped her head and leaned it against Dad's shoulder.

"We sure do," he said, eyes bright. "And right now, they say it's time for this wedding to get started."

The ache of missing Gwen eased from Kristen's chest, replaced with bubbles of excitement. It was time for her wedding. To Clay Norris, the man she'd fallen in love with in high school, the man she was meant to be with.

She stared into the distance a moment, thinking about the rich-brown color of his eyes, the line of his jaw, the way his muscles had filled out since in high school. So handsome—and so much more.

A man who'd turned his life upside-down to care for his sister's girls.

A man who'd worked hard to build his own company, and who had kept on working, even when he had the additional responsibility of his nieces.

A man who knew her flaws and secrets and loved her anyway.

A man who she couldn't wait to call her husband.

"It took Clay and me a while to get here, but I think

we'll be very happy indeed." She stepped toward the door and raised her bouquet like a torch. "Let's do this!"

Clay stood in front of the altar, facing the crowd seated in the church.

He must have been out of his mind to have suggested a big wedding. If the response cards were right, there were five hundred and fourteen people in the sanctuary, and almost every one of them was looking at him.

Dad, who had sat down early in the front row to save his strength for the reception, smiled encouragingly, brown eyes twinkling. A couple of rows back, Kristen's Uncle T.J. winked. His wife, Patsy, was busy shutting off her phone. Near the back, Grace Cassidy was still being seated.

Everyone else—every single other person in the room—was staring at him. Like that row of the Hamlins and their friends. Nate and Tess and Stacey and Seth and Stacey's father, George. Every one of them, peering at him as if he were a bug they were trying to identify.

He ran a finger inside his collar and shot a glance at Lucas, his best man.

Lucas had already told him that he and Samantha, who only recently got engaged, planned a small ceremony at the Lake of the Ozarks. "It's her second marriage," Lucas explained.

Most likely, Lucas had been smart enough not to suggest a big wedding.

"It's all good, man." Lucas patted his breast pocket. "I haven't lost the rings."

Clay hadn't even thought of that. If they got to the part

of the ceremony where he and Kristen were supposed to exchange rings, and there were no rings— "You're sure?" His voice gave a telltale quaver.

Lucas reached his hand inside his jacket and nodded. "Chill. You look as if you're about to pass out."

All three of the other groomsmen—Kristen's cousin Hank, and Glen and Gareth from the office—chuckled. Some friends they were, enjoying his misery.

"I wouldn't be so quick to laugh if I were you, Hank." Lucas pushed his long hair back over his shoulders. "Have you realized you're the only one of the Hamlin cousins who's still single? I'd say your days are numbered."

Hank went silent.

Clay and the other groomsmen laughed.

The music changed. There was a movement behind the open double doors at the back of the church. Something passed too quickly for Clay to identify.

Then Mom appeared, escorted by Kristen's cousin Jack. She proudly carried Lark, stopping every few feet to turn from side to side to show her off.

Not that Clay could blame her. Lark looked really cute in her little red dress.

Eventually, Mom made it to the front row, where she sat beside Dad.

Next, Earl Ray escorted in Kristen's mom, who was carrying Lea. Cara's smile was just as bright and proud as Mom's. Apparently getting two granddaughters was a pretty important part of the wedding.

Cara sat across the aisle from Mom, and, when Lea called out for her sister, Cara pointed to Lark, only a few feet away. For now, at least, that seemed to be enough. If the girls fussed, the two grandmothers had a plan ready to move side by side.

Kristen's niece, Emma, came in next, meticulously dropping red rose petals every couple of inches down the white runner.

Then one by one, Kristen's bridesmaids entered. Samantha, then Becky, then Deirdre, and finally, Abby.

Nerves twisted in Clay's stomach. Why did this have to take so long, with people coming in one at a time? His eyes locked on the double doors at the back, and his ears strained, wanting to hear the first few notes of "The Wedding March."

But they didn't come. At last, when Clay thought he couldn't wait a second longer, the pianist added a flourish at the end of a song, paused, then began the familiar melody.

Kristen walked through the double doors on her father's arm.

Clay's mouth went dry.

She was beautiful. More beautiful than she'd been in high school. More beautiful than she'd been yesterday. More beautiful than any woman on earth.

Her veil was back, and she looked straight at him, soft pink lips tipped up in a smile that he'd remember all the days of his life, a smile that shot straight into his heart.

This beautiful woman would be his wife.

He may have been afraid to marry her back in high school but not today. Today he wanted nothing more than to say the words that would join them as man and wife for the rest of their lives.

Moments later, she was at his side, her fingers clasped

in his, her eyes sparkling as she gazed up at him.

He felt as if his chest might burst.

"Dearly beloved," Pastor Corey said, "we are gathered together today to join this man and this woman in holy matrimony."

Yes. It was really happening. The pastor talked on, giving some type of mini-sermon about love, but Clay had trouble focusing. All he could think about was Kristen.

"Clay," Pastor Corey said.

Clay jerked his head toward the pastor.

"Do you take Kristen to be your wedded wife, to live together in marriage? Do you promise to love her, comfort her, honor and keep her for better or worse, for richer or poorer, in sickness and health, and forsaking all others, be faithful only to her, for as long as you both shall live?"

Clay squeezed her hands tightly. "I do."

The pastor turned to Kristen.

"Kristen, do you take Clay to be your wedded husband, to live together in marriage? Do you promise to love him, comfort him, honor and keep him for better or worse, for richer or poorer, in sickness and health, and forsaking all others, be faithful only to him, so long as you both shall live?"

She beamed at Clay, face glowing. "I do."

He squeezed her hands again.

Then Pastor Corey blessed the rings.

Clay took Kristen's ring from the pastor and looked down at it.

In the middle of the wide gold band, the jeweler had crafted a narrow braid of rose, white, and yellow gold. That thin yellow-gold band was the same band Clay had given

Kristen all those years ago, a band now braided to make it stronger, just as their love now was stronger than it had been when they were teenagers.

"Kristen," he said. "This ring, with its braid of three colors of gold, represents my love to you yesterday, today, and forever. I give you this ring as a symbol of my love, and with all that I am, and all that I have, I honor you, in the name of the Father, and of the Son, and of the Holy Spirit." He held the ring toward her hand, and she stretched her shaking fingers apart, allowing him to slide it on.

Then she took his ring, a ring the jeweler had created to look similar, only larger and more masculine. "Clay, I give you this ring as a symbol of my love, and with all that I am, and all that I have, I honor you, in the name of the Father, and of the Son, and of the Holy Spirit." She slid it onto his finger.

Pastor Corey looked past them. "Will all of you witnessing these promises do everything in your power to uphold Clay and Kristen in their marriage?"

"We will," the crowd thundered.

"Let us pray," the pastor said, and he bowed his head, asking God to bless Clay and Kristen and to help them grow stronger in their love and in their faith. Then he looked back at them. "Kristen Ann Hamlin and Clayton James Norris, having witnessed your vows of love to one another, it is my joy to present you to all gathered here as husband and wife." He turned to Clay. "You may now kiss the bride."

Heart pounding, Clay drew Kristen into his arms and brought his lips to hers.

From this moment forward, they would walk their lives together. Raising Lark and Lea. Celebrating the good times. Working together through the bad.

Finally, finally, the marriage that should have happened ten years ago had taken place.

Truly, God had blessed them when he led them to find love once more.

All of Sally's books are available in paperback and e-book from Amazon. For a complete list, or to sign up for her author newsletter and get a free novella, please visit her website at www.sallybayless.com.

A NOTE FROM THE AUTHOR

Dear Reader,

Thank you for reading *Love Once More!* I am so blessed that there are people who enjoy my books! It fills my heart with happiness to be able to be an author.

I really had fun writing this story, especially the scenes where Clay struggles as a new parent! Although I loved being a mom of young kids, it was much harder work than I expected, even after time to prepare when I was pregnant. The thought of being dropped into it without warning... Please know that if you're raising young children, I admire you for all you do.

As always when I write a novel, I learned a lot with this book, especially about what it's like to have twins. I wanted to make the story more realistic, so I asked a dear friend from church who raised two lovely young women the same age as my daughter to read an early draft. She gently pointed out the places where I had Clay doing the impossible with his twin nieces. For instance, in my original draft, I often had Clay carrying both of the girls at once, one in each arm. Then he'd open the door of his townhouse, walk out to his car, and put one girl inside in her car seat. I never thought about the fact that he wouldn't have a free hand to open the door! Plus, I learned that it's hard to carry two babies at once because if one lurches in any direction, you can't stop them. Yikes! I'm even more impressed by my friend and every other parent who raised twins. And triplets... I don't know how parents survive!

Anyway, I hope you enjoyed reading of Clay's struggles. More importantly, I hope that if you struggle with guilt over something from your past as Kristen did, or if you face control issues like Clay, you found encouragement. Our God is big enough to forgive and big enough to take on any problems we bring him.

Dear reader, please remember today and every day just how much God loves you!

If you enjoyed this book, I'd be grateful if you would write a review on Amazon or Goodreads. Those reviews are the best advertising around, and you wouldn't believe how fun it is to get feedback!

I love to hear from readers! If you'd like to say hello, please visit my website at www.sallybayless.com, where you can email me or find me on social media.

If you'd like a free copy of another sweet Christian romance set in the little town of Abundance, please sign up for my author newsletter at www.sallybayless.com. You'll get a link to download the holiday novella *Christmas in Abundance* for free in ebook or PDF!

A sample of the next book in this series, *Love Meant to Be,* is included just a few pages ahead.

May God bless you,

Sally Bayless

Acknowledgments

The more books I write, the more grateful I am to the people who help me. I could not do this without them. Any errors that slipped in despite their best efforts are my own.

First, I'm deeply grateful to the experts who so willingly answered questions about their field or life experience, allowing me to make my books more real. Robert A. Holm, Jr., D.O. FACEP, reviewed the medical issues in this story. Carrie Saunders, Tiffany Doherty, and my son, Michael Bayless, answered numerous questions about computers, the structure of a computer gaming business, and gaming itself. Lynda D. Johnson, Psy.D., helped me better understand the personality traits of my heroine. Kim Mather taught me so much about life as a parent of twins. I had no idea how easy I had it when I came home from the hospital with one baby!

I am also blessed to have two critique partners, Susan Anne Mason and Tammy Doherty, fellow writers who offer suggestions to improve my stories, as well as advice on how to handle life as a writer. With this book, I am especially grateful to Sue, who offered advice that helped me make the process of taking a book from first draft to being ready for my editor faster and more enjoyable. If she offered the same advice with the last book and I stubbornly ignored it, we won't mention that!

My beta readers—Betsy Anderson, Kristina Gerig, Janice Huwe, Jona Moberg, and Stephanie Smith—are so vital to my writing process. They point out the parts of a story that don't make sense, the sections that drag, and the characters that don't appeal. They clarify my thinking and my writing, helping me get the manuscript ready for editing. Thank you all!

The best editors, I believe, are born teachers, full of encouragement. They understand what you meant to say but didn't, and they make small, surgical changes to fix the problems. My editor, Christina Tarabochia, is one of the best. She made this story so much better—while letting it still be mine—and was an absolute joy to work with.

The beautiful cover of *Love Once More* was designed by Jenny Zemanek of Seedlings Design Studio. I cannot tell you how much I love her work and how blessed I feel that she creates the visual images that go with my stories.

Thank you to my husband, Dave, and daughter, Laurel, who encouraged me as I wrote this book. Your hugs and kind words keep me going when I struggle.

Finally, and most importantly, thank you, Jesus, for loving me, for offering me salvation, and for guiding me along this path. If my stories encourage even one person in their faith journey, I've achieved my dreams.

ABOUT THE AUTHOR

After many years away, Sally Bayless lives in her hometown in the Missouri Ozarks. She's married and has two grown children. When not working on her next book, she enjoys reading, watching BBC television with her husband, doing Bible studies, swimming, and shopping for cute shoes.

Chapter One

Meredith Lawson stepped onto her front porch and gazed up into the late afternoon sky.

Snowflakes poured down, as big and fluffy as popcorn. In less than an hour, her drab yard, leafless trees, and even the muddy field across the road had been transformed into a world of sparkling white.

She buttoned her old brown work coat, dug gloves out of the pockets, and tugged on her navy knit cap.

Duke, her German shepherd, raced off the porch and stuck his face in the snow, then lifted his head, black nose now frosted white. He let out a woof and bounded across the yard.

The vet might say Duke was a mature dog of nine, but he was still a puppy when it snowed.

Meredith pulled her phone out of the back pocket of her jeans, snapped a photo of Duke, and texted it to her sister, Ava, with the message "Happy New Year!"

Within seconds, her phone rang.

"Happy New Year to you as well!" Ava said. "Those flakes look enormous."

"They are."

"I'm so jealous." Ava let out a soft, pouty groan. "Here

in Atlanta, it's rainy and gray. I wish I was still with you in Missouri."

"I wish you were too." Somehow, ever since Ava drove back to Georgia two days ago, things that Meredith hadn't noticed before stood out like lonely lighthouses in her life. The silence of the house at night. The meals alone in front of the TV. The fact that she ran her dishwasher half empty simply so bits of food wouldn't get dried onto the plates and silverware. Even sitting with her aunt and uncle at church this morning, she'd felt alone.

Still, she didn't want to discourage Ava from pursuing her dream at culinary school. Dreams were important. And speaking of dreams... "Even though you're missing the snow, I've got news that will brighten your day. If I can get a loan from the bank, I think I can make the plan for the restaurant work."

Ava squealed. "Really? You can buy Uncle Harris and Aunt Ruby's place?"

"I think so."

"Oh, sis, that would be amazing." Ava's words echoed with longing.

Meredith's heart warmed. It would be so wonderful to be able to do this for Ava. So fun for them to work as a team, with her growing organic produce in the greenhouse and Ava cooking it in her restaurant.

Of course, buying Ruby and Harris's place would mean the loan would need to be sizable. And she wouldn't have much money left over each month after the payments. Certainly not enough for any exotic vacations. Not that she got away for vacations, with the greenhouse demanding all her time. But she and Ava had looked at rental space, and there was nothing at all suitable locally. Plus, buying her aunt and uncle's farmhouse next door wasn't just a good idea. It was the least she could do for Ava.

Plus, rejoining the properties made sense.

After all, the five acres she and Ava owned, along with the land where her aunt and uncle's house sat, had once been part of the same parcel, right outside the little town of Abundance. The property had only been divided after Grandma and Grandpa Carlton died when Meredith was five. They left Uncle Harris twenty acres, including the house, and left Mom twenty acres, plus their savings. Mom and Dad sold all but five acres and used the proceeds and the savings to build their own home and start the greenhouse business. Uncle Harris and Aunt Ruby stuck with traditional farming and, over the past three decades, had added six hundred acres to their land.

Meredith might find Uncle Harris difficult to be around, but she had to admit he was a good businessman.

Now that he and Aunt Ruby were retiring and moving south, if she could buy part of their land, the three acres with the house and yard, it would make a fabulous restaurant. Unlike the more modern, one-story ranch-style house her parents had built, the old Carlton family farmhouse had real historic charm. It was two and a half stories, built in the Queen Anne style, with a roomy wraparound porch and—best of all—a turret. Just the look of the place would attract customers from the city.

"Buying their house for the restaurant would be perfect." Ava sighed. "You could continue with the greenhouse, and once I finish culinary school, we could run the two businesses together. Farm to table, the ultimate in locally sourced food."

Meredith studied the big house next door. The more she played with the idea, the more she liked it. "I've been crunching the numbers all afternoon, and I think it will work. I just came outside to take a break because the snow is so pretty."

"If I was there, we could celebrate by building a snowman, like we always used to for the first real snow."

"We could. This snow is perfect. Wet enough to stick really well."

"You'll have to build it without me," Ava said. "Send me a picture."

Meredith pushed some snow back and forth with one foot. Building a snowman wouldn't be the same without her sister, but... "Okay. It's quite nice out here. Too nice to go right back inside." Besides, the beauty of the snow was exactly the kind of blessing she tried to take time to appreciate.

"I'll be waiting for the picture. And envisioning the menu for the restaurant. Thank you so much for trying this. I love you, sis."

"I love you too." Meredith hung up, tucked her phone back in her pocket, and scooped up a handful of snow. "C'mon, Duke, we've got a snowman to build."

Fifteen minutes later, the snowman was coming along well. Duke hadn't been nearly as much help as Ava, especially when it came to lifting the middle ball of snow on top of the bottom one. Still, Meredith had gotten the three snowballs stacked right in the middle of the yard where she and Ava had built their snowmen for years, ever since they were little, before Mom and Dad died.

Even during the four years that Ava had worked in a restaurant in Kansas City, she'd come home for her days off, for holidays, and for the first big snow. And next year, after Ava finished culinary school and moved back home, she and Meredith could continue their snowman-building tradition together.

Meredith brushed some snow away from the flowerbed by the front porch, gathered up a few pieces of mulch, and used them to create eyes and a cheerful smile.

Now she just needed Grandpa Carlton's fedora and a carrot for a nose.

"I'll be right back," she told Duke as she went inside.

Zach Gilcroft neared a curve on the narrow blacktop. He eyed the road, tightened his grip on the steering wheel of the rented Toyota, and carefully applied the brakes.

The car slid, its tires no match for the snow that had quickly piled to four inches.

He pressed more firmly on the brakes and, after a second, the anti-lock feature kicked in, putting him back in control of the vehicle.

Whew. He let out a silent breath, then glanced over at his thirteen-year-old daughter, Hailey, in the passenger seat.

Seatbelt on, long blond hair pushed back over her shoulders, she was smiling at her phone, oblivious to the road conditions. Probably thumbing through the photos she'd taken of that horse.

Kayla, the girl Hailey had met at church this morning, had been so nice to invite her over to see her horse. That one kind action had made such a difference. Most of the time they'd been here in Abundance visiting family for Christmas, Hailey had been just as unhappy as she had been back in Phoenix. Until she'd met Kayla.

Getting Hailey cheered up even for an afternoon was a big deal. So big that Zach had been reluctant to pull her away and had stayed, visiting with Kayla's parents, after he arrived to pick Hailey up. They probably should have left sooner.

Cautiously, he rounded the curve to where the road straightened.

Good thing he knew this stretch of County Road 1400 so well. He'd been out here in the snow many times as a teenager, driving Dad's pickup with a load of firewood in the back to make it easier to steer, when he visited a friend who'd lived a mile past Kayla's house. These days, though, at thirty-five, he was old enough to know to head home when the snow started to come down heavy.

Yet he'd lingered, foolishly hoping that one fun afternoon might somehow make up for the fact that Hailey was facing the evils of middle school without her mom to offer guidance.

Hailey set her phone on her lap. "Dad, do you think there's any way I could have a horse in Phoenix?" She looked over at him as if she didn't already know the answer was no.

A *no* that was hard for Zach to get out every time they had this conversation. He loved his girl so much. Every day she reminded him more of her mom, with her big blue eyes and golden hair. If only Jillian were still alive to see their daughter growing up.

And to help him handle the murky waters of parenting

a thirteen-year-old girl, a girl who had—after she seemed to recover from her mother's death—been so full of life. Until last year when she started middle school. Now, except for discussions about horses, Hailey was sullen and withdrawn.

"Buying a horse would be hard, princess." Zach caught her eye and shook his head. "With where we live, we'd have to board it, and I'm not sure how often you'd be able to get out to see it." He tried to keep his nights and weekends clear, but running his own energy business didn't allow nearly the amount of free time Hailey would want to spend with a horse.

"I bet we can find a stable close to town, and I can take the bus there after school to go riding."

Ride without him or another adult there to keep an eye on her?

That wasn't happening.

But somehow he had to find a way to get her past seventh grade. Truly, he was desperate enough to let the horse live in their garage and tell her she could ride it around their quarter-acre backyard in the suburbs and—

The car hit a slick spot and veered toward the right shoulder of the road.

Zach's pulse kicked up a notch, and Hailey sucked in an audible breath.

He steered into the skid, then eased the vehicle back toward the center of his lane.

"How far"—Hailey's voice wobbled—"are we from Grandpa's place?"

"About three miles." He tried to sound confident. He'd like to give her a reassuring look as well, but after that skid, he didn't dare take his eyes off the road. "We just have these two big curves."

Curves that, even now, seventeen years after he'd graduated high school, still weren't banked right. He crept along, staying in the tracks from other cars as best he could.

Finally, he got back to another flat, straight part of the road. "We're in the home stretch now, Hailey. We have that little hill up ahead and after that we'll be on a road that's plowed."

"Good." She went back to her phone. "Although I'd rather be stuck in a ditch here than go back to Phoenix."

Her voice had that hopeless note again, the one that cut right into his heart. So much for cheering her up with a visit to a horse.

She let out a long sigh. "I can't believe I have to deal with Desert View Middle School again in only two more days."

Zach winced, gave the car a tiny bit of gas, and—

It fishtailed and spun out.

A thud sounded outside Meredith's house.

She put her gloves back on, grabbed the carrot and fedora, and opened the front door.

For a second she stood motionless, mouth open. The fedora and carrot fell from her hand, silently plunging into the snow on her porch.

There, in the middle of her front yard where her snowman had stood, was a light-blue sedan. The lower sections of her snowman were shattered. The snowman's head, fully intact, sat on the hood of the car with its smile still in place. And a tall, dark-haired man in a black jacket was climbing out of the car with his head angled to one side as if he couldn't quite take in what had happened.

Duke raced over, barking at top volume.

"Hush," she told the dog. "He's all bark," she called to the driver. "Really, a big love." She shut the front door and dashed over. "Are you hurt?"

"We're okay. I'd slowed almost to a crawl, but I couldn't stop before..." He gestured to the snowman's head on the hood of his car. "I'm afraid your friend sustained pretty serious injuries."

A young teenager climbed out of the car, hands covering her mouth, turquoise gloves the exact shade as her puffy coat. "Dad, you decapitated it!" A note of wrought-up emotion rang in her words, a note that tugged at something inside Meredith, reminding her of when Ava got upset when she was younger.

"Don't worry. I can fix it." Meredith lifted the snowman's head off the hood of the car and set it on the ground beside her. "I'm simply glad you're both are okay. I'll build a new base for Mr. Snowman and do...well, a...a head transplant."

For a half-second the girl seemed unsure of how to react, then she gave a small smile.

Meredith grinned at her. Good, just like with Ava, a little humor helped.

The man walked closer and his scarf slipped down, revealing a face with a strong jaw and familiar blue-gray eyes.

Eyes that sent a tingle through Meredith's chest.

"Thank you," he said. "For being understanding." His gaze held hers, as if adding unspoken thanks for how she'd lightened the mood.

But there was no glimmer of recognition in his eyes.

Maybe that was too much to expect.

"I'm sorry I ended up in your yard." He gestured to the muddy ruts behind the wheels of his car. "I'll be happy to pay to have new sod put down."

She brushed his offer aside. "Really, there's no need. I'll throw out some grass seed when it warms up."

"Are you sure? I feel like I should—" His eyes narrowed. "Wait a minute. I remember you. We went to school together. You're...Megan, isn't it?"

She pressed her lips together and mustered up a polite smile. "Meredith, Meredith Lawson. And you're Zach Gilcroft."

"Yeah." He tipped a head toward the girl. "This is Hailey, my daughter."

She'd heard he was married, living in some city out west, and was a pretty big deal. From the looks of things, it was true. She didn't know much about men's clothing, but those boots the girl was wearing cost $300.

So Zach was rich, married, and probably living a lifestyle she could only imagine. No wonder he barely remembered her. She was just plain old Meredith Lawson. Five foot four, fifteen pounds overweight, with brown hair and brown eyes. Whether it was when she'd had a crush on him at eighteen or today at age thirty-four, she was nothing memorable.

He opened his car door. "At least let me move my car and help with the, uh, head transplant."

"What? Oh, you don't need to—"

"I insist. The snow seems to have stopped, so the roads aren't getting any worse."

A minute later he'd backed the car into her driveway and begun rolling a snowball in the yard.

His daughter waited by the car, petting Duke.

Zach pointed to the place where the original snowman had stood. "Should we put him here?"

"Sure." She rolled her own snowball toward the spot. Zach's snowball was already larger. Clearly, it would be the base.

He angled his head toward the house. "I see those two big greenhouses out back. What do you grow?"

"Organic microgreens and a few bedding plants, especially flowers. What do you do?"

"I'm co-owner of a business in Phoenix in the energy sector, funded by venture capital."

That certainly sounded more impressive than growing baby radish and cabbage plants.

"We've been home for more than a week visiting family, but we fly back tomorrow." He smoothed the side of his snowball, flattening out a lump. "School starts in two days, and I need to get back in the office. It's pretty busy, being an entrepreneur and a single parent."

Meredith stopped rolling her snowball. "Single parent?"

"My wife died when Hailey was seven."

Oh. Poor Zach. Poor Hailey. Meredith glanced over at the girl, who was deep in conversation with Duke. It didn't matter how old she was, a girl needed her mom. "I'm so sorry."

"It's okay," he said gently. "Here, let me." He took the second snowball from her, easily lifted it into place, and added the head. "Does that look good to you?"

"Even better than before. Thank you." She added

branches for arms, then dashed to the porch, dug out the carrot and hat, brought them over, and positioned the carrot nose so that it pointed slightly up.

Zach took Grandpa's fedora and set it atop the snowman's head at a jaunty angle. Then he patted the snowman's shoulder. "Sorry about the incident, old fellow, but now you're as good as new." He turned to Meredith. "I guess we should get back on the road. If you're sure about the sod?"

"Seriously, do you know anyone in Abundance who puts down sod?"

He shrugged.

"Besides, I'm a farmer. If I can't get a little grass to grow, I need a different career."

He tipped his head in acknowledgment. "Then I guess we'll head back to my dad's place." He looked toward the car. "We should take off, Hailey."

The girl hugged Duke, waved, and got in.

Zach hesitated, then turned back to Meredith. "It's been nice seeing you." He caught hold of her hand, dwarfing her small navy glove with his big black one. "I miss people like you, living out in Phoenix."

A zing of warmth shot through her chest. "Have a good trip home." She stood there, waving, as he pulled onto the county road and drove away. The warmth in her chest fizzled out at the thought of how far away Arizona was.

There was no use getting excited over a chance encounter with Zach Gilcroft. He was out of her league. His time in Abundance was limited. He had big deals to put together in the energy sector.

And she had a loan to secure.